GONE FISHIN'

Sam and I shone our lights across the water. The water bubbled away with the nicoji but nothing more, nothing bigger. There were so many, so easily taken.

"Let's get one more net," he said.

I nodded. The help swam past Sam. We started pulling in the net.

And the water stopped boiling. All the noise in the treetops quit, suddenly, as if the silence had been commanded. I looked back, but could see nothing on the shore or in the water.

The help suddenly dropped the net, swam to me, and bunched up around my legs. They'd never done that before. We'd always held the net together till every one of us got on the raft or on shore. It was something new then, out there.

"Sam—" I said.

Something dark rose out of the water in front of him.

"Run!"

Nicoji

M. SHAYNE BELL

BAEN BOOKS

NICOJI

A Baen Books Original

Baen Publishing Enterprises
P.O. Box 1403
Riverdale, N.Y. 10471

ISBN: 0-671-72034-1

Cover art by Don Clavette

First printing, January 1991

Distributed by
SIMON & SCHUSTER
1230 Avenue of the Americas
New York, N.Y. 10020

Printed in the United States of America

For my Mother and Father

Not life, but a good life, is to be chiefly valued.
                    —Plato, Crito

I

I got out of the shower and dressed while I was still wet so that maybe I'd cool off while I walked down to the company store. It was evening and quiet. The store was quiet.

But the ship from Earth had come in.

Vattani was opening a wooden crate with the back of a hammer, and Marcos and Fabio, Vattani's two little boys, were kicking through piles of white plastic packing around his counter. Vattani smiled at me and motioned proudly at his shelves: filled, some of them; restocked, as much as they would be till the next ship.

"Peanut butter!" I said. I grabbed a can of it from the display on the end of the counter. The can was bulged. The peanut butter had frozen in the unheated hold on the way out. But the can felt full. "I'll take it," I said, not asking or caring about the price. Vattani looked at me doubtfully but put down his

1

hammer and keyed in my purchase. I thought of—
Morgan, was it?—who said if you had to ask the
price you couldn't afford it. Well, I couldn't afford
the peanut butter and I knew it so I didn't bother
with the price. Besides, they had me. The company
had me. What was another twenty or thirty dollars
on my bill?

I put the can on the counter and went after the
staples Sam and I needed. That's when I saw the
company "boy" sitting in the shadows by an open
window next to the racks of boots and underneath
the hanging rows of inflatable rafts nobody bought
because they'd get punctured and the three butterfly
nets nobody wanted after the company quit bringing
up naturalists. He tapped his gun against his leg and
watched me pick up a five-pound sack of rice and a
two-and-a-half pound sack of beans. He moved his
chair so he could look at me when I went down
another aisle to get a loaf of bread and a jar of
vinegar that had an expiration date Vattani hadn't
changed. He chuckled when I grabbed a bag of
raisins Vattani's wife had dried from the native gagga
fruit.

I held out the bag. "Want some?"

He laughed. "We've got apples and bananas in the
company house, Jake."

I shoved some raisins in my mouth. "You don't
know what you're missing."

"I tried 'em, once."

I thought of different replies to that, communica-
tive things like shoving fistfuls of gagga raisins down
his throat.

"How's the college application?" he asked.

My best friend and I had come up, one year out of
high school, to earn money for college. I turned and

walked back to the counter. "Trouble with shoplifting, Vattani?"

"Less of it. You got your nicoji frozen?" Vattani keyed in the prices of the food I'd picked up.

"Just got in. Sam and I'll eat first."

"Ship leaves in the morning—early. You'll work all night?"

"Sure, work all night."

Vattani stuffed my food in a plastic bag. "You'd better, you and Sam. You missed the last ship, and the price has gone down since then—five cents less per package, now."

"It's the only ship we missed this year. It came early."

"But you missed it, so I had to extend your credit, again. How are you going to pay me back?"

I just looked at him.

"You eat fast and get to work."

I put my right hand on the counter and stared at him. Marcos and Fabio quit kicking the shredded plastic and looked up at us. Vattani waved back the company boy and finally lit the tile under my hand to add forty-six dollars and twenty-three cents to my bill of credit. Then he handed me the groceries. I walked out and let the door slam, listened to the bells over it jangle while I walked down the dirt street.

But I had a can of peanut butter from home, from Earth.

And the sky ahead of me was red on the horizon where the sun was.

Manoel stopped me just down the street from the store. "Dente," he said in Portuguese, pointing to his teeth. He'd never learned much English. "Raimundo."

"Anda já," I said. He took off down the alley that led to Raimundo's house. I followed.

The company had let Raimundo's teeth rot. Raimundo had asked Sam and me to come help him with his teeth just after we'd gotten in—he thought two Americans would know more about dentistry than the Brazi guys he'd come up with. We didn't. But he was in so much pain I took a pair of electrician's pliers and pulled out the incisor he pointed to. Since then, he'd asked only me to pull his teeth.

Raimundo was sitting on the one step up to his door, holding the right side of his swollen face. He had a pair of pliers tucked between his knees, and he'd set alcohol, aspirin, a scrap of clean cotton, and a pocket knife at his side. I put my sack of groceries on the step and looked at him. He handed me the pliers and pointed at the third bicuspid behind his upper canine: black, rotted out in the middle. It must have hurt for weeks. "How can you stand waiting so long?" I asked. But I knew. The company kept promising to bring out a dentist, and a dentist could save Raimundo's teeth if they were still in his mouth.

"Pull it, Jake," he said, his speech thick. He tried to talk out of only the left side of his mouth.

"Let me wash my hands and these pliers."

He grabbed my arm. "Just pull it. Now."

I knelt in front of him. "You take any aspirin?" I asked.

"Six," he said.

Which meant he was hurting bad. He'd generally throw up if he took more than four aspirin—his stomach couldn't handle it. But the company didn't stock any other kind of over-the-counter pain killer. I opened the thinnest blade on the pocketknife, stuck it in the alcohol, and laid it on the cotton. "That's all the cotton you've got?" I asked.

"Manoel packed up the rest," Raimundo mumbled.

That surprised me. Evidently they had their raft packed and ready to go again, though they'd gotten in only a day before Sam and me. No sticking around town for them. "Lean back," I said. Raimundo leaned back against the door frame so he'd have something to push against when I started pulling. "Hold open his mouth," I told Manoel, mimicking what I wanted him to do. He stood left of Raimundo, stuck his fingers between Raimundo's teeth, and held the jaws wide apart. Raimundo grabbed the step with both hands and closed his eyes. I grabbed the tooth with the pliers and pulled hard and fast, to get it over with for Raimundo.

The tooth shattered. Raimundo tried to stand up, but I shoved him back down. Manoel growled Portuguese words I didn't understand—he'd gotten his fingers bitten—but he held on and opened up Raimundo's mouth again. I pulled out the parts of tooth. Only one root came. "I've got to get the other root," I said, and I used the knife to work the root loose enough to grab with the pliers. I pulled it out and laid it on the step with the other pieces of tooth. Blood spattered my arms. Manoel let go of Raimundo's mouth, and Raimundo started spitting blood. I tore off a chunk of cotton, shoved it up where the tooth had been, and had Raimundo bite down.

His hands were white, he'd held onto the step so hard. "You hurt me," he mumbled.

"I'm sorry," I said. "I did the best I could."

He looked at me. Manoel wiped the knife clean on the hem of his shirt.

I set the can of peanut butter on the table Sam had hammered together from crates Vattani threw away behind his store and listened to Sam whistle while he showered. I was shaking. I'll never pull another tooth, I told myself.

I opened the bathroom door and walked in. Sam stopped whistling. "That you, Jake?" he asked from behind the shower curtain.

"Yes," I said. He started whistling again.

I wiped steam off part of the broken mirror Sam and I had salvaged from the trash heap north of town and looked at all my teeth. They were fine, no cavities.

It was my turn to cook. I went back to the kitchen, dumped three handfuls of beans in a jar, washed them in tepid water from our distiller, and set them to soak on the counter for supper the next night. Then I dumped water and a handful of gagga raisins in a pan and let the raisins plump up while I took a clay bowl and walked out to the freeze-shack for some of the nicoji.

The freeze-shack smelled musty, sweet, like the nicoji. "Light on," I said. I heard a rustling in the shadows and flipped on the light. The help had all scurried under boxes or stacks of burlap sacks. Three help peeked out at me.

"Sorry, guys," I said. The help hate light, even the dim light Sam and I had strung in our freeze-shack.

"It's Jake," some of them whispered. "Jake."

I walked to the far wall where we hung our sacks of nicoji and lifted one down from its hook. It was wet and heavy. I set it carefully on the dirt floor and untied it. Nicoji were still crawling around inside. I put my hand in the sack, and a nicoji wrapped its eight spindly legs around my little finger. I lifted it up. It hung there, its beady eyes looking at me. I flicked it in the pan and picked out eight more nicoji that were still moving, since they'd be the freshest, set the pan on the floor and started to tie up the sack, thinking we shouldn't eat too many ourselves, not now, but then I thought why not? We'd had a good catch. Even Vattani would be proud of Sam and me.

Not that it mattered how well Sam and I did.

So I put four more nicoji in the pan, threw one or two nicoji in each corner of the freeze-shack, and hung the sack back on its hook. The help waited till I switched off the light to scramble out after the nicoji.

Sam was still in the shower. I banged on the door. "Supper, Sam!" I yelled. Whenever we first got back in town, he'd stay in the shower just letting the water run over him, trying to feel clean; then, after he'd taken all the water in the rooftop storage tank, if it hadn't rained, we had to go to the well half a mile away for cooking water and to the company bath-house if we wanted a bath—five dollars each.

I dumped the water off the raisins, poured in a cup of vinegar, sprinkled sugar and a dash of salt over that, and turned on the heat underneath the pan. When the raisins started bubbling, I washed the thirteen nicoji, chopped off their heads and stiff little legs and tails, gutted them, rinsed the blood off the bodies, dumped them in with the raisins and vinegar, and set them to simmer. The photograph of Loryn, my girlfriend back home, had fallen out of the windowsill onto the stove. I dusted it off and stuck it back in the window.

Sam padded out from the shower, still wet, towel-ing his hair dry. When he saw the can of peanut butter he just sat down and held it.

"It's been two years," I said.

We ate our nicoji over rice and, though the nicoji had made me a slave, I still loved the taste. "They never get 'em like this back home," I said, "fresh."

Sam nodded. We finished the nicoji and carried the peanut butter and bread to the veranda and sat on the steps. The gravitational wind was blowing, and it felt cool, off the sea. We sat facing into it. The moon was so big, it didn't pull in just tides: it pulled the atmosphere along with it, and we could count on relief from the heat at least twice a day. I tore the bread into thin pieces. Sam pushed up the tab on top of the can, broke the seal, and carefully peeled back the lid. I wiped the peanut butter stuck to it onto a piece of bread, tore the piece in two, gave Sam half, and we ate without a word.

One of the help wandered out, dragging the garbage sack from the kitchen. The help were famous for scrounging through garbage sacks and trashheaps. This help had on someone's greasy old shirt that hung in tatters, open. Whoever had thrown it away had cut off and saved all the buttons.

The help dumped out the garbage and rummaged through it looking for the heads, legs, and tails I'd cut from the nicoji we'd had for supper. Little eight-legged "ants" had swarmed all over the nicoji hard parts. The help let a few ants crawl on his fingers, and he watched the ants run up and down his hand. He ate the ones that started up his arm. Eventually he settled back to eat the nicoji, ants and all, watching Sam and me. Suddenly he stuck his fingers in the peanut butter. "Hey!" I yelled. I swatted his hand away, but he lifted it up with a look of horror on his face. He sniffed the peanut butter on his fingers, wrinkled his nose, and looked at Sam and me eating peanut butter on our bread. He tried to shake the peanut butter off and finally ran to the street and rubbed his fingers in the dirt till they were clean. He came back for the nicoji and walked away, disgusted, leaving the garbage scattered. Sam and I shoved the garbage in the sack and sat back down.

The night had cooled off. There were clouds around us, and lightning, and when it rained it wouldn't matter that Sam had taken all the water. The moon was rising. It filled a third of the sky, shining red through the clouds.

"You boys still eating?"

It was Vattani walking home with his two sons, holding their hands. "Go help your mother home from the bayou," he told them. The boys ran off. Senhora Vattani washed other teams' clothes in the bayou. Sam and I washed our own clothes, to save money, and Senhora Vattani used to hate us for cheating her out of work, at least till we started bringing her new plants from the pântano for her garden.

Vattani marched up to our veranda.

"You let my friend vagabundo buy a can of your peanut butter," Sam said. "Muito obrigado."

"Vagabundos—both of you," Vattani said. "The ship will leave in three hours. Other teams have already taken their nicoji to the company house."

"You told me the ship would leave in the morning," I said.

Vattani shrugged. "I was wrong. Ships keep their own time."

Ships keep the company's time, I thought.

"Thanks for the warning," Sam said.

I wrapped the peanut butter in a towel to keep off the ants and grabbed our butcher knife to cut the nicoji with. Sam used his pocketknife. I got our two buckets, one to fill with disinfected water to rinse the nicoji in after we'd gutted them, the other to throw the guts in. We went out to the freeze-shack, pulled down our sacks of nicoji, and set them by the freezer. The freezer was a rectangular machine that misted the nicoji with water and packed them in square, five-pound blocks that were wrapped in plastic and lowered into liquid nitrogen which, at minus 195 degrees Fahrenheit, flash-froze the nicoji, forming ice crystals too small to rupture the cells, preserving the color, nutritive value, and taste. The company shipped the nicoji to a station above Earth where they were graded, UNDA inspected, given a final packaging, and shipped down to market a great luxury.

We'd hung dim, red lights over the table where Sam and I sat to do our cutting. After we turned on the freezer and adjusted the nitrogen pump, we turned off the other lights in the freeze-shack and the help came out. Sam and I had twelve help following us around just then. We'd had as many as thirty. They'd take turns feeding nicoji bodies down the hole on top of the freezer till the weights registered five pounds and a red light started flashing; then they'd jump from the stool and reach their leathery little hands around Sam and me very carefully, very quietly—holding their breath, almost—and snatch the piles of heads, tails, and legs. They didn't like the guts as much as the hard parts. We could hear them munching and chittering in the corners all night every night we worked the freeze-shack. By morning they'd be sick from eating so much.

"Slow down," Sam said. "Leg." He pointed with his pocketknife to a bit of leg I'd left on the nicoji I'd just cut. The company inspectors had opened a package from our last shipment and found a tiny bit of chitinous leg. They docked half our money for that. You couldn't train the help to reject a nicoji that still had part of a leg or tail—they liked the stuff—so you had to make sure yourself. Some teams had so much trouble with the inspectors that they worked together, one team to cut, the other to inspect what had been cut. Sam and I weren't that good yet, hadn't started making enough money to be in danger of paying off Vattani and buying a ticket home.

One of the help started parading around the freeze-shack rattling the two peach pits we kept in a can. I got up and took the can away from him and hung it back on its nail. Sam and I'd each gotten a peach our first Thanksgiving out but didn't plant the pits. It was too hot here, though when we were going to get someplace on this planet cool enough to plant peaches I didn't know.

"I got a letter," Sam said when I sat back down.

I looked up. I hadn't, again. Even Loryn hadn't written for seven months.

"My family got the nicoji I sent for Christmas," Sam said.

It was soon Christmas, and the company would ship nicoji at reduced rates to our families so they would think we were making lots of money and were all right—sent the packages with company versions of our letters.

"Think Vattani got his camera fixed?" I asked.

Sam shrugged. Vattani had had a camera our first year out, and Sam and I had cleaned up, rented clothes in Vattani's store to dress up in, and had our pictures taken to send home—we'd sat in the back of Vattani's store in rented clothes holding up handfuls of nicoji we'd caught ourselves. The company'd loved it. We'd been out two months.

Sam started sucking his finger. "Something bit me," he said.

"No nicoji," I said.

He nodded. He stirred the pile of nicoji in front of

him with his knife. One started crawling away, and
Sam stabbed it and held it up on the end of his
blade—a nicoji shark: a carnivore that had evolved
into looking like a nicoji. It had been in heaven,
trapped in that sack with thousands of nicoji, and it
was fat. Sam flicked it to the ground. One of the help
stomped it with his heel to make sure it couldn't
bite, then started tossing it in the air. He'd throw it
so hard it would hit the ceiling and slam back down
on the dirt.

Another help started squealing and jumping up
and down—the freezer was out of plastic to wrap
nicoji in. I ran for some plastic while Sam turned off
the freezer and made the help stop pushing nicoji
down the chute. I brought back three boxes, loaded
one into the freezer, and we started up again. You
couldn't train the help to go after plastic.

"Got enough plastic?" Sam asked.

"Most of last month's," I said.

Sam laughed. It was another way the company
kept us. We had to pay rent on the freezers and go
to Vattani's store for plastic, liquid nitrogen, and
company-approved disinfected water to mist the nicoji
with.

Sam started humming the tune the company played
on its ads back home—"Make a million; Eat nicoji.
Spend a million; Beat the times"—and the rain started:
a few drops hit the tin roof of our freeze-shack like
bullets, then a downpour came in an explosion of
sound that made me remember Javanese rock con-
certs. The help covered their ears and ran under
crates, sacks, and our chairs, chittering loudly, trying
to be heard over the rain. But the rain could fall for
hours and Sam and I had a deadline to beat, so I
kept cutting nicoji and Sam stood up to feed nicoji to
the freezer.

The help quit chittering, suddenly.

I looked up. Sam looked up, and then we heard a pounding on the door. I ran to open it, and Sam switched off the freezer.

It was Raimundo, wet to the skin. He stepped just inside the doorway, brushing water from his arms, his pants dripping on the dirt floor. I pushed the door shut.

"I owe you," Raimundo said to me. "I've come to pay you back for helping me with my teeth."

I didn't know if he meant he was going to beat me up for the pain I'd caused him, or what. He walked to where Sam sat, and I followed. "Turn on the freezer," he said. He wanted noise. I thought the rain made enough noise, but Raimundo wanted more. Sam turned on the freezer.

"A new company's set up base on the mesão," he said.

We just stared. The mesão was a huge mesa rising out of the pântano two weeks south of us—solid land to build on, but days away from nicoji marshes, we were told, and out of our concession anyway. The company had its concession only till scientists decided whether the help were sentient or merely imitative, and it could keep its part of this world only if the help weren't sentient. I wondered if the coming of this second company meant ours had finally bought off the scientists and had their "decision."

"The new company's Brazilian registry and will buy your contracts and give you citizenship. It pays well. Its town has cinemas, more stores than one, good doctors, and women."

"How do you know?" I asked.

"I met one of their teams in the pântano. They had new equipment—prods that shocked nicoji out of the mud before the tide."

"And they told you this—about the cinemas and the women?"

"Do I look like a fantasist? Do I look like my brain is full of lagarto poison?"

I looked at Sam.

"Manoel and I are poling south to this new company. I spit on American Nicoji for keeping me here three years and letting my teeth rot."

He spat on the floor. I hoped, for his sake, that there was a new company with a dentist. "Come, too," Raimundo said. "You won't need your insurance, then."

Sam laughed.

"Do you still have your insurance?"

I nodded. The option to buy life insurance from firms not owned by the company was the one real benefit the company-controlled union allowed us. Sam and I had named each other the beneficiaries of our policies.

"So if Sam dies, you get to go home?" Raimundo laughed, asking me.

"And vice versa," I said.

"Aren't you afraid he will kill you in the night?" Raimundo asked Sam, pointing his thumb at me.

Sam smiled.

"*If* they let you go home," Raimundo said.

Everybody wondered if they'd really let us go home, where we could talk and dry up their supply of workers. I knew only one guy who'd left: Ben Silva. He'd scrimped and saved and one day made enough from a catch to pay off Vattani and buy a one-way ticket halfway home. That was good enough for him. They'd made him wait three days before letting him up to the ship, and he sat the whole time on the steps of the company house, afraid they'd leave him if he wasn't ready the minute they called.

He hadn't bought another thing, not even food, worried he wouldn't have enough money for something he touched that they'd charge him for and that they'd cancel his ticket before he could borrow money to pay off Vattani again. Sam and I took him some food on the second day. He said he'd write us a letter and say "the nicoji here tastes like duck liver" which would really mean he'd made it home in one piece, alive. We never got a letter.

"Will you come?"

I looked at Sam. We were both thinking the same things. We'd been Americans all our lives, and it might be fun to be Brazis for a while—the average person had three different citizenships in his lifetime because of company transfers. We even spoke a little Portuguese. But getting American Nicoji to sell our contracts was the problem. If it wouldn't, we'd be in big trouble when we got back here. And if we broke contract and stayed with the new company anyway, we'd have to stay with them forever no matter what they were like. Breaking contract would ruin our work records. Only renegade corporations would hire us after that. It was also nearly hurricane season, and we usually stayed close to the company town then. Besides, Raimundo had been quick and free with his story, and we'd learned not to trust anyone who was easy with information. Our first month out, an older team had given Sam and me directions to a nicoji hole they knew about, and we'd followed their directions to one of the worst holes in the pântano. I wondered if Raimundo was setting up an elaborate joke on me to get even.

"Does this company have a station?" I asked.

"Claro que sim, Jake—of course."

"Why haven't we seen it in the night sky?"

"They positioned it a few degrees below the horizon. American Nicoji already had the spot above us."

Sam and I just looked at him.

"The new company pays experienced guys *more*—they located so close to us, on the very edge of our concession, to draw us all off to work for them."

I looked down and scuffed my right shoe on the ground.

"Oh, I get it," Raimundo said. "Don't trust me. Don't come with someone who's had the way pointed out to him. But when I do not come back from the pântano, think of what I said and head for the south edge of the mesão. We'll party in the new town."

He kicked a nicoji tail to the help crouched under my chair. "Ten cents less per package, this ship," he said. He turned and walked to the door. I let him out and watched him run under the eaves of our house and up the street, splashing through the rain and mud.

"Vattani said five cents less," I told Sam.

If Raimundo's story were true it meant a way out—a new company that would buy our contracts gave us a place to start over. If it paid a fair price for nicoji, Sam and I could earn passage home someday.

We got back to work. Most of the help crawled out from under the sacks and boxes and chairs after the rain stopped. I wasn't paying much attention to anything but my thoughts—just automatically cutting off nicoji heads, legs, and tails; gutting the bodies and rinsing them; stacking the bodies to one side and sliding the hard parts to another; thinking of movie theaters and dentists—when one of the help started screaming. Sam switched off the freezer, and I jumped up. The help stuffing nicoji down the chute had his hand caught; had probably dropped a nicoji down the chute after the red light started flashing and tried to grab it back. I ran to his side, and he quit screaming once he could see that Sam and I knew what had happened to him. He was shaking so badly that the stool he stood on shook, and when I leaned against him to look down the chute, he rubbed his head on my shoulder.

"Hand's caught in the wrapper, Sam, and bleeding."

Sam ran for the alcohol. I flipped the wrapper setting to retract and pulled back the wrapper's arms. The help flipped out his hand and jumped down from the stool. Before he could run away, I grabbed him and pulled the melted plastic from his hand. Sam came and dumped alcohol over the cuts. The help howled. I smeared on an antibacterial cream that must have felt good because he calmed down while I bandaged his hand. Sam started cleaning the freezer. Two of the help's fingers were broken, and he'd have bad bruises. I made little splints for his fingers and sent him off with four uncut nicoji in his good hand.

We worked till half past midnight, then put on our insulated gloves, boxed up our packages of nicoji, and carried them to the inspectors. Sam and I were the last team in line. Eloise Hansdatter was just ahead of us, gun strapped to her leg, careful to watch us walk up, make sure who we were. The few women up here had to be careful. She was telling a team of Brazis about a scam of lagarto that had crawled onto the lower branches of the tree she was sleeping in. "Poison was rank on their breath," she said. "I started to hallucinate just breathing the fumes—saw talkative naked men all around me in the trees. I had to kill the lagarto just to make the men shut up." The Brazis laughed. I smiled at Sam. Eloise worked alone

and would not stop talking when she was in town
because for weeks at a time she had no one to talk to
but herself. Even so, you had to like her.

"Freeze all your nicoji?" she asked Sam and me.

Sam laughed.

"Thought not," she said. "Me either—which made
my help happy: they know I'll give them what's left
when I'm out of here."

She didn't mean just out of the company house—
she meant out of the town. Eloise never slept here.
She'd take out her raft, drift down different bayous,
and spend the night guarded by her help.

The company had strung one light bulb over the
door, and the guys standing in the light were swat-
ting bugs. Something dropped into my hair and
crawled inside my shirt and down my back. I started
squirming, and it started biting. "Something's biting
my back, Sam!" I said.

He got behind me, shoved his boxes against my
back, and smashed whatever was biting me. "Why
did they put up this light?" I asked. No one had ever
kept a light outside before.

"My help couldn't stand it," Eloise said. "They're
off in the shadows. When it's my turn to go in, I'll
have to go get my boxes from them." She'd worked
with the same group of help ever since she'd come
up, and they always carried her boxes to the company house for her. They were jealous little devils
that would hiss at you if you sat too close to Eloise
and throw trash at you if you stayed too long in the
freeze-shack she ran with two of the other female
teams. But they only treated you that nice if Eloise
actually let them know she didn't mind that you
were there. If she did mind, or if the help thought
she was in any danger, watch out. Just before Sam
and I came up, two guys had tried to jump Eloise,

and her help practically bit them to death before she could pull the help off and keep them off—one of the guys had an eye chewed right out of its socket and he'd had to start wearing a patch. For her sake, I was glad Eloise had her help. Guys talked about poisoning them so they could have a little fun with Eloise, but no one ever tried it.

Agulhas, tiny bugs with eight needle-sharp suckers spaced evenly on their bellies, started swarming over our feet and crawling up our legs. Eloise tried to keep them brushed off her legs and ours, but she couldn't do it—there were too many bugs. That was it for me. "Turn out the light!" I yelled. Other guys and Eloise started shouting the same thing.

A company boy shoved out through the door. "Shut up!" he yelled.

"The light's attracting bugs," I yelled back.

"Then complain to your union rep when he comes next month. He insisted you guys needed this light."

The union rep hadn't asked us about putting a light outside in the dark.

"Think of this as your bonus for being last in line," company boy said, "more bugs to swat." He laughed and turned to walk inside.

"Just turn it out!" I yelled.

"And what will we tell your union?" He swatted his neck, looked at his hand, and rubbed it on his pants.

"Tell the guys in there to hurry," Eloise said.

"Oh, you want me to tell the inspectors they're too slow? You want them to hurry and maybe not figure the right price for your nicoji but at least get you inside and out of the bugs?"

Nobody said a word to that.

*　　*　　*

Sam and I finally got inside and onto a bench where we swatted the agulhas on our legs, and sat with our cold boxes steaming beside us on the bench, and under our feet. I pulled off my shirt and had Sam try to see what bit me at first, but he'd smashed it so bad he couldn't tell what it was. He brushed off my back, and I shook out my shirt and put it back on.

A company boy walked up and down the aisle in front of us, leering, swinging his billy club onto the palm of his hand. The company boys needed clubs. The company house saw trouble.

"Next."

We set our boxes on the counter. The inspectors took them to a table and tore into one, tossing random packages of nicoji onto scales and then into a microwave. They cut open the thawed packages, and nicoji juice spurted out over the inspectors' plastic aprons. One fat inspector kept shoving our raw nicoji in his mouth four at a time, chewing and swallowing. He started into another box.

"Hey!" I yelled. "That's *one* already."

He jerked his thumb in my direction. "You guys get the special treatment after last time."

Sam grabbed my arm. I could hear the company boy walking up behind us, slapping his club onto his palm. I wanted to shove the club down his throat, but I knew better than to try it. The inspectors had our nicoji.

They tore open packages from each box. When they finished, the fat inspector stuffed his mouth full of our nicoji again, counted the packages left whole, thought for a minute, then sputtered a price. A different inspector keyed the money into our account and printed out a receipt. Sam put it in his shirt pocket. We turned to leave.

"This way, farm boys."

Company boy stood in front of us, pointing down a hallway with his club. Farm boys? At least I'd had a job before coming up here—at least I hadn't been a thieving street thug.

"Yeah," I said, and I started to brush by. I always walked out the *front* door.

He grabbed my shirt collar. "You hard of hearing? I said this way." He tried to shove me in the direction he wanted me to go. Six more company boys ran up. Before I could do anything, Sam grabbed my arm and pulled me down the hall. The company boys followed. I shoved Sam away from me, mad that he'd stopped me, even though I knew fights only got us trips to the correction field and made us poorer after we'd paid for damages and the company boys' medical bills.

Eloise staggered out from a room at the end of the hall, holding the back of her right wrist. Two company boys shoved her through a door and out of the building. The company doctor met us in the room Eloise had been in. He'd flown down from the station. He hardly ever flew down. "This won't take long," he said. "It's for your safety, sons."

He called everybody "son" though he looked so small and scrawny he probably couldn't father anything.

"What's for our safety?" Sam asked.

"These implants—locators," he said, holding one up. "Help us find you if you get lost in the pântano."

He was going to implant a locator on the back of our wrists.

"They're really quite simple," he went on. "The bottom of each locator is coated with a mild acid that quickly destroys the underlying skin, allowing the locator to replace it. The surrounding skin eventually bonds to the edges of the locator, making it a permanent, if shiny, part of your wrists—quite a comfort, I'm sure, when you'll be . . . away from here."

Sam and I stared at him.

"These locators run on minute amounts of power drawn from the natural electrical impulses in your bodies, so they quit functioning if you're killed or if they're removed."

A warning: don't cut them off. They'd have a fix on your last location and come looking. The doctor stepped up to a chair. "If one of you'd please sit here and let me disinfect your wrist, we'll get started."

Neither of us moved. Two company boys grabbed my arms and dragged me toward the chair. "Scared of a little pain, Jake?" one sneered. "Don't worry. We'll hold you like your mommy used to when the doctor'd give you shots in the ass."

"Freeze you," I said. I broke away, slammed my fist on the guy's nose, and heard it snap. He fell into the doctor, and they both fell in the chair. Sam kicked the table and knocked down the implanter, scattering locators all across the floor. The other company boys ran in. I knocked one down, but two grabbed my arms and shoved me up against the wall. The guy I'd hit on the nose, his face bloody, kicked me twice in the stomach. Someone hit the back of my head with his club, and I fell to the floor. I couldn't get up. I started smashing locators with my fist, but I felt a sting in my leg and the room went black.

II

I came to, covered with agulhas, lying in mud in the circle of light in front of the company house. On the back of my right wrist, bloody, was a locator. It felt tight in the muscle when I moved my hand. I tried to sit up but then dropped back, dizzy from the drug they'd put me out with.

"Hey, one of them's awake," somebody yelled from back by the company house. I heard steps splashing through the water toward me. I turned to see who was coming, but all I could see were his legs. He kicked Sam in the ribs. Sam rolled over next to me, sprawled an arm across my chest. A company boy crouched down, unbuttoned Sam's shirt pocket, and pulled out our receipt. "This will cover half the cost of what you two pulled in there," he said.

He stood up. "Get out here! These two are waking up."

I heard guys running through the water. I tried to

23

sit up, but I couldn't. I kept blinking, trying to see. Two guys pulled me to my feet, and two others pulled up Sam. They dragged us down the street and into the correction field south of the garbage dump.

"Put 'em in here."

They tore off our shirts and shoes and made us crouch down into narrow metal boxes and clamped our wrists above our heads and our ankles to the floor. Some guy stood to one side and recited legal stuff at us—about how the company was empowered and obligated to keep law and order, about how we'd known this when we'd signed contracts with the company, and how we'd agreed to abide by its rules and regulations and accept its punishments.

"Let me out!" Sam yelled.

They were making examples of us: look what happened to Sam and Jake when they tried to get out without a locator. Better get the locators on your wrists. What's acid eating a little of your skin compared to this?

I heard the doctor talking: "Hearts are OK—I checked them when they were out. No danger with these two."

"Son of a bitch!" I yelled. "You castrated, excised, son of a—"

They slammed down the box lids and turned on water.

"Let me out!" Sam yelled.

We had no light in the boxes. They filled the boxes with so much water I had to tip my head back to keep my nose out. The doctor lifted up the lids and looked at us, then dropped them back down. He and the company boys stood around the boxes, talking.

"There's something alive in here!" Sam yelled.

A company boy laughed.

"Get it out!"

I heard Sam thrashing around. Something settled onto *my* shorts and started crawling up my stomach. Its eight, feathery legs tickled across my skin. I tried to hold myself very still. Whatever was on me had stopped moving and clung to the hair on my chest. After a while, it crawled onto my neck and up under my chin, just at the edge of the water. I couldn't stand it. I shook it off, and it settled back down onto my stomach and bit me. I could feel it sucking blood through the skin. I thrashed around in the water and tried to shake it off, but I couldn't. "It bit me!" I yelled. "Get it off."

"Two twenty-five," the doctor said. "Write that down."

He lifted up the lid. "Just got to get a blood sample," he said. He drew blood out of my neck. He took blood from Sam after he got bit. "Nothing to worry about, boys," he said. "You're just helping me with a little research. Back in an hour to check your blood." All legal, according to our contracts: criminals could be used in nonlethal scientific experiments. The doctor dropped down the lids, and we heard him and the company boys walk away.

The doctor checked our blood at three hourly intervals, then drained out the water. He left the lids open, and in the waning red moonlight I could see the bloodsucker. Its head was buried in my skin. The eight spindly arms around its head clung to my belly, and its bloated body had flopped down against my stomach. The doctor looked in at me, then soaked a piece of cotton in alcohol and touched that to the back end of the blood sucker. The bloodsucker pulled out its head, fast, and the doctor tore it off me, threw it in the mud, and treated the bite. Then he got the bloodsucker off Sam and took care of him. He closed the lids and left us shivering in the wet boxes.

The help found us sometime before dawn. I heard them chittering. "Lift up the lids," I said.

"Jake!" one of them said. "Jake!"

The lids were locked down. "Wait for us by the house," I told them. But I didn't know if they'd wait for us, and we needed them. "Eat the nicoji we left in the freeze-shack," I told them. "It's yours."

We wouldn't have frozen it. The company paid only a third of the normal price for packages that came in after the ship had gone—barely enough to cover the cost of plastic wrapping and liquid nitrogen. They claimed it wasn't fresh. The help ran off.

It rained most of the day, so it never got too hot in the boxes. The company boys pulled us out that night, after twenty-four hours. Sam and I couldn't walk. They dropped us in the mud. A company boy threw our gloves, shirts, and shoes in the water beside us and stomped off, splashing water in our faces. I grabbed our gloves and held them on my chest so they wouldn't get wet inside. After a while I pulled Sam up. "Let's go," I said. But we didn't go home. We staggered down the streets through red moonlight to Raimundo's house. He'd told us the truth about there being a new company. American Nicoji didn't put locators on us for our safety, to help us if we got lost. They wanted to keep track of us, keep us from defecting south to the new company.

Raimundo was gone.

We decided to sleep in our own house that night and head out in the morning. The help were waiting for us. They hadn't been able to get the sacks of nicoji down from the hooks, so we still had nicoji to eat. I took down a sack and gave it to the help.

"And we've got this to finish," Sam said, picking up the can of peanut butter I'd wrapped in a towel.

But the towel was covered with ants.

Sam dropped the towel on the floor. The can was thick with ants. Sam took out his pocketknife, scraped off the top layer of peanut butter where the ants were, and flicked the ants off the sides and bottom of the can. I brushed off the table. We sat and ate the peanut butter with our fingers.

In the night, the help who had gotten his hand hurt crawled on top of my chest and patted my face till I woke up. "Yeah?" I whispered, trying not to wake Sam. The help held up his hand. "Being better," it chittered.

I knew it would be. The help had such fast metabolisms—they healed faster than anything I'd seen.

"What you want me do nice you?" the help asked.

"Let me sleep."

He patted my face. "What you want most? What you want most, Jake?"

I closed my eyes. "To go home," I said.

He scampered down off my chest and hardly made a noise as he ran out across the straw sleeping mats Sam and I had woven.

I lay there and thought of home. I remembered one day, in particular: the day that started Sam and me toward this place. Sam and I had climbed into a truck with Loryn, my girlfriend, to eat lunch. We'd been running potato harvesters while Loryn drove one of the trucks we dumped the potatoes into. It was a cold day, and the sky was overcast and grey. It looked as if it might snow.

We pulled off our gloves and hats and opened our sacks. We had the same things for lunch: roast beef sandwiches, potato chips, apples, hot chocolate. Loryn sat in the middle. "Hitachi Farms got their last spuds in at 11:00," she said. She heard things like that in the pits when she dumped her potatoes.

"Beat us again," Sam said.

"They beat everybody, again," Loryn said. "CitiCorp and UIF don't expect to get done till next week. They're hoping for snow."

The potatoes wouldn't freeze under a blanket of snow. They could still be dug.

"We'll finish today," I said.

We worked for Westinghouse Farms. In the spring, we'd tried to get on with Hitachi, but the Supreme Court had struck down Idaho's intrastate labor laws and Hitachi had brought in cheap contract labor from California and didn't hire local help. All the corporate farms were watching Hitachi's profit margin. If it was good enough, every farm would switch to contract labor, and Sam and Loryn and I'd either be out of work or we'd have to sign five-year contracts with one of the agricultural labor pools and forget doing anything else. You couldn't get ahead on contract labor. You'd have to sign up for another five-year stint, then another and another till you died. So every Idaho farmhand worked hard, trying to make our farms beat Hitachi.

From where Loryn had parked the pickup, we could look down over the dry farms to Alma, the county seat, built on bluffs above the Snake River. The clouds above the city had broken, and Alma looked blessed in the light, the white houses and churches shining, surrounded by dark fields. But the clouds closed up again, and it started to snow. The snowflakes melted on the windshield, the hood of the truck, and the ground. I downed the rest of my hot chocolate, shoved my half-eaten sandwich back in my sack, and looked at Sam. He had two more bites of his sandwich to go. Loryn just held hers. "Trouble," she said.

I looked up from pulling on my gloves. A Westinghouse pickup pulled to a stop in front of the truck. Sam and I climbed out. Loryn slid over behind the wheel. Floyd Johnson, one of the foremen, climbed out of the pickup. So did Doug Phillips, from Hitachi. Loryn climbed down from the cab when she saw Doug Phillips. The other drivers got out of their trucks and hurried over.

"Hitachi bought us out," Floyd said. No explanation. We'd had no hint Westinghouse was selling out.

"I hope I can welcome you into Hitachi," Phillips said. "We got Hitachi equipment and teams headed here to finish digging these spuds, but we could use all of you running the old Westinghouse equipment. Just go down to the pits first and sign the contracts we got waiting there."

"Five years?" I asked.

"Standard."

I looked at Sam and Loryn.

"We'll take everybody but you, Sam," Phillips said.

Because Sam had sent away for a copy of *Corporate Feudalism* after the county library wouldn't order it in. It was all I could figure. The book said we were no better off than feudal serfs who gradually, and probably without realizing it at first, if ever, gave up their freedoms in return for physical protection. Relatively recently, our ancestors had once again given up the freedom to control their lives—had let corporations in effect buy them—this time in return for economic well-being. Corporations now had the land and the wealth and hence the power, and most men and women had become merely productive or unproductive units tallied in offices continents away. We were serfs, again, serving a corporate aristocracy. The first serfs cast off their chains after a thousand years of wearing them. When would we find the courage and vision to cast off ours, the book asked. Sam had passed that book around to too many people, and when Westinghouse found out about it they'd nearly fired him. Now Hitachi wouldn't take him.

"You'll all get paid for the work you've done here," Floyd said.

Loryn, Sam, and I drove back into Alma. Loryn and I wouldn't sign Hitachi's contracts, and none of us knew what we were going to do. We passed the Hitachi equipment and workers headed for our fields. One of their harvesters got caught in a rut in the muddy road and veered into our truck. We skidded off the road into a ditch. The cab filled with freezing water, and we couldn't open the doors because the ditch banks were snug against the truck. I held my breath and tried to kick out the windshield, but it wouldn't break though I kicked it, and kicked it, and kicked it—

I sat up. It was still night. I'd gone to sleep and started dreaming. We hadn't been forced into a ditch to drown. Sam and I ended up here. Loryn got work with a feed-supply franchise, but it didn't pay much and in her last letter she said she might be getting a new job. She hadn't said what. I wondered what she was doing. My stomach felt tight like it always did when I thought about signing contracts with labor pools.

Sam was gone. I heard someone in the freeze-shack, so I stumbled out there, rubbing my eyes, blinking in the light when I opened the door and walked in. Sam looked up and smiled. He was sitting on the floor, getting ready to drain the liquid nitrogen from the freezer. "Just in time," he said. "I need help with this nozzle."

"What are you doing?"

"Packing up everything we've paid for."

I laughed. We hadn't talked about going to the new company to check it out, but we hadn't needed to. We were going, and we both knew it, hurricane season or not. We'd head south as far as we could without upsetting American Nicoji, then we'd cut out the locators and head for the new town. If we didn't like what we saw, we could always come back, face the correction fields and fines.

Sam had me hold a wrench clamped on the bolt below the nozzle so the hose on the nitrogen can wouldn't turn while he screwed the nozzle in place. Once done, he pulled the drain lever, and we sat on the ground with the can between us, listening to the nitrogen hiss into it.

"I dreamt it was snowing," I said.

"Here?"

"Back home."

We looked at each other.

"You scared?" I asked.

"Just about hurricanes. I can take the rest."

Hurricanes scared us. One had slammed into the coast three hundred miles north of the company town two years ago, and we'd had waves forty feet high. The company evacuated us up to the station. I did not like to think how high the waves would get under the storm itself.

"We might have the help for company," Sam said. The help always left us at the start of hurricane season. They'd go south with us as long as we went south, but if we turned north, east, or west it was goodby for three months. We thought they probably went to the mesão to wait out the storms. Now we'd find out if that was true.

"I want to chance it," Sam said.

So did I. "Where are the help?" I asked. We needed them to carry stuff down to the raft.

"I shooed them out before I turned on the light," Sam said.

I hurried outside and looked around. I couldn't see any help, so I took down a sack of nicoji and scattered nicoji over the ground. The help immediately came out of the shadows. I let them eat, then Sam and I handed them our nets, fish trap, cooking gear, and clothes. They chittered off through the trees, happy to be going, happy we were going in the dark. And they'd be happy we were going south. They couldn't carry the heavy stuff—the plastic and the cans of liquid nitrogen and the waterproof chest—so Sam and I ended up carrying those and the medkit and guns. I wrapped my picture of Loryn in a scrap of plastic and put it in my pocket. Sam got the mirror and shower curtain from the bathroom. Normally we had to take everything with us when we left or expect it to be gone when we got back, so it didn't look odd for us to pack up everything we owned. Anybody who watched us would think we were just heading out again to catch nicoji, but with luck Sam and I were saying goodby to this place and that did not make me feel sad.

I took a plastic bag we'd gotten in Vattani's and walked behind the freeze-shack to pick a bagful of alma leaves. Alma was a pungent little plant Sam and I grew on the wood slats of the freeze-shack's back wall. The leaves were an almost-black dark green, as long and wide as my fingers. We always took a bagful with us into the pântano and dried them on the raft. The Brazis had convinced us to do this: they thought the leaves were rich in iron and vitamins. We'd crumple the dry leaves over our beans and rice; it gave them a kind of nutty taste. I felled the bag with alma leaves and turned to see what was left of the orchard we'd tried to grow.

The mango tree was still alive, waist high now. The company had given us a mango once at Christmastime, and we'd planted the seed. The apples were all dead. They'd been our biggest failure. The help loved to chew on the saplings. We couldn't stay up all night to make them stop, so we'd given up on apples. The two avocados were only as high as my head but their branches were touching, so I started to think maybe Sam was right and we'd planted them too close together. But we were Idaho farm boys—what did we know about avocados? The Brazis couldn't tell us how to plant them. They were city boys used to buying avocados in a feria, so Sam and I just stuck the seeds in the ground as far apart as looked right to us and hoped for the best. Now we might never know how they'd turn out.

The help had been "planting" again. I kicked eight tin cans and a frayed length of wire out of the dirt past the avocados. We couldn't keep such trash cleaned out of the garden. The help would put it right back. When we'd water or weed in the evenings, the help would pour water over their cans and sit and stare at them as if they expected something to happen. They just didn't believe, yet, that you first had to grow food from plants and then put it in cans.

Something was glittering in the little mango tree. I walked over to see what it was. The help had put pottery shards on all the branches. I wondered what kind of fruit they expected to grow from that, or whether this was part of some religious ritual with human trash.

The help had dumped our gear on the raft and were chittering in the trees. The raft's logs felt cool under my feet. Sam's and the helps' and my feet had worn the logs smooth, and we hardly ever got slivers anymore. The raft was longer than it was wide and held together with three-sided crosspieces driven through notches we'd cut top and bottom in the ends of each log. It was sturdy and not really tippy once you learned how to handle it. We set the two cans of liquid nitrogen towards the front of the raft for balance, since the back end was a little heavier, and packed everything else in our waterproof chest. I put my picture of Loryn in there.

Sam untied the raft and jumped on. I poled us out on the bayou. Sam grabbed his pole, careful of his sore wrist, and we were off. The help followed in the trees. After two minutes we could not see the lights of the company town, could hear only the regular thumping of the generator, and that, too, faded quickly. Red moonlight skittered on the water. Otherwise, the bayou was dark. The leaves of all the trees around us started rustling—the gravitational wind was blowing off the land, cool on the back of my head, in my hair. The tide was starting out. Sam and I were alone, again, in the pântano—Portuguese for *swamp*; that's all the Brazis had called it: swamp. So many Brazis had come up at first—before American Nicoji bought out Nicoji de Tocantins, the Brazilian corporation granted the original monopoly up here—that their names for places stuck. The maps in the company house showed tens of thousands of miles of pântano. It was so flat that even where we were, one hundred miles from the sea, when the moon pulled the tide in through the mass of vegetation, the water covered all the muddy land. We'd sleep on our raft tied to the top of a tree or in the trees themselves. The help would crowd with us on the platforms we made in the branches, not sleeping, since they slept in the day, but watching Sam and me while we slept.

The trees started shaking and a roar swept over us: a ship had taken off. We watched it climb into the sky, red-orange glares under its wings. Two help fell from the trees into the water. One grabbed my pole, and Sam pulled the other onto the raft. We lifted them back up to the branches. I could see the help with the hurt hand still up there—he'd hung on. His white bandage flashed through the trees ahead of us till dawn began to light the bayou and the help crept into the shadows to sleep. They'd catch up with us. They knew the route. We had no open water to cross for two days, so they didn't have to keep up. But when we came to open water, in the daylight, we'd have to bundle them up out of the light, put them on the raft with us, and pole them across to the next grove of trees.

Late in the afternoon, it started to rain. The help had come down to sleep on the raft, but now they sat up and peeked out from under the sacks they held over their heads and stuck their tongues out to catch the cool rain. It rained harder and harder, so Sam and I decided to find shelter and wait it out.

We poled our raft up against the roots of an old tree. The roots towered over our heads. We turned on our guns, listened to them hum for the three seconds it took them to warm up, then fired into the shadows under the roots. Nothing bellowed or splashed into the water, so we used the guns to burn through enough roots to let us pole the raft under the rest of them to the calm water against the trunk.

It was dark under the roots. Before Sam could pull the lights out of the chest, the help swarmed into the roots to look around. The help with the hurt hand came back and tugged on my shorts. "Got nothing here, Jake," he said. "Nothing."

"Fine," I said. Sam and I shined the lights around anyway. Some guys told stories about waking a sleeping scam of lagarto when they went under roots like this. Sam and I'd never had anything like that happen. A few times we'd heard something around the tree swim away from us. That was all.

So we sat there in the dark, shining our lights, making the help screech when we'd shine the lights in their eyes. The forest canopy above us and the roots let very little rain drip down. It thundered, and the sound of it boomed out across the pântano.

I started thinking about Alberto Goldstein, the Brazi Jew who got under a tree like this once and found a perfect Star of David growing in the bark. He took it for a sign that he was going home. He told us he didn't plan to stay in Brazil—he'd go to Israel, and after that, if he could manage it, to one of the Israeli stations in the asteroids. Nice as all of us goyim were, he said, he'd spend the next Passover with his people in Jerusalem.

He disappeared one month after that. He was working with two other Brazis. Cliff Morgan and Doug Jones found the Brazis' raft tied to the side of a tree below a platform they'd built. Up on the platform was all the Brazis' gear, packed in tidy piles, their guns laid out in the sun to recharge. No sign of the Brazis. No sign of a struggle. Cliff and Doug looked for them for two days and finally gave up, took their gear back to the company town, and gave it to the Brazis' friends.

I shined my light up the tree trunk. No Stars of David grew there. Just muddy, black bark. Sam took a nap, but I kept shining my light around, looking. Soon the rain lifted, and we floated the raft back out on the bayou. The help climbed up to the forest canopy and followed us along there, it was that dark under the rain clouds.

When the sun started down and the water began to rise, we were in the right place. We laid our poles across the raft and let the raft rise up among the empty boles of a great grove of mature trees. Only young trees had branches below the night waterline. Sam and I had a platform in an old tree thick with branches growing straight out across the water. Some teams got used to traveling at night, but Sam and I stuck to the day so we could see. We weren't sure enough of the things that hunted in the dark.

I tied our raft to the tree, and Sam and I climbed up to the platform, twenty feet above the water. Somebody had slept there since we'd last used it. They'd left the platform covered with leaves. The leaves had rotted in the rain, and ants were thick in the rot. I stepped out on the platform, but Sam pulled me back. "Booby-trapped," he said. He pointed to a branch on the outer edge of the platform. It was cut partway through.

"Who'd do this?" Sam asked.

I hung onto a branch and stomped on the log. It snapped and dropped into the water. Sam and I stomped on each log, and half of them broke in two.

"I didn't like this place anyway," I said.

"Who wants to sleep with ants?" Sam asked.

We dumped the rest of the logs in the water to get rid of the ants and built a new platform on the other side of the tree. Sam climbed to find the wide leaves we slept on. I let down our fish trap and pulled up one nicoji and a long slimy thing with eight stubby legs that flapped around in the trap till I threw it out. The nicoji surprised me, but only one came up so I decided no big colonies had moved in nearby. The third time I dropped the trap I brought up six sadfish. Sam and I laughed at their melancholy faces and ate them. By the time we finished washing our dishes and tying everything down on our raft, it had been dark for an hour.

Our help came chittering up through the trees. They leaned down from the branches to smell us, then scampered around the platform and the raft. I opened the waterproof chest, pulled out the bottle of gagga raisins, and gave some to the help. They loved the raisins.

Sam took out his glasses and flashlight and read a few pages from his one book, *Pilgrim's Progress*. He'd read that book five or six times—twice to me out loud. The wife of our first company inspector had given it to him. It had bored her. When we settled down to sleep—a flashlight in one hand to scare off the littler things that might crawl up after us, our guns strapped to our sides for the rest—the help settled down around us to watch.

In the night, something bellowed, far off, a hollow sound like a foghorn's, deep and huge. The help patted our faces to make sure we were awake, listening. They were terrified, but they made no sound. We heard nothing else unusual for half an hour, and

I was drifting off to sleep when it bellowed again, closer. Sam and I sat up. The help climbed quickly and silently into the branches. I occasionally saw pairs of their round eyes looking down at us. The help with the hurt hand inched down the tree to the water and rubbed mud and slime over his white bandage, to hide it. I thought we ought to take it off if he was going to do that, but he climbed up the other side of the tree and disappeared. We heard nothing else. Sam and I finally lay back down. I kept thinking of all the things we'd seen that the scientists had never seen, and of all the things we'd heard but never seen.

We got up in the dark when the wind started and the tide turned. The water hissed away through the trees. We were quiet then—night things were still out—and we had to be careful not to let our raft get tangled in branches below the nighttime waterline. Our raft had got caught, once, thirty feet above the mud, in a snag of dead and dying branches that hadn't yet fallen off the trunk of a young tree just starting to grow above the waterline. We foolishly tried to shove the raft free with our poles—and let the water drop farther and farther away below us till we could see mud. We couldn't cut the raft free, then. We were afraid the fall would break it apart. So we tied the raft to the tree trunk to keep it from floating away when the tide came back or from falling to the mud if the dead branches it was caught in broke away, grabbed our stuff, and spent the day in the part of the tree above the waterline. In the evening, when the water came up under the raft, we cut it free, floated it up on the tide, then over to a mature tree that wouldn't still have branches below the nighttime waterline.

But we didn't get caught this time. By dawn we'd almost dropped down, and in the light we felt safer. We set our guns in the light to recharge.

My hand with the locator felt stiff and sore. Sam kept rubbing his. I wondered what would happen after we'd gone as far south as we dared go with the locators on and we cut them out. I wondered how long it would take to get to the new company town. "Women, Sam," I said.

He smiled. "More than one, I hope," he said.

I laughed and remembered the "shore leave" the company'd sent us on when we were out one year. They'd flown us up to their station and given us a tiny room together. The fridge was stocked with fruit from home—apples, oranges, even a peach. We sat on the beds to eat the fruit, and someone knocked on the door. I opened it. A pretty girl stood there in a tatty white dress with a red sash around her middle, barefoot. "Oh, there are two of you," she said, and her face went red. The company was so cheap it had sent one girl for the two of us. We had her come in. She ate an apple, and we laughed for a while. "Well," she said when our conversation lagged. She smoothed out her dress and looked at us. I couldn't do anything. The girl was willing to take on both Sam and me—it was her job—but I was just a year away from Loryn, and Loryn had promised to be true to me, and I'd promised to be true to her. I'd even carried Loryn's picture up with me in my pocket. So I left the girl with Sam and went to the observation deck to watch clouds blow over the seas below us and to look at my picture of Loryn. "Yeah, women," I said to Sam.

I wondered what Loryn was doing now, and whether she was thinking of me.

*   *   *

We traveled south for a week to the nicoji colony Sam and I'd discovered on our last trip—the best we'd ever found. It was on a huge hummock rising seventeen feet out of the pântano—a mile square, Sam and I figured—and when the tide was out hundreds of thousands of tiny, black holes covered the mud below the trees, holes that marked where the nicoji burrowed down for the day. When the tide came in and covered most of the hummock, the nicoji swarmed out. Since only Sam and I knew about the colony, it hadn't been overharvested, and in three nights we'd catch more nicoji than our raft could carry south to the new company town, a decent catch that would pay our way.

We got to the hummock about midday, so Sam and I tied up the raft and lay down on our stomachs to sleep since we'd have to work hard all night. The help scampered out from under the sacks we'd covered them with and clambered up the trees to the shadows. On their way, some poked their hands down nicoji holes and tried to pull up a nicoji. The first few caught one or two—muddy and gasping in the air and light—and carried them up the trees to suck them clean, spit out the mud, and eat them. The rest had a harder time. The nicoji sensed the vibrations of the help walking on the mud and burrowed deeper and at angles from their original tunnels. The last help off the raft didn't catch any nicoji.

Toward evening, I woke up and then woke Sam. The water was rising and the wind was blowing. We floated up with the tide and poled our raft toward the center of the hummock to a place the water didn't cover—a dry place twenty feet square—and tied our raft to a tree on the shore. We'd dug three pits there that filled with water where we kept our nicoji alive in burlap sacks till we were ready to go.

Sam and I stripped down to our shorts and started stringing out our nets. The help came up through the trees, slowly, climbed down and chittered around behind us on the grass. It was worktime now, and that never made them happy.

"Fix net? Sam and Jake fix net?"

It was the help with the hurt hand. He was picking up sections of the net and inspecting it.

"Yes, we fix," I said, and then I laughed. I was talking like the help.

"You got hole here."

He held out a section of the net to me and, sure enough, he'd found a hole. I got our hemp from the raft and mended the tear.

When the sun was nearly down, the water around us started to boil: the nicoji were swarming to the surface to go after bugs that sailed on the surface tension. The nicoji never jumped out. They just stirred the water and sucked the bugs under. We watched the water carefully, and the help were watching it, trying to see if anything had swum in around the island hunting for something more substantial to eat than nicoji. The water looked fine. Sam and I took opposite ends of the net, our twelve help picked up the middle, and we waded into the water, mud squishing up through our toes.

The nicoji hardly swam away from us. Sam and I waded up to our chests in the water and the help swam bravely, holding their sections of net in their teeth and keeping it from getting tangled. When we started back for shore, dragging in the net, it got so heavy Sam and I couldn't pull it and we had to let some of the nicoji go. After we got the net on shore, the nicoji swarmed out and tried to crawl to the water, their tails arched high over their backs. Sam and I scrambled after them, filled two burlap sacks, and dropped the sacks in the pits. We broke the necks of all the nicoji sharks we saw to cut down on the competition. The help sat and shoved whole handfuls of nicoji in their mouths, gorging themselves contentedly.

The water looked fine. We watched the help, and they seemed willing to go again, so we went, this time on the other side of the island. By the time we'd dragged that net to the beach, dumped the nicoji in sacks, carried the sacks to the pits, and straightened out our nets, it had been dark for half an hour. Sam and I shone our lights across the water. The water bubbled away with the nicoji but nothing more, nothing bigger. We'd usually drag in two or three nets, then pole out the raft, watching and taking turns using a smaller net to catch nicoji. Wading through water in the dark was too dangerous. "Time for the raft," I said.

"But look at the nicoji," Sam said.

There were so many nicoji so easily taken.

"Let's get one more net," he said.

I nodded. If something came after us, it usually got tangled in the net while we climbed on the raft, or on shore, or up a tree. So we went. But this time we only waded out till the water came up to our bellies. The help swam past Sam. Sam and I started pulling in the net.

And the water stopped boiling. All the noise in the treetops quit, suddenly, as if the silence had been commanded.

Sam and I kept hold of the net—letting the nicoji

swim out underneath and above it but keeping the net between us and whatever had come hunting— and started walking backwards toward shore, slowly, disturbing the water as little as possible. I looked back but could see nothing on the shore or in the water behind us.

The help suddenly dropped the net, swam to me, and bunched up around my legs. They'd never done that before. We'd always held the net together till every one of us got on the raft or on shore. It was something new, then, out there.

"Sam—" I said.

Something dark rose out of the water in front of him.

"Run!"

Sam turned to run but the thing lashed out at him, and he screamed and fell in the water.

I stumbled to the raft for my gun and waded out after Sam. Sam was floundering in the water. I splashed up to him, and he hung on around my waist. "Its tongue's around my leg!" he yelled. I held my gun ready to shoot whatever had his leg, but I couldn't see anything. It was under the water. I started dragging Sam to shore, and it rose up, dark and huge. Lagarto. It was a lagarto with its hallucinatory poison on the needles in its tongue. It had been waiting for the poison to work before pulling Sam to its mouth and teeth. It roared and lunged for Sam's foot.

I shot the lagarto in the head. The light shaved off its forehead and snout, cauterizing the wound so there was no blood. It slumped down in the water, dead, but still holding Sam with its tongue. I pulled the light through the water to cut the tongue, sending up clouds of steam. The tongue snapped loose. Sam and I fell back.

I pulled Sam to the muddy shore, part of the tongue still wrapped around his leg. Sam sat up and tried to pull off the tongue, but I grabbed his hands. "Don't touch it!" I yelled. I wound a scrap of burlap around my right hand, tore off the tongue, and threw it in the water. Lagarto needles had punctured Sam sixteen times. Four had broken off in his skin. Red streaks ran up his leg already. I knelt in the mud, wrapped burlap around my fingers, and pulled out the four needles, then took Sam's pocketknife, cut his leg, and started sucking and spitting out blood and venom, fast, trying not to swallow anything. "Help us!" I called to the help, but not one would come near Sam and me.

Sam started hallucinating, pointing, mumbling something about a woman in white with a red sash around her waist and a leaking can of oil. I looked where he pointed and saw such a woman standing back in the huddle of help, but she wasn't holding an oilcan—she was holding a dog, and she wore red slippers, not a red sash. "You're wrong, Sam," I said. "She's got red *slippers* and a little dog, too." As soon as I said that, I realized what was happening, and I slapped my face and stumbled to the raft. I was hallucinating now; I'd swallowed some of the poison. But lagarto poison in my stomach would only make me sick and crazy, not kill me. I had to give Sam a shot of antibiotic and antivenin before I went out of it. By the time I found our medkit, Sam had crawled partway to the raft, knowing what he needed. I ripped open the kit and spilled the syringes and vials in the mud. My eyes weren't focusing. Our vials of medicine were held in a padded metal case, and I had to open it and look closely at each vial before I found one that read *Instituto de Butantã*, the antivenin center back in São Paulo that developed our medicines. I tore the plastic cap from a syringe, shoved the needle in the antivenin, and filled the syringe. I grabbed Sam's arm and stuck the needle in it—but my own arm stung and I realized I'd shot my own arm, so I pulled out the needle and pinched Sam's arm; mine didn't hurt so I knew I had Sam's. I gave him the shot. I wanted to give him another since I didn't know how much I'd shot in my arm, but I couldn't find the right vial again, and then the woman put down her dog and started walking towards me, smiling, holding out her hand—

I came to my senses just after dawn when I threw up. I could see it wasn't the first time Sam and I had vomited. I was holding Sam's head in my lap, patting his cheeks as if I were one of the help.

The help were gone, off to the shadows. Why had they run from the lagarto, I wondered? They'd seen Sam and me kill twenty lagarto. And why had they given no warning?

Sam's leg was swollen and red. He was sleeping deeply, sweating. I put down his head and staggered back to the raft after the cloth we kept for bandages, thinking I had to make some kind of bandage for Sam's leg. I remembered where the girl had stood, and I couldn't help looking for tracks. There were none. There were no dog tracks. But I looked at the mud flat where the water had been the night before and saw the carcass of the lagarto, partially eaten. Who knows what had crawled around Sam and me, feeding on that thing in the night?

When I found the cloth and started back for Sam, I heard a rustling in the tree above me and looked up. The help were all there, in the shadows. Help-with-the-hurt-hand climbed down the branches towards me, shading his eyes from the light.

"Sam die?" he asked.

"No. Sam's alive, barely."

I started off for Sam, but the help started cooing sadly, as if they were disappointed. I looked up again.

"You not get insur-nance then, Jake? You not go home?"

It took a minute for that to sink in. The help had all been in the freeze-shack when Raimundo talked to Sam and me about our insurance, and they must have understood that I'd get to go home if Sam died. Then I remembered Help-with-the-hurt-hand waking me up in the night to ask what I wanted most—and what I'd answered. "You bastards!" I yelled. I picked up a stick and threw it at them. They clambered higher in the branches, chittering confusedly. I kept throwing sticks, and they finally climbed into other trees and hid in the shadows.

I dumped alcohol over Sam's leg, and that woke him up. He swung his arm over his eyes to keep off the light. "Where is she?" he asked.

"In Kansas," I said. I smeared an antibacterial cream over Sam's leg and bandaged it. I'd have to keep changing the bandage and the cream, and I hoped I'd have enough of each to keep Sam going till I got him to a doctor. I picked our syringes and vials out of the mud, washed them off, gave Sam a shot of antibiotic, and put the medkit back on the raft. I dragged the raft down to the water and tied it to a tree, went back for our bags of nicoji and dumped them on the raft. When I went back for Sam, the help crawled into the tree above him, chittering.

"Where you go?" one called.

"*You* go to hell!" I shouted. But I thought about that and changed my mind. "No," I said. "Go back to the old company. You deserve it."

I knew they couldn't understand the irony of what I said, that they'd never understand my actions, but I didn't care. They'd slop across the mudflats to get off the hummock, then wander back to wherever it was they lived. When they got hungry enough they'd find some Brazi team to work for. The Brazis could have them. I dragged Sam onto the raft, untied it, and poled us out on the bayou, heading south.

III

I thought about the locators on our wrists sometime before noon when I threw up again. "Sam," I said, "we've got to cut these off."

Sam was awake then, lying on his back, one arm sprawled over his eyes to keep off the sun. "Cut what off?" he mumbled.

"The locators."

He moved his arm so he could see the locator on his right wrist. We'd already gone so far south we'd probably reached the limits of the company's patience. If we kept going, they'd come looking.

"These will quit transmitting when we cut them off—but they'll have a fix on our last position. They'll try to stop us, fast," Sam said.

"I know." I also knew what else Sam was saying: he'd not be much help to me while we tried to get to the new company.

And we couldn't turn around. Sam needed a doctor, and we were closer to the new company town. It would take longer to get back to the old. So we had to go on. I had to get Sam there. Which meant we had to cut out the locators. I couldn't trust the company to help Sam if we just kept going till someone came after us. I remembered Paulo Toscano, the guy whose partner had gotten so sick he didn't dare move him. Paulo'd seen a company helicopter flying over the pântano on a survey run, and he'd built a fire and called it over with the smoke, thinking they'd been saved. But the company boys made Paulo get in the helicopter and leave his partner—since he was nearly dead, they said, and wasting time or money on him was no use. The company bosses claimed such a thing had never happened, that Paulo's partner was already dead when their boys got to him. But Raimundo and I believed they'd left him to die. Paulo and his partner were making money and were probably going to be able to buy tickets home. Sam and I weren't making money, but I couldn't be sure the company would help Sam. Paying the medical bills of somebody seriously ill could cost more than bringing out a new guy from Earth. I did not want to wake up back in the company town, having been knocked out by one of their drugs, and realize they'd left Sam. So we had to cut out the locators.

I laid my pole across the end of the raft and grabbed our medkit and an old burlap sack. Sam took his pocketknife out of his shorts and pulled up a long, sharp blade.

"Let me do it," I said.

He shook his head.

"Look, I'll do it. My hands are steadier."

He handed me the knife. I cut off a long strip of burlap and wrapped it tight around Sam's forearm as a constriction band. I opened the medkit, tore off a chunk of cotton, and handed it to Sam. "Keep the blood wiped away so I can see."

He nodded and took the cotton.

I sat cross-legged, grabbed his hand, and put it on my left knee where he'd have something to hang onto while I cut open the back of his wrist. Skin had grown to the locator, like the doctor said it would. I looked at Sam. "This will hurt," I said.

He nodded. I stuck the knife blade in our bottle of alcohol, shook it off, then cut across the bottom of the locator and up the outside edge in two quick movements. Sam clenched his fingers into a fist, and the muscles in his whole body tightened. Blood oozed up through the cuts I'd made. Sam dabbed away the blood. I used the knife blade to pry back the locator, but it was hooked on: a thin clamp wound down around one of the bones. "Sam—"

"Just hurry it, Jake!"

I cut down after the clamp and scraped along the bone, trying to pry the clamp loose. "The locator's clamped to a bone," I said.

"Just get it off."

The doctor had said nothing about clamps. Sam was breathing hard, and his face was white. I thought he was going to pass out, which would have been good, considering what I was doing to him. But he kept dabbing up the blood. Blood ran across his wrist, over my knee, down my leg.

The clamp came loose. I bent it back, but the locator was still stuck in the skin. I cut along the top edge and wiped off the knife. Sam dabbed away his blood. Then I saw that the inside edge was next to the radial artery. If I cut that, not even the blood coagulator could stop the bleeding. Two weeks into the pântano was no place for a tourniquet. My hands started to shake.

Sam looked at me, hard. "Finish it, Jake."

I wiped off the knife and cut. Sam dabbed away the blood, both of us breathing hard. The locator dropped off. I had not cut the artery. I threw the locator in the water.

Sam sat looking at his wrist. The locator had left a bloody wound an inch square. It bled, bad, even with the constriction band.

"I've got to disinfect it," I said.

Sam nodded and wiped the sweat off his forehead with his other hand. We had only alcohol, so I dumped some on a clean piece of cotton and started dabbing it where the locator had been. Sam sucked in his breath and held it. I took off the constriction band, pressed fresh cotton against the wound, and had Sam put pressure on it while I took the can of coagulator from the medkit and shook it. "Take off the cotton," I said.

Sam pulled back the cotton and blood flowed out across his wrist. I sprayed it. The blood bubbled, turned black, and hardened. Sam lay back on the raft and closed his eyes.

"You OK?" I asked. He didn't answer. I tied a pressure bandage tight on his wrist. Sam and I looked at each other. "That's one," I said.

Sam nodded.

"I don't think I can do my own."

"I'm right-handed," Sam said. I'd cut the locator out of his right wrist. He wouldn't be able to use the hand. "I'll try to do it left-handed."

"You just keep the blood wiped away," I said. I hadn't meant for him to volunteer. I didn't want him digging left-handed in my wrist when he was sick. If somebody had to do a left-handed operation, it would be me.

Sam sat up and helped me tie a burlap strip around

my arm. I grabbed my right knee with my right hand, hunched down, and cut the skin along two sides of the locator. My hand shook so bad I had to stop and hold my wrist and close my eyes. Sam tore off a chunk of cotton and tried to dab up the blood. I pushed his hand away and cut the skin along the other two sides of the locator, then sliced down through the muscle, following one side of the clamp, afraid of cutting an artery. I could see one of my arteries. I could see my blood pumping through it. I pried the clamp loose from the bone, pulled the locator out of my wrist, and threw it in the water. Something dark flashed up from the muddy shallows, swallowed the locator, and sank out of sight behind us. My knee was white, I'd held it so hard. I had bruises on it for days where my fingers had been.

"You look bad," Sam said. He grabbed the bottle of alcohol, thinking he'd at least disinfect the wound for me, but when he went to pour the alcohol on a clean piece of cotton he splashed alcohol across my wrist by accident. I stood up and sat back down and stood up again, holding my wrist. Sam started coming at me with the cotton, anyway. "That's enough!" I said. I sprayed the wound with the blood coagulator, tore off the constriction band, and had Sam help me tie a pressure bandage on my wrist. I put the medkit back in the chest, and, one-handed, poled us out on the bayou and away from there, as fast as I could.

By night, Sam was hallucinating again. I'd given him all the antivenin I dared, and I'd given us both shots of antibiotics after I cut out the locators. But he wasn't doing well. I let the raft drift up among the trees while the water rose, and I tied the raft to the trunk of a big tree. My walking around the raft started Sam babbling.

"Maria!" he shouted. He pointed at the water and tried to stand up, but he couldn't put any weight on his sore leg. I held him back so he wouldn't fall in the water.

"Let me go, Jake. It's got Maria."

"Maria's in the company town, not here, Sam."

"It's got her! She's drowning."

"You saved her already. She's not drowning. Look at the water: it's calm."

He held onto my arms, breathing hard, blinking at the water. All at once he let go and lay back on the logs, looked at me and kept breathing hard.

Sam had saved Maria Vattani. One afternoon, we'd heard Marcos and Fabio shouting for help. We ran down the street to the bayou. The two boys were on the rocks where Senhora Vattani washed clothes, pointing and shouting. Senhora Vattani was in the water. "Maria!" she screamed. Maria was her eight-year-old daughter. Sam got to the edge of the rock first and jumped in the water.

I jumped in, too, but Senhora Vattani was floundering. I pulled her to the side. Marcos and Fabio grabbed her arms. Then Sam broke out of the water, with Maria. He shoved her on the rock and started giving her mouth-to-mouth resuscitation. Senhora Vattani pushed him away and gave Maria mouth-to-mouth herself. Maria coughed and threw up and started crying. Senhora Vattani picked her up and ran for the company house to call down the doctor on a shuttle.

Sam turned me around. "Look," he said. Something black had risen to the surface, dead. The boys pulled it out. It was long and thin, with a big mouth and no teeth. "It had Maria," Sam said.

Sam was holding his leg. Blood oozed out from between his fingers. "Maria stabbed my leg with her stick doll's arm," he said. "I had to take the doll and stab this thing's eyes before it would let Maria go."

I patted Sam on the back. He didn't own a pocket-knife, then. Sam started dragging the creature to the company house. I helped Fabio and Marcos off the rocks and gathered up Senhora Vattani's clothes so the tide wouldn't take them.

The other teams in town crowded around the steps of the company house, and officials came out and took pictures because the creature was new.

"It hasn't been named," one official said. "You can name it, Sam."

"Maria should name it," he said.

When the doctor got down from the station, he decided Maria was fine, just scared, and he came out to disinfect Sam's leg. Senhora Vattani carried Maria out to name the thing lying in the street. Maria wouldn't look at it, but when her father told her she'd be famous for naming it, that that animal would be called by her name forever, she looked at it and called it an afogador, Portuguese for "drowner." Fabio and Marcos kicked it and beat it with sticks till one of the company boys grabbed its tail and dragged it to the trashheap. "It's starting to stink," he said.

An official came out with a recorder and had Sam make a deposition for the company history. Everybody stood around and listened to Sam tell his story and laughed when he said he had to stab the afogodor's eyes with the arm of Maria's stick doll. When the story was told, Senhora Vattani picked up Maria, had Marcos and Fabio carry her wash, and hurried away. We thought she had gone home.

But she called to Sam from her husband's store when we walked past. She came out and handed

Sam one of her husband's best pocketknives, with a
V carved in the handle. Senhor Vattani did not argue
about it.

Sam had his right arm over his eyes and was
breathing hard. I went to the other end of the raft,
kicked the little fish trap over the side to see what it
would bring up for supper, and started looking around
through the dark trees. I did not like staying all night
on the raft. A hundred things could come up under
the raft after us. I checked the LED display on my
gun. The gun was three-quarters charged.

I wasn't going to get much sleep.

And I started missing the help. They'd watch Sam
and me all night with their sharp little eyes and wake
us up if something was coming. I wondered where
they'd gone. Home, probably. Maybe to the mesão
to wait out the hurricane season.

The trap was still empty. I untied a sack of nicoji,
stuck two nicoji in the trap, and dumped the trap in
the water again. After a while, the line started moving. I pulled in the trap. "Paulistas, Sam," I said.
There were four Paulistas: ugly little fish somebody
from Rio must have named. They cooked up in a
hurry. I put them in a clay bowl, sprinkled salt over
them, and walked back to Sam. He ate one of the
Paulistas, and I got him to eat a couple of fried
nicoji, too, but then he absolutely would not eat
anything else. I dropped a water-purification tablet
in a bowl of water and waited while it fizzed and
disinfected the water and condensed out the salt and
dirt in granules along the bottom of the bowl. The
granules looked like snow falling in a snow-dome
someone had shook up and was letting settle. I had
to be careful to pour off just water when I poured the
water into another bowl. I made Sam take a drink.

After that he went to sleep, holding his wrist where I'd cut out the locator.

I sat down and tried to eat, but after two bites of fish I had to lean over the side of the raft and throw up. I wanted to abandon supper as hopeless, but I'd made Sam eat, and I knew I had to keep up my strength, and I couldn't allow myself to get dehydrated. I took another bite of fish and drank some purified water, then closed my eyes and took deep breaths till I knew I wasn't going to throw up. It took time to work lagarto poison out of your system, to get your stomach to accept food again. But I would probably feel better in the morning. I looked at Sam.

The embers in our tin firebox started smoking, so I dumped them in the water. I scraped the extra food over the side and let it drift away so it wouldn't attract things to our raft. Then I stood and looked at the sacks of nicoji. The nicoji would attract anything hungry, but we had to keep them. Sam and I might need to eat the nicoji, and we'd definitely need the money they'd bring us in the new town.

I sat for an hour watching Sam sleep and watching the trees and water. I kept hearing a soft cooing in the tree next to us. Then I heard a coo above my head, in a deeper tone. I shined the light above me and saw fruit hanging on the branches here and there, round and green with a red band at the bottom. They looked like Christmas tree ornaments. I stood up to look at one more closely, and when I touched it, it cooed. This tree evidently attracted seed scatterers with sound, not sight or smell. I wanted to try eating the fruit. I thought one with the deepest coo would be the most ripe, so I listened for the lowest coo and picked that fruit. It was so ripe the juice squoze onto my fingers. But when I bit into it, it tasted bitter, sharp. I spit out the pulp and threw the fruit in the water. But all night I could listen to the fruit coo.

The raft kept drifting back and forth between the branches. When I started to get sleepy I walked around for a while, but that disturbed Sam. I started pulling myself into the tree and letting myself back down, softly, trying to stay awake. Once I climbed as high as I could go and looked out across the pântano. Treetops stretched away around me in all directions and looked almost flat from where I sat, as if they'd been trimmed, black in the red moonlight. Far off, south, I could see the mesão.

Before dawn, when the water started hissing away through the trees, Sam woke up. "Jake," he whispered.

I crawled over next to him. "Yeah," I whispered back.

"Thanks," he said. He had a hard time keeping his eyes open. "Thanks for getting me away from that lagarto. I thought it was going to bite off my feet. You'd have had to shoot me, then."

I just looked at him. He was in his right mind.

"Slap me around if you need to. Make me behave."

"I've been slapping you around—you just don't remember."

He smiled and held up his left hand. I grabbed it with my left hand—our right hands were too sore. But his hand went limp. He'd drifted off again. I untied our raft and let it drift down with the water.

I'd stayed awake all night, but I couldn't rest till I got Sam to the mesão. After I guided us into the middle of a wide bayou flowing south and the water had dropped down as far as it was going to, I realized

I was hungry. A good sign, I thought. I laid my pole across the end of the raft, set our guns in the light to recharge, then built a fire in the firebox and put the wire mesh grill over the top. I walked back by Sam and opened a sack of nicoji. Most were still crawling around, but I saw three dead ones. I threw out the dead nicoji, then held the sacks over the edge of the raft to let the nicoji get wet to keep them alive longer. I picked out ten lively ones; cut off their heads, legs, and tails; gutted them; and put them on the grill. Then I opened the chest and got out the bowls. Sam opened his eyes when he smelled the nicoji cooking. Another good sign, I thought. When the nicoji were done, I put them in a bowl, salted them, and turned around to carry them back to Sam. "Breakfast," I said, and stopped.

Sam had one of the guns.

"Put it down," I said. I set the bowl of nicoji on the logs.

"I'm going to throw away the guns, Jake. We might accidentally kill something with them."

He had the other gun in his lap.

"You're out of your mind, Sam," I said, but I knew he was actually dredging up religious stuff he'd learned years ago. I didn't know what I'd do if he threw the guns in the water and ruined them. We'd be lunch for whatever carnivore decided we looked tasty, and the raft would serve us up like a platter.

"We shouldn't kill," Sam said.

"Where would you be if I hadn't killed the lagarto that tried to eat you?"

"That's not the point. Life is important, all life."

"Right. So my life is important, Sam, and so is yours. We won't keep them very long without the guns."

He held the gun in his hands over the water.

"Jake, believe me in this," he said. "Don't hate me after it's done. Try to understand why it's necessary."

I wanted to rush him, save at least the gun in his lap, but I thought if I kept him talking I might be able to walk up to him step by step and save both guns. I took one step forward. "What about the roots?" I said. "What about when it's raining, and we want to get out of the rain under the roots? If you throw away the guns, we won't be able to cut our way under anymore. We'll have to sit in the rain."

He frowned and thought for a minute, but finally looked at me as if I were stupid. "The roots are alive, Jake. The trees are alive. Why do you want to hurt them?"

I took two steps toward Sam, but he put the butt end of the gun in the water and grabbed the second gun, ready to throw it. I stopped, fast.

"What about the dead trees that clog up the bayous?" I said, trying to keep him concentrating on my words, on reasons for keeping the guns. "What if I can't cut through the snags? The raft would be trapped behind them. We'd be trapped here forever."

"The tide would lift us up past the snags at night."

"We can't travel at night."

He sat thinking about that, holding the butt of the gun in the water.

"You know the water's too deep at night, Sam. I couldn't pole us along. We have to travel in the daytime, and in the daytime we face snags in the bayous. I'm not killing anything if I'm just cutting through a snag so we can pass by."

"We could make paddles and use them at night."

"You can't help me paddle, and I can't paddle the raft from just one side. We'd go in circles." Besides, he was forgetting how dangerous it was to travel at night. I took another step toward him.

"Jake," he said, warning me. But he'd thought of no answer to refute me.

"What if we have to repair this raft—or build a new one if this one gets wrecked?" I said. "How would we cut down the trees to get logs?"

"I wouldn't want you to cut down trees."

"Dead trees, Sam. I'd only cut down dead trees for logs."

He put the guns back in his lap and held onto them. "Are you saying you won't kill living things anymore, Jake? If you are, it wouldn't be bad, I suppose, to keep the guns to cut through snags or build rafts out of dead trees."

I ran to him and jerked the guns from his hands. "You're out of your mind," I said. He tried to grab the guns, but I shoved him down and strapped both guns around my waist. "You're sick, Sam. What if you change your mind in two minutes and decide you've been spiritually commissioned to kill all lagarto in the pântano? Would you mistake me for a lagarto and burn off my head?"

"Don't be stupid."

"You're sick."

"We've killed too many animals, Jake. If we had the faith of Buddha, we'd throw ourselves to the lagarto so the lagarto might live."

"Neither of us is a Buddha, Sam." Sam used to claim he wished he'd been born Japanese or Mongolian so he could understand the universe and not have a crippled Western mind. I'd gone with him once to a Zen temple in Idaho Falls. José Melendez, a wrinkled Mexican with a Fu Manchu mustache, met us at the door and bowed, had us sit on red mashed-down pillows, poured us tea in tiny cups, and tried to act movie-oriental. Sam donated six dollars to the temple, and José looked at me as if he expected me to donate something, too. I just poured myself more tea. The phone rang, and José went to answer it. Sam jabbed me in the ribs and told me no one ever pours his own tea and that I had to give José some money or he wouldn't give us a lecture. When José came back, I handed him three bucks which was more than I thought any lecture of his would be worth. José shoved the money in his pocket and started lecturing Sam and me in bad English on patience and the necessity of drawing on one's inner resources in times of both calm and trouble. He talked for about three minutes. Then he had us carry our pillows to a back room and sit facing a bare, white wall. "Sit aquí till you feel pacífico, at peace," he said, and he left. I sat still for eight minutes then looked at Sam and started laughing. Sam didn't laugh, and he didn't smile. "You're not taking this seriously, are you?" I asked. No answer. Sam just faced the wall and sat very still. My legs went to sleep after half an hour, and I had to kneel down. Then I put my legs straight out in front of me. Finally I stood up. "Enough peace," I said. "Let's get out of here." He wouldn't go. "See you later," I said. I carried my pillow to the reception room and told José adiós. Sam faced the wall for six hours and claimed that once I'd left he'd had a spiritual experience.

If he'd ruined the guns, he'd have given both of us the ultimate in spiritual experiences. We'd have gotten to see what the life after this one was like.

I got the bowl of nicoji and took it to Sam.

"I don't want to eat," Sam said. "You killed those nicoji."

"We don't have anything else to eat but gagga raisins; and besides, you're mixing Hinduism with Mexican Buddhism. It won't work."

"I'll throw up."

"You have to eat. How do you expect to get better?" I tore a nicoji apart and shoved some meat in his mouth. He swallowed and kept it down. I made him eat two more nicoji while he lay there on his back, but after he swallowed the last bite he leaned over and threw up on the logs. I sat back and looked at Sam. His stomach was red, it had contracted so hard, and his leg was swollen. I got an old piece of burlap from the chest and scrubbed the raft clean. When I finished, I pulled two more nicoji off the grill.

"Try again, Sam," I said. "Fight to keep it down this time."

But he wouldn't eat more nicoji. "I *am* sick, Jake," he said.

He wouldn't eat any gagga raisins or drink any water.

"You have to drink water," I said. "You can't get dehydrated." I helped him sit up and drink from a bowl of water I'd put a water-purification tablet in, but he threw up as soon as he finished. He lay back down and looked at me. I felt his forehead, and it was hot.

"Damn it, Sam, you've got a fever." I pulled the thermometer from the medkit and shoved it in his mouth. After a minute I took it out. It read 102.8.

The raft was drifting toward the east shore. I took my pole and shoved us back into the current. As we rounded the bend, we drifted through a cloud of tiny, black insects that swarmed all over us. Ovandos, the Brazis called them, short for flying eggs—a misnomer: the ovandos weren't adult insects ready to lay eggs; they were larvae frantic to pupate. I had to spit one out of my mouth, and Sam sneezed twice and rubbed his eyes. "Hold your nose, Sam!" I yelled. Seven or eight ovandos flew in my mouth. I spat them out, dropped down on the edge of the raft, fished a handful of moss from the bayou, wrung it out, and tossed it on the coals in the firebox. I sat next to the firebox waiting for the smoke and smashing as many ovandos as I could. Ovandos burrow into a living host's flesh through open wounds where they pupate into adult eating machines that can chew through tendon and bone. I once saw a Brazi whose hand was being eaten away by ovandos. Black trails of digested flesh covered the hand below the skin. The doctor couldn't kill the ovandos. He had to cut off the hand. But then he discovered ovandos in the Brazi's arm, and the doctor had had to cut off sections of the arm, inch by inch, till he was certain he'd cut above the ovandos.

The moss started smoking. I picked up the firebox and walked around the raft. The smoke drove most of the ovandos upriver. I swept off three crawling over the bandage on Sam's wrist, then smashed them, and unwrapped the bandage to make sure none had gotten in the wound. Sam looked at me when I started to wrap his wrist again. "None got through," I said.

He grabbed my arm. "Give me the peanut butter," he said. "I could eat that and keep it down."

I finished tying his bandage and looked at him. "We finished the peanut butter two weeks ago—back in the company town."

He let go of my arm and looked at me. "You've eaten more of it than I have, Jake, so I should get what's left."

"It's gone, Sam!" I pulled handfuls of moss from the bayou and laid the moss on the logs in case we drifted through another swarm of ovandos.

Sam stared at me the whole time. "I'd feel better if I had some peanut butter," he said.

I laughed. "So would I. If we had some, I'd give it to you." I arranged the two cans of liquid nitrogen and the sacks of nicoji around Sam's head, ripped open an empty burlap sack, and draped it over the sacks and cans so Sam's head would be out of the sun. It made a little cave two feet high. I took a scrap of burlap, wet it, folded it, and put it over Sam's forehead. "Keep this wet," I said. "It'll make you feel better."

"Just give me the peanut butter."

"Sam!"

"I paid for half of it."

"We've got no peanut butter on this raft."

"I've seen you get the can out of the chest and eat the peanut butter with your fingers. You thought I was asleep. I wasn't, Jake." He looked at me with an expression of triumph on his face.

I dragged the chest up next to him. "Eat any peanut butter you find in here," I said.

"Oh, so you hid it somewhere else." He wouldn't look in the chest.

"Where else would I hide it? We're on the raft, Sam."

He just looked away, out across the water. "Please, Jake," he said.

With his fever and the poison making him crazy, I didn't know if Sam would know peanut butter if he had it. I looked at our jar of gagga raisins. Why not? I thought. I mashed some raisins in a little water in a bowl so they'd have more of the consistency of peanut butter and handed Sam the bowl. "You win, Sam," I said. "Here's the peanut butter."

He put a spoonful of the gagga paste in his mouth and swallowed it. "Thanks, Jake," he said. "If I'm ever taking care of you, you'll only ask once for whatever you want."

I started to say "Go to hell, Sam," but I looked at him eating his raisin paste. I will not get angry, I thought. He's sick. I picked up my pole and started shoving the raft downstream. Sam kept eating the raisin paste. Suddenly he grabbed the side of the raft and threw up in the water. His vomit drifted away behind us. He'd knocked the clay bowl into the water and he tried to grab it out, but it sank. Sam washed off his face, lay back, and rubbed his eyes.

"You OK?"

He nodded. The fork was still on the raft, down between two logs. I picked it up, swished it through the water to clean off the gagga paste, and put it back in the chest.

"I'm sorry, Jake."

"Don't be sorry about getting sick."

"You gave me the last of the peanut butter, and now it's gone."

"Don't worry about it."

"I should have let you keep sneaking it out of the chest; at least it would have done somebody some good."

I kicked the chest into the center of the raft and wet Sam's scrap of burlap again. "Keep this wet, huh?"

He nodded. He could reach the water just behind his head over the side of the raft. Twice that day he wet the burlap. I had to freshen it for him the six or eight other times I thought of it.

I poled us down the bayou for half an hour, then threw out the rest of the cooked nicoji, afraid the ovandos had burrowed into them, sat down by the firebox, cooked three more nicoji, and made myself eat them and drink some water. I felt well enough after that to realize I was dirty. We had soap, but there was no time for bathing. I started poling us south down the bayou as fast as I could.

Before noon, I gave Sam another shot of antibiotic. He looked at me when I shoved the needle in his arm, but that was all. He closed his eyes again and was probably asleep. Just as I pulled the needle out of his arm, I saw floating lagarto dung drift past the raft, and I knew a scam of lagarto had to be close by. I hoped they had eaten well the night before. "Wake up, Sam," I said. I dropped the syringe in the medkit, pulled my gun out of the chest, and checked the LED display. The gun was at full power.

"Sam," I said. I didn't see any lagarto, yet. Lagarto could lash out across the raft with their tongues and pull things off—including Sam and me—or grab the logs with their teeth and tear the raft apart. "We've got trouble, Sam." Sam didn't stir. I let the raft drift with the current and knelt down, watching the water and the roots on both banks. Nothing. The heat above the water made the air shimmer. "Sam," I said. I shook his good leg.

And saw a lagarto. It was under the roots of a rotting tree on the west shore. I could see only its eyes and the top of its head, but the eyes were open and looking at me. I slowly lifted my gun and aimed it at a spot between the eyes—but before I could fire, the lagarto sank down in the water and disappeared. Only ripples were left fanning out in rings from the spot where the lagarto had been. I fired anyway, and the water exploded under the roots and shot up in clouds of steam, but I didn't hit the lagarto. Roots splashed into the water and bobbed there.

"Sam!" I said. "Wake up!" We'd drifted straight across from where the lagarto had been. I didn't know where that lagarto was. The Brazis told stories of lagarto big enough to come up under a raft and knock it over.

The raft drifted under shadows, and I looked up. The trees had grown together over the top of the bayou, and the leaves and branches thirty feet up shaded us and cooled the air. I sat very still while my eyes adjusted. Something bumped the bottom of the raft, gently. It bumped it again, under my feet. I aimed the gun down between the logs and considered shooting, but didn't. I'd break the raft apart.

Then I saw lagarto in the roots around me, on both sides of the raft, swimming out toward us.

"Sam!" I yelled. I shot and killed a lagarto coming from the east. It slumped down in the water and turned belly up. I shot one coming from the west but must have hit only its leg. It bellowed and lashed out with its tongue but backed off.

Something hit the bottom of the raft, hard, and knocked me sprawling. I held onto the gun and sat up as a lagarto rose out of the water behind us, lunged over the back of the raft, wrapped its tongue around a can of liquid nitrogen, and pulled it under the water. Sam sat up so fast the burlap sack covered his face. He pulled off the sack and crawled forward.

Liquid nitrogen suddenly burst out of the water and seethed on the surface. The lagarto had bitten the can. It rose to the top and thrashed in the water behind us. The can was frozen in its mouth. The entire face of the lagarto and its throat and lungs must have been frozen. I tried to shoot the lagarto, to put it out of its misery, but I missed and it sank in the water before I could shoot again.

The lagarto I'd shot in the leg swam back and grabbed the side of the raft in its teeth and started shaking it up and down, knocking off the sacks of nicoji and my pole and the chest and knocking me onto my stomach. I dropped the gun and it slid toward the water, but I grabbed it and shot the lagarto in the head. I shot it again and again and hit the outside log and scattered sparks over the water. The lagarto stopped shaking the raft and looked at me while its eyes glazed over and its jaws tightened— dead, but locked on the raft.

Great, I thought. Why couldn't it have let go of the raft?

Then I saw the medkit. I'd left it open by the chest, and vials and bandages and sterile syringes lay scattered all over the raft and on the water. I scooped a handful of syringes and the blood coagulator out of the water and found the medkit itself and shook the water out of it and started putting everything back in—at the same time trying to watch for lagarto. I found the bottle of water-purification tablets and the thermometer and the bandages and sun screen and tape and alcohol and the half empty jar of antibacterial cream.

But I didn't find the little metal case that held the antibiotics and the antivenin.

I pulled the chest onto the raft, and my pole, and hooked the two sacks of nicoji and pulled them over to the raft and dragged them back on. The nicoji were squirming in the sacks.

But I couldn't see any vials of medicine, or the eye drops, or the scissors. There was nothing else on the water. I pulled open the medkit and looked inside again, but the medicines were gone. The antibiotics were gone.

I turned the chest right side up and opened it and pulled out a light and shone it under the roots all around us but I couldn't see the medicines.

The dead lagarto's hind legs snagged roots on the

west bank and swung the raft around. We slammed
into the roots. The burned lagarto smelled like fish
thrown in a hot dumpster and left to rot for five days.
I grabbed my pole and beat on the lagarto's head and
pried up on its mouth till it broke loose and slumped
down in the water. Then I poled us back up the
bayou to where we'd been attacked. I saw no more
lagarto. The water was quiet.

And I saw no medicines. The metal case had sunk
with our antibiotics and antivenin. Why hadn't I put
the medkit back in the chest when I'd taken out my
gun? No, I didn't have time to pack things neatly
before every lagarto attack, but I should have paid
attention to the medkit. Sam needed the medicines.

"There's two more lagarto!" Sam said, pointing.

I spun around, but only our raft floated on the
surface of the bayou.

"They'll come up under the raft!" he said, and that
was a possibility—one we could do nothing about.

"Let's get rid of the nicoji," Sam said.

"No," I said. "A lagarto will come for us as fast as
it will for the nicoji." I watched the water and held
my gun ready and looked for the little medicine case.
Eight scarlet borboletas fluttered out from under the
roots of a tree and circled up the trunk into the
leaves, but no lagarto came out. It had either been a
small scam or most of the lagarto had eaten well and
preferred sleeping to eating Sam and me.

I wiped off the thermometer and shoved it in
Sam's mouth. His temperature had climbed to 103.4.
I purified some water and made him drink it, and he
kept it down.

"Why did the Brazis call those things lagarto?"
Sam asked.

"Who knows what they've mutated on the Ama-
zon," I said. For an hour I poled us around the spot

where we'd been attacked, looking for the medicine. I cut down the roots and poled us up against the trees, hoping to find the case of medicines floating, somewhere, thinking that since the bottles of medicine had a little air in them they'd keep the metal case floating. But I didn't see it. It had sunk. I finally gave up and started poling us down the bayou again. Now, faster than ever, I had to get Sam to doctors in the new company town.

In the late afternoon, I tied the raft to the tallest tree I could find and climbed up to get a bearing on the mesão.

It was still far away. At least two days.

Something was flying over the treetops a mile north of us, weaving back and forth across the pântano. I watched it till I could hear the regular thump of its rotors: a helicopter. The company was looking for us. I considered building a fire and letting the smoke bring them to us so they could maybe take Sam back to the doctor, but I decided against it. I remembered Paulo Toscano.

I climbed back down, turned on my gun, and burned through the roots in front of the raft so I could get it under the roots and hide it. Nothing came charging out. Nothing splashed into the water under the tree. I poled the raft into the hole I'd made in the roots and shined a light around. It was dark under the tree and dripping with muddy water. That was all. I saw nothing alive there—no lagarto—so I poled the raft in. If the help had been with me, they'd have rushed up into the roots and explored the whole root system in two minutes, told me if there was anything to worry about. I just kept shining the light around and listened to the helicopter pass us by, following the twistings of a bayou a quarter of a mile east.

A big drop of water hit the back of my neck and ran down my spine. I shivered and hunched my shoulders so my shirt would soak up the water.

"Don't leave me, Jake."

Sam was awake. I crawled over to him.

"I'd die, Jake. The help wouldn't stay with me."

The help aren't here, I thought, and I missed them for the third time. "I'm not leaving," I said. Sam's eyes were closed, and he was breathing hard. "You OK?" I asked.

"Don't leave me," he said.

"I'm staying right here. I'm not leaving."

He tried to open his eyes and look around. "Jake?"

"I'm here, Sam."

"We can't ever go back."

"Maybe not." I didn't like thinking about the punishments the company would devise for us after we'd tried to defect, but we'd face them if we had to.

"Don't leave me."

I grabbed his arm so he'd know I was there. "I'm right here," I said. "I'm sticking by you."

"Promise me."

"I promise, Sam. I won't leave."

He seemed to go to sleep then, fast. He was not doing well at all. This can't be happening, I thought. Not to Sam.

I'd heard stories of men who, for one reason or another, couldn't go on, men who'd quit working and simply disappeared. Some had supposedly wandered across the hundreds and hundreds of miles of pântano to the mountains that rose up on the western edge of the continent. I hadn't believed those stories. I'd thought they were simply accounts of what men wished they'd done. If they were all true, more men than the company had ever brought up had gone AWOL.

But one morning a year ago, Sam and I smelled smoke. We were afraid another team had followed us to spy out our nicoji holes, so we went to investigate. We found a little hummock that rose up above the night waterline, and on it someone had built a fire. The embers were still smoking. The grass was trampled around the fire, and we could see where at least two men had slept in the grass. On one side of the fire, the grass had been torn out of the ground, and someone had made a stick arrow and laid it on the bare dirt, pointing west. That arrow could have meant anything—one team trying to tell another the way they'd gone, two guys leaving behind a record of their passage, maybe just a joke.

Then I kicked a hatchet out of the grass.

The hatchet was made of chipped stone and fire-hardened wood tied together with a gut string dried from some animal's intestines. The stone was a metamorphosed sedimentary rock—a form of quartzite—not the porous igneous rock common in the pântano. We had no idea where such rock could have come from, and we'd never seen other teams with homemade stone tools or heard of anybody making them. I'd wondered ever since if some guys had, in fact, gone AWOL and wandered far enough west to find metamorphic rock.

Something bumped the side of the raft, and I shined my light on it. A boot. Chewed. I pulled it out of the water—but threw it right back.

The bones of a rotted foot were still in it.

I tried to shove us out on the bayou, fast, but I got the raft caught in the roots. I couldn't hear the helicopter, and I hoped it was gone. But if not, and if I had to get us under a tree again, it would be under a different tree.

I started cutting down roots with my gun so I could free the raft. Bits of human trash were caught here and there in the roots: scraps of rubber raft, a sleeve from a blue raincoat.

We were where the naturalists from Duke had been killed. That was all I could think. All it could be since none of our guys had boots like the one I'd picked up. The naturalists had come to get help specimens—they needed females, had plenty of males—but they'd been attacked by forty lagarto. Six naturalists got eaten and the rest climbed trees, but they'd lost everything—radio, food, guns. They'd left the captured help screaming in cages on the rafts, and the naturalists watched while lagarto tore the cages apart and ate the help. The lagarto then camped under the trees the naturalists were in, wallowing in the mud by day, swimming through the water at night, waiting for the naturalists to fall.

It took the company a week to find them. Only five guys were left. Duke sued, said the company should have prepared them more, protected them more, found them sooner. After that, American Nicoji wouldn't bring up any more naturalists. If the labs needed help, the company would send them, they said, but on their own ships, using their own people, so nobody'd get hurt and there'd be no chance of lawsuits. Besides, they insisted, the scientists should be able to determine whether the help were sentient or not using the specimens they already had. How many hundreds did they need?

American Nicoji had sent its helicopters to kill all the lagarto in the area where the naturalists had been attacked. Nobody wanted lagarto with a taste for human flesh.

But the lagarto had come back to this area, and I was scared. I couldn't drive off forty lagarto. I'd have a hard time getting Sam into a tree if I had to. I wanted to get away—get as far south as we could go.

I cut the raft free, pulled the roots off the front of it, and started to pole it out on the bayou. As we floated out I saw, caught in the roots above my head, a muddy clump of blonde, human hair. I knew it was human. The bottom end was still braided and held together by a white, plastic clasp.

IV

I poled us south, fast, all the rest of that day, and saw no more lagarto. I was so busy watching everything around us that not till the wind began blowing and the water started rising did I notice Sam was worse. I lifted him by the shoulders and shook him. "Wake up!" I said. He opened his eyes and looked at me, but his eyelids closed and his head fell back. I laid him down. I didn't know what to do. He'd slept all afternoon, and I'd thought that was good so I hadn't tried to wake him to make him drink water or eat. Now he couldn't wake up. His fever had climbed to 104.1. I thought he might be slipping into a coma. Lagarto poison did that, before it killed people, if so much poison got in their systems that safe doses of antivenin couldn't counteract it. And he needed antibiotics, and I didn't have any to give him. Why hadn't I put the medkit in the chest?

This can't be happening, I thought again.

I wet the scrap of burlap, refolded it, and put it back on Sam's forehead, for all the good it had done him. His fever had just kept climbing. I took his pulse. Even his wrist was hot. But that gave me an idea. I couldn't remember if I'd read about it or not, or if it would work, but I grabbed whole burlap sacks, shoved them in the water till they were sopping wet, and wrapped Sam's wrists, armpits, neck, ankles—anywhere blood vessels were close to the surface—hoping it would cool his blood and lower his fever.

The water kept rising. I grabbed my pole and guided us up among the treetops, shoving us away from dead stumps and the branches of young trees, but there were so many branches—another blunder. I hadn't paid attention to Sam when he'd needed it, and now I'd spent too much time with him. I'd let the raft drift away from the bayou into a dense grove. If the raft got caught below the night waterline, we were in trouble.

It grew dark below the leaves. I took out my gun and the light and shone the light around and kept trying to steer the raft toward the biggest breaks, using the gun to cut down branches, wondering what I'd do with Sam if the raft got caught. The water lifted us till the branches were so thick I couldn't stand up straight or cut away the branches fast enough. I gave up and threw my pole across the end of the raft, pulled out our rope, and started tying it around Sam's chest, thinking I'd have to pull him into a tree and tie him there, when I realized the water had stopped rising. There was a sudden quiet. The water lapped the edges of the raft. The tide was in. I tied the raft to a tree, sat down, and shone my light up through the branches. I saw nothing in them.

I shone the light on Sam. He hadn't moved. I splashed more water over the sacks I'd wrapped him in and sat down and heard a little dog barking behind me on the other end of the raft. I turned around, and the girl in the white dress and red slippers was there with ham sandwiches and potato salad and chocolate cake packed in a picnic basket. She held it out to me. "Hurry and eat, Jake," she said. "Then you can go to sleep while I keep watch."

"You're not real," I said. "*I've* got to keep watch." I reached out for the food anyway, but she wouldn't give it to me.

"I can't feed people who don't believe I'm real," she said.

"I'm hungry."

She gave a ham sandwich to the dog. "We're all hungry," she said.

And I woke up. I looked at Sam and looked at the dark water patched with red moonlight and looked at my hands. I'd gone into REM so quickly. I had to stay awake. I splashed water over my face and more water over the sacks I'd wrapped Sam in. I wondered how long I'd slept. My mother had given me a waterproof watch before I'd left Earth, but I had had to barter it for food at Vattani's.

"Gotta eat," I said out loud. I dumped the fishtrap over the side and let it dangle in the water till I thought I saw the line move. I pulled up the trap, but it was empty. I baited it with three nicoji, tossed it back in the water, and almost fell in with it. I grabbed the edge of the raft, then lay back on the logs and covered my eyes with my hands. I felt dizzy. Lagarto poison, I thought, and no sleep for two days, and hard work, and not enough to eat. I didn't know if I could stay awake again all night. I sat

up slowly and pulled in the trap. It had only the
nicoji in it. I gave up getting something to eat with
the trap and built a fire in the firebox, fried a handful
of nicoji, ate them with gagga raisins, and drank a
bowlful of water. I tried to get Sam to drink some
water too, but he just choked and coughed and never
opened his eyes. I didn't know what to do for him,
and we were still a day away from the mesão.

I changed the bandages on Sam's leg and wrist and
cleaned up after my supper. By then it was full
night. The raft rocked up and down on the water. I
splashed water over Sam again, then shone my light
through the trees. I saw nothing except leaves and
branches. I crawled over next to Sam and sat there
with my gun in my lap listening to him breathe—

And heard soft singing. I turned on my light,
shining it toward the sound, and caught a flash of
white in another tree. The singing stopped. I turned
off my light and listened for the music to start again,
but it didn't. I heard only the wind off the sea
sighing in the leaves. I climbed the tree above our
raft, and the wind felt cool on my face. I found a
thick vine and jerked on it again and again. It didn't
come loose, so I wrapped part of it around my right
arm and swung across the open water to the tree
where I'd seen the flash of white.

It was the girl with red slippers, again. Her black
hair was blowing in the wind. She'd climbed nearly
to the treetop. Her little dog ran around on a thick
branch below the one she sat on, and he barked and
barked at me as I climbed up toward them. The girl
only looked down at me once. I pulled myself onto
the branch with the dog, and he rushed to the far
end and growled, his eyes bright yellow in the shad-

ows. The girl took an oilcan out of the picnic basket and started pouring oil in cracks in the bark. "Why are you doing that?" I asked.

She looked at me as if I were stupid. "These trees get stiff if you don't oil them," she said.

I tried to remember what kind of tree got stiff if it weren't oiled, but I couldn't remember. I thought I should at least offer to help. "I'll oil the cracks down here by this branch," I said, reaching up to take her can, but she wouldn't give it to me.

"No, Jake," she said. "You've got to do something about the things in the trees. I told you I'd keep watch."

"What things?" I asked.

"Look around us," she said. I looked and saw black things climbing stealthily up toward us through the shadows. I'd left my gun on the raft, so I didn't have anything to fight with. I started trying to break off a branch from the tree, but that upset the girl. "We've got to oil it first!" she said. She leaned down and tried to pour oil in the cracks in the branch, but I couldn't wait for her oil. The black things were getting closer. The branch was green and hard to break. I kept pushing and pulling it back and forth, which made oil from the can flip all over the girl's arms and my legs and not in the cracks at all. One of the black things reached down and grabbed the oilcan from her hand. I had to break off the branch. I gave it the hardest jerk I could—

And woke with a start. It was hot. There was no wind off the sea. I don't know how long I'd been asleep and dreaming—not long probably. I was still sitting up.

Then I heard something in the tree above Sam and me.

I turned on my gun, and flipped on the light. Something stirred in the leaves above us, something dark, I couldn't see what. This was no dream. It climbed up in the tree, and I heard nothing after it stopped moving except the gentle hum of my gun. I kept shining the light around us, hoping the light would scare away whatever was up there.

It didn't. After a while I heard it moving in the shadows. It clambered through the branches to a point above the opposite end of the raft from Sam and me, above our box of gear, the nets, and my pole. I heard rustling in that direction and in three other trees—more than one of whatever it was was up there.

I aimed my gun at the shadows, but waited to fire till I heard movement again. "I don't know what you are," I said, "but some of you are going to die." I crept slowly toward the other end of the raft, my gun in one hand, my light in the other, ready to shoot at the first clump of branches that moved or rustled—

When something dropped down onto the raft behind me, by Sam. I spun around, waving the light, trying to see something to shoot at—and saw one of the help. It rushed back up in the tree. I lost sight of it in the branches and leaves. Everything was quiet again. Nothing moved.

Except me. I crawled back by Sam and turned off the light. "Come down," I said.

Nothing happened. I began to wonder if it *had* been one of the help that had gone around with Sam and me, or if it was part of a different group. I didn't know what it would be like to meet wild help.

"Come out," I said, not knowing if it could understand me.

Nothing happened for a long time. I just sat quietly next to Sam. Finally one dropped down on the other end of the raft and crouched there, not moving, stiff and tense. The raft bobbed up and down. I sat very still. Another help dropped down, then another. Twelve dropped onto the raft altogether. When the last help hit the logs, the help started chittering nervously.

"Do you know me?" I asked. When I spoke, they stopped chittering and looked at me. One climbed up in the tree again, but after a minute he dropped back down. Two help took steps in my direction, making the raft bob. I held out my hand and let them smell it.

They were our help. One still wore the black scraps of a bandage on his hand. I wondered if they'd followed us or if Sam and I just happened to be going the direction they were going. They chittered after they smelled my hand and realized it was definitely me. Help-with-the-hurt-hand sat down in front of me, and I carefully pulled off the scraps of bandage.

"Why you left us? Why you left us, Jake?" he asked. He was rubbing his fingers where the bandages had been. They were sticky from the tape.

"Sam's still alive," I said. "You didn't kill him. Can you understand that I didn't want him to die, that going home wasn't worth that to me?"

They chittered among themselves, then stopped and looked at me. "Why?" Help-with-the-hurt-hand asked.

I closed my eyes. How could I make them understand? "Sam is my friend," I said, finally. "Do you understand the word *friend*?"

"Help friends to Jake."

"The help should be Sam's friends, too."

They scratched their heads. "Jake not want go home?"

"Jake wants to go home. So does Sam."

"In-sur-nance only take Jake."

"Damn the insurance!"

Three help stood up. One hissed at me.

I moved closer to Sam and turned on my gun. "I want Sam to live," I said. "If the help are friends to Jake, the help will be friends to Sam, too."

Help-with-the-hurt-hand held up his hand that had been caught in the freezer. "Jake make hand feel good. Jake give help nicoji. Jake leave help in freeze-shack, not shoo out."

So I'd happened to come out on top of a tally they kept of the good things Sam and I did for them. "Sam gives you nicoji, too," I said. "He lets you go through our garbage. And don't you remember the day he boiled leaves in our pan and made a ball?"

The help wrinkled their noses.

"Sam was very good to you then."

One help pounded the logs of the raft—help laughter. The rest only looked at me. Sam had made the ball back in the company town. I could smell Sam's boiling leaves two streets away. When I'd walked in the kitchen, Sam had smiled. "I thought this plant looked rubbery," he said, "and it is!" Green plant goo covered the stove, the floor, and the table. We never could clean all of it off the pan. Sam shaped his "rubber" into a ball and sent it through the freezer. It came out hard, and it even bounced, though not very high. He and I played catch with it till dark. The help came out then and watched us. "We could have teams," Sam said. "We could teach the help to play ball." He threw the ball to one of the help, but the help ran away, shrieking. "Come back!" Sam yelled. I found the ball in the shadows and threw it to Sam. He threw it back. It was getting sticky— thawing as we threw it around. Dirt and grass stuck to it. I threw it to Sam. He dropped it on the ground and rolled it to one of the help. The help picked it up and bit it—then dropped it and spit and started scraping his teeth with his fingernails. Another help picked up the ball, hefted it, and threw it at a third help's chest. That help threw it back, harder. A fourth help grabbed the ball, but the ball stuck to the fur on his hand and he had to shake off the ball and kick it. Sam and I laughed. All the help wanted to throw the ball, then, but only to other help. We never got them to throw it to us. It was soon too dark to see, so Sam and I went inside to bed. The help played with Sam's gooey ball all night till it disintegrated.

"Sam helps me catch nicoji," I said. "No help can do as much as Sam. What would I do if he were gone? Sam cooks better food than me. And Sam can talk to me. He knows my family. He knows my home. I wouldn't kill Sam so I could go home."

Two of the help looked at Sam. "Sam sleep?" one asked.

"Sam's sick."

They all touched the wet burlap I'd wrapped Sam in and patted his face, feeling his beard. He never stirred.

"I want to help Sam get better," I said. "I want to do this good thing for him."

"Sam hot."

"I'll kill all of you if you hurt Sam again."

The help stood up and looked at me as if I'd gone mad. "Help not hurt Sam," one said, as if I had no reason to think otherwise. "Help watch Sam. Help watch Jake."

That sounded like repentance and an invitation to sleep. I hoped I wasn't dreaming again. I wanted to sleep. I wanted to trust the help again. I didn't know why they'd come back—except that they wanted nicoji and empty tin cans and the medical attention I could give them. But I needed them, too. I needed them to keep watch while I slept—but even then they were exploiting me: they could wake me up and I would protect them.

"Help not want make Jake mad."

"Maybe so," I said. I turned off my gun. I needed the help, for now, for whatever reasons they'd come back.

The help chittered amongst themselves, looking at Sam and me. One came up and patted my face. Then they all had to. "You got beard, Jake," Help-with-the-hurt-hand said. "Beard."

"Do I look like you, now?"

They pounded the logs and rocked back and forth when I asked that.

"What you do? Why you not go house?" one asked.

"I'm taking Sam to a new house on the mesão. The people there can make Sam better."

"You go light?"

"Light?"

Five help stayed on the raft, watching Sam; I climbed up through the tree, following the other seven. In order to see out over the treetops, we had to climb so high I was afraid the small branches we were on would break.

"See light?"

We clung to the treetop, waving back and forth, and I could see a light. It was on top of the mesão, shining steadily: the new company. While we looked at it, a ship took off. The red-orange glare of its engines climbed into the sky and disappeared.

I went to sleep with the help sitting all around Sam and me, watching. I felt safe. But in the night, I opened my eyes and saw a ghostly face hovering three inches from mine: it looked something like a help, but its eyes were wider and didn't blink, ever, and its face glowed with a soft, white light. I could see through the skin, see organs in the head floating down through a thick fluid toward me and bunching up around the eyes while the thing stared at me. I couldn't move. "This is a dream," I told myself, so I wasn't afraid. The help were gone, and I started to wonder if I had only dreamed that the help had come back or if this thing was a dream. I shook my head, and the thing above me jerked up in the air and hovered there—it was three to four feet long and had arms, and legs, and a torso, and white transparent wings like an insect's that let it hover above me. I felt the wind from its wings brush my skin, and I smelled sulfur in that wind. I'd never smelled any living thing in the pântano that smelled like sulfur. Three of the sulfur-men hovered over Sam. They'd reach down one at a time to touch Sam's hair. I sat up. "Get out of here," I said. "Leave us alone." The sulfur-man above me hissed and bared his teeth. He had long, sharp teeth, solid white—not transparent. I turned on my gun, and when I did I realized I was not dreaming, but they were gone, that fast, just gone and I couldn't see in the dark they left behind. I turned on the light and shined it through the trees. The help were there, cowering in the branches. I hadn't dreamed them, either. "Why didn't you wake me?" I asked. I couldn't believe they hadn't woken me up. I didn't know what to think of them. I wondered why I'd decided to trust them to watch Sam and me. They said nothing. "What were they?" I asked. The help just came back down on the raft and wrinkled their noses when they smelled the sulfur on the air and brushed Sam's hair and held onto him and onto me and wouldn't say a word.

I tried to stay awake, but couldn't, and ended up sleeping the rest of the night. I didn't wake till the water started to hiss away through the trees. Sam hadn't moved. I shook him. "Sam," I said. "Sam?" He didn't move. His breathing was shallow.

I had to get him to a doctor.

The help just looked at me with their eyes wide in the dark. I shoved the two sacks of nicoji in the water to get the nicoji wet and keep them alive, then set the dripping sacks by Sam's head. The sacks squirmed. The nicoji crawled around inside the sacks till the sun came up and heated them and made them go to sleep. I untied the raft. We floated down with the water and dropped below the branches. I held my pole ready and pushed us away from the tree trunks, guiding us toward the bayou. The help stayed awake with me, watching the trees flow past, waiting till the light drove them under the empty sacks to sleep.

We floated through the dark trees for a quarter of a mile. The help began walking around the raft, touching the water over the side, chittering. They'd stop by the sacks of nicoji, scratch their heads, and walk on. I laughed and untied one sack. They crowded around, and I let them grab handfuls of nicoji for breakfast. The ones who got to the sack first shoved their mouths full of nicoji and crowded back for more. "Hey," I said. I swatted their arms and lifted the sack above my head. Eventually they settled down around the edges of the raft and munched on the nicoji, watching me. I tied the sack shut and set it with the other. It was good to have the help back.

The raft bumped against a tree trunk. I shoved the raft around the tree and must have pushed too hard. One of the help dropped his nicoji in the water. He dove in after them and came up sputtering, nicoji in both hands. The others crowded around him and helped him onto the raft. But instead of chittering and touching his wet fur, they put the nicoji under their feet and looked past me. I turned around. A white froth drifted on the water ahead of us, nothing more.

"Stop raft," one help whispered.

I'd learned to do what the help said when they said to do it, so I shoved the raft in among three tree trunks spaced closely together and tied the raft to one. The help seemed upset with the noise I made, though I'd tried to be quiet. "What—" I whispered.

The help—all twelve—clamped their hands over their mouths and looked at me. The froth was closer, bobbing gently on the surface. I stood quietly with the help and watched the froth and said nothing. It was still dark and hard to tell whether the froth itself was alive and coming toward us, or if it marked the passage of something below the water, or if it was just froth. Whatever it was, I wanted it to hurry so we could get to a bayou before the water dropped out from under us and left us stranded on the mud.

But it came straight for us. One help touched my leg and pointed behind me. Patches of white were floating all around us on the water.

"Sam," the help whispered, pointing up. "Tree."

Instead, I took out my gun, turned it on, let it hum for three seconds, and fired at the closest patch of froth. The beam cut it and made a bubbly white seam through the middle, but the two halves rejoined and kept coming, slowly, toward the raft. There was nothing below the froth—evidently the froth itself scared the help. The help waved their arms and tried to grab my gun, to make me stop shooting and be quiet, but they didn't chitter. Five help clambered up the tree I'd tied us to. The others ran for Sam and tried to lift him.

We were fifteen feet below the lowest branches. "What is it?" I asked, not caring about the sound. The froth knew we were there.

"Sam!" the help insisted. "Climb!" They were patting Sam's face, trying to wake him up.

I looked all around us. I wanted to try to float away. We couldn't stop to climb a tree—I had to get Sam to a doctor. But the froth had surrounded us. I grabbed my pole, stuck it in the froth, and dragged a gob of it to the raft. It clung to the pole when I lifted it up. The froth smelled earthy, like dried leaves after the snow melts, and faintly, underneath that smell, like sulfur. Sulfur again. Was some kind of sulfur-based life endemic to this area of the pântano? I'd never heard anyone talk about such things.

The froth started to flow up the pole toward my hands. I swished the pole through the water, but the froth clung to the pole. I couldn't dislodge it. I tried to scrape it off against the side of the raft, and the help chittered at that. "Jake," Help-with-the-hurt-hand said. "Stop, Jake!" The froth flowed across the log into one patch of white and started for my feet. I scooped it up with an old sack and threw it out on the water.

The water, as far as I could see, was now covered with white froth. We couldn't get through it. I stepped on the log where the froth had been, and my foot started stinging. I rubbed it, and my hand felt prickly and odd.

"What is this?" I asked.

Four more help had climbed the tree. The froth around us started edging closer, touching the ends of the raft. "Tree!" one of the last help said.

"All right," I said. I pulled a fifty-foot length of rope out of our chest and gave an end of it to one of the help. "Get up the tree and hang onto this. Go!"

It shimmied up the tree into the shadows. I locked the chest shut, then tied the other end of the rope under Sam's arms. Help-with-the-hurt-hand pulled my hair and pointed down: the froth was under the raft and oozing up through the cracks between the logs. I didn't want it to get on Sam. I hurried to finish tying the knot, and made sure it was secure.

I untied a sack of nicoji and threw the nicoji on the froth around the raft, thinking they might slow down the froth, give it something to eat besides Sam and me and the help. I untied the other sack. "Throw out the nicoji," I told Help-with-the-hurt-hand. He stuffed three nicoji in his mouth, then started throwing out the rest. I turned just as the eleventh help started up the tree. I grabbed his arm, and he bared his teeth at me and hissed. "Hold the rope when you get to the top," I said. "Have the others hold it with you. I've got to climb up the rope."

I let him go. Help-with-the-hurt-hand was dragging the sack of nicoji around the edges of the raft, throwing one handful of nicoji on the froth and eating the next. The froth surrounding the raft and under it broke apart, foamed over the nicoji, and bunched up around them in balls that seethed over the surface of the water, slamming into the trees, each other, and the raft.

I yanked on the rope. It fell down around me. "You've got to hold it!" I yelled at the help. "Come back and get your end."

Help-with-the-hurt-hand shoved a handful of nicoji in his mouth, took one end of the rope, and shimmied up the tree. The mass of froth among all the trees around us flowed forward, surrounded the raft, and went under it and over the outside logs. It started coming up through the cracks between the logs again. I got froth on the bottoms of my feet, and my feet stung. The balls of froth covering the nicoji bobbed to the surface of the froth layer and rolled stickily there, back and forth.

Help-with-the-hurt-hand slid back down the rope. "Help hold rope now," he said. I yanked on it, and it seemed firm. "I'm coming up," I shouted. I tucked my shirt in my shorts, then shoved two handfuls of nicoji down my shirt so I'd have something to give the help when I got to the top, stepped past Sam and started up the rope, hand over hand. The help could never learn to tie knots. If they couldn't hold the rope with me on it, Sam and I would be trapped on the raft.

I was halfway to the branches when Help-with-the-hurt-hand started screeching and jumping up and down: the froth had covered all the logs and there was nowhere left for him to stand except on Sam's chest. He'd thrown out all the nicoji. "Come up," I yelled, and I tried to climb faster. Help-with-the-hurt-hand sat on Sam's chest and beat the froth with an empty sack.

I grabbed the branch the help were on. It wasn't strong enough to hold Sam and me and the help. "Get off this branch!" I shouted. The help vanished above me. I climbed into the branches and pulled myself onto a thick branch higher up, clamped my legs around it, and pulled on the rope. Sam sat up and grabbed the rope. My pulling on it must have hurt. Froth covered Sam's back and the hair on the back of his head. Help-with-the-hurt-hand held onto Sam's chest. The help dropped back down onto branches all around me and sat shading their eyes, looking at Sam and Help-with-the-hurt-hand. I pulled on the rope again. "Help me," I said.

The help just stared at me.

"I need help!" I said.

The help chittered at that and threw leaves down at the froth.

"Grab the rope!" I said, but they wouldn't. Bastards, I thought. They could see the nicoji were gone and thought they might not get anything out of helping Sam and me but work. "I'll give you nicoji," I said. The help couldn't understand the contempt in my voice.

"Nicoji gone," one help said.

I reached down my shirt, pulled out a nicoji, and threw it at the help. "I've got nicoji down my shirt," I said. "You'll get them if you'll help me pull Sam up here."

The help chittered and scratched their heads and finally got on the branches above me, grabbed the rope, and pulled. Amoral, I thought. The help are amoral, self-centered, and alien. Five pulls had Sam off the raft. Help-with-the-hurt-hand climbed over Sam's head and started up the rope. "Come up the tree!" I shouted. The rope was so heavy, and I

wanted Help-with-the-hurt-hand off the rope, but he
ignored me. I waited to pull the rope till Help-with-
the-hurt-hand was in the branches. He rubbed his
hands on the leaves and bark, blowing on them and
shaking them. What was the froth doing to Sam? I
pulled on the rope again and got Sam one foot higher.
None of the help had pulled with me. "Pull!" I said.
I pulled Sam up another foot, then the help pulled
on the rope and didn't move Sam at all. "Pull when I
pull!" I shouted. They stopped pulling and started
chittering. "I'm sorry for shouting," I said. "But pull
now."

We pulled together. Sam came up two more feet.
The white froth had oozed over everything on the
raft. It started up the tree we were in. "Pull!" I said.
Two more feet. "Pull again." Sam was only a few feet
below the lowest branches. Four help let go of the
rope and dropped down below me, screeching and
pointing at Sam. "Help me!" I said, but they wouldn't.
"Pull!" I shouted, but I was the only one pulling. All
the help rushed to the lower branches and stretched
down, trying to reach Sam.

My arms hurt from pulling on the rope, but Sam
wasn't a barbell I could drop when my muscles started
to burn. "Help me pull!" I shouted. The help squinted
at me once and reached back down for Sam. I kept
pulling up the rope, hand over hand. One help
grabbed Sam's hair and yanked on it. Sam shook his
head, but the help wouldn't let go. The others grabbed
his ears, then his shoulders and arms. I pulled him
into the branches. The help tore off leaves and started
wiping Sam's back, neck, arms, legs, and hair. They
followed him through the branches as I pulled him
up to me. "You've got to help me lift him onto this
branch," I said to the help. I didn't dare let go of the

rope to grab his arms. Four help crowded around me and held Sam's shoulders and arms. I grabbed him, and we lifted him onto the branch. I shoved him back against the trunk and tied him to it so he wouldn't fall off. His eyes were open, and he'd grabbed the rope under his arms. His skin was red wherever the froth had touched him. "We're in trouble again, Sam," I said. He nodded and tried to say something, but all he could do was lean over and throw up on the froth below us. The help scattered through the branches. As far as I could see a solid, white mass covered the water and oozed up the sides of all the trees around us. I tore off handfuls of leaves and wiped the froth from Sam's feet. "Bad stuff," I said. Sam nodded.

I pulled out the nicoji and gave them to the help, left Sam tied to the trunk, and climbed down to try to burn the froth from the trunk. It was nearly up to the lowest branch. I turned on my gun, let it hum, and fired. The froth bubbled under the beam, turned to liquid, and ran down the trunk, but the rest kept coming.

I trained the beam of my gun on the bark above the froth. The bark smoked and would not burn—it was wet. When it cooled, the froth flowed over it. I couldn't keep the bark hot all around the trunk long enough to stop the froth. By the time I heated the bark on one side, it would be cool on the other.

The help started throwing sticks at the froth, and that gave me an idea. I broke off a small branch, burned it into flame with the gun, and dropped it. It bubbled on the froth at the base of the tree, but the froth opened up around it and the brand sank in the water with a hiss.

I couldn't stop it.

I climbed back up to Sam and the help. "What can I do?" I asked.

"Other tree!" one help said, pointing. "Other tree! Other tree!" they all said. Only nine help were still there. Three had already gone.

"I can't move Sam to another tree," I said. "I couldn't get myself to another tree from here."

The help squinted at me, quiet. Then you're dead, I could almost hear them thinking.

I looked down. The froth was in the branches, covering bugs and leaves. "Go," I said. "Get in the other trees." I fired my gun at the branches below us and started them on fire. I climbed all around the tree, burning branches and leaves. The smoke rose up in the sky, visible in the dawn. I coughed, and my eyes hurt. Sam coughed, too.

And the red power's-low light started flashing on my gun. It needed to recharge in the sun, but it wasn't light enough yet to recharge. I didn't have time to wait for it if there had been light. Sam's gun was in the chest on the raft. I untied Sam from the tree trunk, climbed to a higher branch, and pulled Sam up after me. Six help were still with me.

"Go," I said. "Get to safety."

"Try go other tree," Help-with-the-hurt-hand said.

"And fall into that?" I said, pointing. "What would happen to Sam and me if we fell?"

The help didn't know the words to explain to me what would happen. They chittered and kept poking their fingers up their noses which probably meant the froth would flow up our nostrils and smother us.

"Go!" I said. But the help squinted up through the branches and grew very quiet and still. Then they faded away into the shadows. I heard the rotors of a helicopter. The smoke had brought it. I tied Sam to

the tree and climbed up as high as I could go. One of
American Nicoji's helicopters came and hovered above
the tree.

They shone lights in the shadows and found me. I
waved frantically, pointing at Sam and the white
froth. I thought they'd drop a ladder, that I'd somehow climb up it and drag Sam after me, but they
kept hovering, keeping us in the light. I stopped
waving and looked at the dirty, white bandages over
my wrist and Sam's where the locators had been.

No door opened.

No ladder dropped.

After five minutes—enough time to talk with officials in the company town and get an answer—the
helicopter lifted up and flew away to the north.

V

All the help climbed away into other trees. When my gun gave out, I sat waiting with Sam and watched the water drift down to the bayous and the froth rise up through the tree. The sun rose. I was glad for the light. I did not want Sam and me to be smothered in the dark.

But wherever the early morning light filtered down through the leaves to touch the froth, the froth stopped rising. It still flowed up through the shadows, but soon stopped even that. The froth was light sensitive. It started quivering, flowing back down the trunk or dropping from the branches to ooze into the mud. It sounded like a hard rain gradually tapering off to an occasional drip. I sat for a long time, watching, not moving, not having expected to live. Our raft was left hanging against the tree trunk, our gear scattered over the muddy, flat ground where it had floated or dropped. The company would have been surprised to find Sam and me alive that morning. I was surprised.

The help came back, struggling against the light, holding leaves in front of their eyes. "Go, Jake," they said. "Get away this place."

"Can I walk in the mud?"

The help rubbed their legs and chittered and would not look at me. "Raft," they said.

But I had to drag the raft to a bayou. I had to walk through the mud. "Will it follow us?" I asked.

"White dark, not light," one said.

So we had all day to get away. I left Sam tied against the trunk and lowered myself onto the next branch down. It was slimy from the froth and charred black near the trunk where I'd burned it, but it seemed sturdy. It held my weight. I climbed to the next thick branch and kept going till I reached the lowest branches, checking to see how far through I'd burned each branch and whether I could lower Sam onto it.

I sat and looked at the mud. I could see no sign of the froth. Three help had followed me down. "Wait here," I said. "I'll go back for Sam and the other help."

Sam was not conscious. I got him untied from the trunk and lowered him to a branch fifteen feet down. The help followed him, shoving him past branches, pulling the rope closer to the tree trunk and chittering at me.

"Hold Sam on that branch till I get down," I shouted.

The help hung onto Sam. I climbed down to them, then lowered Sam onto one of the bottom branches and tied him to the trunk.

The help cooed at the raft dangling ten feet down. I tied part of the rope to the lowest sturdy branch, slid down to the raft, cut the raft from the tree, and let it crash through the roots into the mud. It landed upside down. Great, I thought. I slid down the rope onto the roots and dropped to the raft. Its underside was slimy and wet and the logs were still rough—nobody's feet had walked over them hundreds of times to make them smooth. I stepped carefully to the edge, trying not to get slivers in my feet, crouched down and poked the mud with one finger. The mud started quivering. I scraped the mud off my finger on one of the logs. Nothing came out of the mud, but the froth was obviously just under the surface, probably staying where it was still wet so it wouldn't dry out. Maybe it wasn't just the light it didn't like, but also the daytime heat.

Three help were inching down the slick tree trunk, making sure of their holds before lowering down to the next. "Jake," they said. "Don't touch, Jake."

But I had to touch it—I had to walk through it and drag the raft to the bayou—if I was going to get us away from here. The waterproof chest was caught in the roots above me. I climbed up after it, worked it free, and dropped it down on the raft. Then I turned it right side up, opened it, and got out Sam's gun. It was fully charged. I turned it on, cut away the roots above and in front of the raft, and threw them out as far as I could. Then I jumped off, heaved the raft right side up, and climbed back on, wiping mud and slime from my legs and feet and wiping my hands on my shorts. The froth in the mud made my feet sting—probably because I'd already stepped in the froth and made my feet tender.

The help dropped down on the raft and soon started lifting up and shaking one foot at a time.

I pulled myself back up the rope and lowered Sam to the raft. The three help already on it caught him in their arms and eased him onto the logs. I grabbed Help-with-the-hurt-hand's arm. "Wait here till the rest of us are on the raft," I said. "Then untie the rope and climb down the tree trunk."

"OK, Jake," he said. "OK."

I slid down the rope, and the other help followed me, carrying leaves to hold in front of their eyes. Help-with-the-hurt-hand tried and tried to untie my knot, but he couldn't. Finally he just gave up and slid down the rope onto Sam's stomach.

I got a knife out of the chest and handed it to Help-with-the-hurt-hand. "See if you can cut the rope free," I said.

He took the knife and ignored me. He was delighted to hold the knife, and he touched each of his fingers to the tip of it, sucking on them when he drew blood and squinting at the knife in the light.

I crouched down in front of him. "You'll have to give me back the knife, now," I said, "Unless you go up and cut down the rope."

"Keep knife?"

"No."

He blinked at that and bared his teeth, but he grabbed the rope, put the knife between his teeth, climbed up, and managed to cut the rope just below the knot. I coiled the rope and laid it by Sam. Help-with-the-hurt-hand took a long time climbing down the tree trunk. He kept poking the knife in holes and biting it and touching the tip to his knees, his stomach, underneath his chin. He handed it back, though, when he jumped on the raft.

The other help were touching the mud and squinting at it through leaves, watching it quiver.

"Not got food now, Jake," one said. "Not got food."

"Too bad we threw out all the nicoji," I said.

Four help squinted up at me.

"White eat nicoji, Jake," Help-with-the-hurt-hand said. "Eat."

"I know," I said. "We bought time with it." One of the burlap sacks lay on the mud by the raft. I picked it up and shook it and threw it down on the logs. The help were squinting at me.

"White eat sack, Jake. White eat raft—eat all logs."

"What?"

Eight of the help stood up. They seemed excited about something, and started touching my legs and tugging on my shorts.

"Eat trees," one said. "Eat trees."

"Eat nicoji! Eat nicoji!"

"Eat lagarto."

All the help pounded the logs at that.

"You guys are crazy," I said. I looked at the mud, realized I had no other options, jumped off and pulled one of the nets back and threw it on the raft. "Help me pick up this stuff so we can get out of here," I said.

But none of the help would get off the raft.

"Not got food, Jake," Help-with-the-hurt-hand said again.

What were they trying to tell me? I knew we didn't have any food. "Look, guys," I said. "When we get to the bayou I'll put out the trap and we'll catch some fish. Now help me get this stuff."

None would. I had to wade out alone, through the mud and froth, and drag back the nets and burlap sacks. The sacks were muddy and slimy. I threw them on the raft. The help picked them up and shook them and pulled faces and would not climb under them to get out of the light. I found our poles and the firebox and the trap. Then I tied the rope to one end of the raft and started pulling it toward the bayou.

The help loved the ride. They bunched up along the front of the raft, holding leaves in front of their eyes, chittering and pointing at me and pounding the logs when I fell in the mud. It became a game of skill for them to see who could stand up and not fall on his haunches every time I pulled the raft ahead. I didn't mind till they grabbed the rope and tried to pull it out of my hands. I made them stop that game.

I was soon covered with mud. My skin started stinging wherever the mud covered it very long, not just the skin on my feet. I rubbed my hands on my shorts. My hands were red and sore.

The froth was digesting my skin.

I jumped back on the raft and tried to rub the mud from my legs, feet, stomach, and hands. The help cooed and touched my red skin. "I need some leaves to rub off the mud," I said.

The help looked at me. I'd pulled the raft against the roots of an enormous, old tree, and I needed leaves, but the help just looked at me.

"Climb the tree and either bring me back some leaves or throw them down."

The help just backed away and watched me rub the mud off my legs and scrape it off my hands onto the logs. I didn't have any nicoji to give the help—they had no reason to do anything I asked. I couldn't buy their help, and that made me mad. I slammed my fists on the logs. "Get off this raft!" I shouted.

The help started chittering, confused.

"Do you want to ride down the bayous? Do you want to keep going around with Sam and me and eat the nicoji we catch? Then get up that tree and bring me back handfuls of leaves. Now."

Help-with-the-hurt-hand suddenly hurried up the tree trunk. The others followed him in a rush. I didn't know if they'd come back. I really had nothing to give them, except rides on the raft which they'd gotten before for free. But they came back, with leaves. I used some to rub my legs and hands and feet as clean as I could get them, then spread out the rest for Sam to lay on over the slimy logs. I rolled Sam onto the leaves and looked at the mud.

One help handed me the end of the rope. He wanted to start playing again. I pointed back at the tree they had just climbed. "Get up that tree and follow me along through the branches," I said. "You make the raft too heavy. You can ride the raft when I get it on the water."

The help just looked at me through slits between their fingers. I knew it was hard for them to climb through trees in the daylight, but I didn't care. I'd told them the truth. "Get!" I said.

Most pretended not to understand me. "Light," Help-with-the-hurt-hand said. "Light."

"I don't care if it's light. You've got to help me."

None moved. I scooped up a handful of mud and threw it at one of the help. It splattered across his back. He hissed and bared his teeth at me and tried to reach behind him to rub off the mud while the other help pounded the logs. I threw mud at two more help, and not as many pounded logs, then. "Get off of here!" I yelled, and I threw more mud. One threw back a handful that splattered across my shorts. All the help pounded the logs, hard, but I was in no mood and had no time for games. I didn't think Help-with-the-hurt-hand would bite me, so I picked him up and shoved him against a thick root. He grabbed on, and I let go. He started to climb back down.

"No," I said.

He stopped and looked at me.

"I need your help," I said. "You know the froth is

in the mud. I have to pull the raft through the mud to the bayou so we can get out of here. You've got to stay off the raft so the raft will be lighter to pull."

Help-with-the-hurt-hand did not climb back down to the raft. He clung to the root and looked at me. I boosted two more help onto the roots, and then all the rest rushed to the roots and climbed up the tree trunk into the branches, chittering and breaking off leaves and twigs and throwing them at my head. They were not happy.

I looked out at the mud. I couldn't see the bayou, it was that far away. Finally I just jumped in the mud again, grabbed the rope, and started pulling.

It took maybe an hour to drag the raft to the bayou. I was in mud past my knees when I finally got there and shoved the raft out on the water. My skin was raw and bleeding. I got our soap from the chest and scrubbed myself clean. The soap stung my skin where the froth had eaten, which meant I stung everywhere but parts of my ears and my bottom eyelids. I rubbed a little antibacterial cream on my legs and feet. The cream was almost gone. I rubbed what was left over Sam's back and legs and neck and threw the empty tube in the water. I tried to scrub the raft clean, and I rinsed out the burlap sacks so I could keep Sam covered, have something to lay the guns on, and leave the help something to crawl under out of the light.

All that time the help chittered up among the shadows in the trees, but when I shoved the raft out on the bayou they climbed down to some tree roots and jumped on the raft as I floated past. They sniffed their burlap sacks and walked on them, kneading the sacks with their toes, trying to wring out the water, then climbed under and went to sleep curled up around Sam.

The raft was still slimy. I kept slipping and falling when I'd pole the raft ahead. But we were moving, getting away from the froth, getting closer to the mesão and a doctor.

The bayous were deeper the closer we got to the sea. That day I sometimes had trouble poling—couldn't touch bottom—and had to let us drift with the current. Dead trees washed out by the tides clogged the bayou's curves, and I had to cut through them with my gun. The standing trees were thicker and taller than what I'd seen before, better able to last against the deeper wash of water onto and off of the land.

And the land changed. It grew rockier. Hills stuck up above the night waterline, covered with trees, and grass curled and black on the tips as if a fire had rushed across it. Even leaves on some of the trees were edged with black and falling off, drifting along on the bayou. I'd never seen anything like that. Nobody'd ever talked about trees losing their leaves here.

But I didn't have to climb trees anymore to see the mesão: it towered above the treetops, enormous, green, flat-topped. The help woke up and started poking their heads out from under the burlap sacks to watch. I heard them chittering under the sacks—about the new land, I thought. But Help-with-the-hurt-hand crawled up to me holding a sack over his head. "Sam," he said. "Sam."

I dropped my pole, stepped over the help huddled under sacks around Sam and pulled the sack from his face. His face was red. I couldn't wake him.

The help kept touching his forehead. "Hot," they said. "Hot."

I took the thermometer out of the medkit and put it in Sam's mouth.

The raft was scraping against roots on the west shore, so I poled us back into the sluggish current. I needed a fast-flowing river, not a convoluted bayou.

I laid my pole back across the raft and looked at the thermometer. Sam's fever measured 105.4. Three help had their hands pressed to Sam's chest. I picked up his wrist and felt his pulse: it was slow; very, very slow.

"Heart stop," one said.

I didn't understand. "His heart stopped for a minute?" I asked.

"Lagarto," Help-with-the-hurt-hand said. "Lagarto stop heart soon."

I looked at Sam. Lagarto poison evidently affected help hearts, and the help expected it to affect Sam's. "How much time does he have?" I asked.

The help squinted at the sun. "Not be dark," one said.

"New house?" one asked.

The new company town was still a day away. "Too far," I said.

One help patted Sam's face and climbed back under the sacks.

This can't be happening, I thought. "We'll be all right," Sam had promised. "We'll have money for college and stories to tell our kids."

Another help patted my legs and pointed. I looked up. The raft was drifting toward a snag of dead trees. I grabbed my pole and shoved it against the tree trunks and pushed the raft around the snag, but the help kept patting my legs and tugging my shorts. I looked up and saw what else he was pointing at.

A helicopter.

Help-with-the-hurt-hand threw a sack over Sam's face, and all the help huddled around Sam and pulled sacks over their heads. The helicopter dropped out of sight behind trees farther down the bayou. I could hear its rotors. I prayed the company boys hadn't seen us and shoved the raft among the roots of an old tree but couldn't get it under. I had to turn on my gun, let it hum for three seconds while we floated on the open bayou, and cut close to the water through five of the big, outer roots, making a hole barely large enough for the raft to pass through. I grabbed the cut roots and dumped them on the raft—the current wouldn't take them far, and I didn't want to mark the tree we'd gone under more than I already had by cutting the roots. I shoved the raft through the hole and kept cutting away the spindly roots farther back till we broke through to the quiet water around the trunk.

The raft bumped the trunk, and drops of water spattered over us. The help rushed out from under the sacks and up into the roots to investigate. "Come back!" I hissed, and I pulled one help out of the roots and held him on the raft. I was scared of going under a tree without letting the help look around, but I was more scared of having the guys in the helicopter see the help. After a minute, all the help came back and huddled around me. Good, I thought. At least we're safe under here. But something splashed into the water and swam away. I fumbled in the chest for a light and shone it around. Nothing else was under the tree. I didn't see anything in the water. Nothing came up under the raft. "Not got worry, Jake," Help-with-the-hurt-hand whispered to me, holding onto my leg. "Not got worry." I wondered what he had seen that he thought I shouldn't worry about. It was dark under the tree. The help stared at me, their eyes silvery in the darkness.

I knelt next to Sam and the help and listened for the helicopter. I could hear only water drip from the roots and thought maybe the company boys *hadn't* seen us, that they'd flown away.

"Looking Sam, looking Jake?" one help whispered.

"Maybe," I whispered back. I didn't know if the company boys in the helicopter were tracking another team that had cut out their locators, or if they were looking for Sam and me in particular. We hadn't left bodies. They'd kill us themselves now, to make sure of the job, and I could imagine the reasons why: the company was the law-keeping force for the men contracted to it, so it was obligated to keep us in line. We'd destroyed company property when we cut out the locators. They'd have fewer nicoji to ship since we weren't going back to town with a catch— profit margins would drop. Most importantly, we were trying to leave their employ, and they evidently didn't want to sell our contracts—not because we couldn't be replaced, but because they didn't want the new company to get experienced workers. They'd make the first guys who tried to defect pay badly for the attempt, on whatever trumped-up charges, so the rest would be afraid to try.

One help was picking at the tree trunk. Suddenly he pulled back his fingers, shook them, and swished them in the water. I shined the light on the trunk. It was dotted with pustules as big across as the tip of my thumb. I crawled over and smashed one open with the light, and a creamy white liquid ran down the bark. It stank of sulfur.

"What is this?" I asked.

The help chittered softly to each other, but would not answer me.

And I heard the helicopter. It flew up the bayou, low enough to make the water choppy under the roots. Our raft bobbed up and down. The helicopter flew so far up the bayou I could hardly hear it.

Maybe they've gone, I thought. Maybe they really hadn't seen us. I didn't know I'd been holding my breath till some of the help exhaled loudly.

But the helicopter turned around and came back.

The company boys had seen us. They probably hadn't shot at us sooner because they had to talk with officials back in the company town and explain the situation.

I stood and held my gun. The help sat looking at me. I listened to the gun hum and contemplated murder, something I had never imagined. If I hit the helicopter in the right places—the base of the rotors or one of the fuel tanks—I could bring it down. I climbed up through the roots and shoved myself into a snag where the company boys couldn't see me, but where I could get a good shot. The helicopter lifted up above the trees, and the sound of its rotors grew faint. I couldn't see it. I sat waiting for it to drop back down into sight, wondering what it was doing and whether I should let it shoot first or if I should shoot first—

But then sparks were in my hair burning down to my scalp, and I couldn't see through smoke, and the tree south of ours was burning. I couldn't hear it burn. The concussion had deafened me. I shook the sparks out of my hair and hit my ears, and the company boys hit our tree. Fire burned up the trunk to the branches. I could hear the help shrieking—far off, it seemed—and realized my hearing was coming back. I'd just been stunned. I'd dropped my gun. It had landed against the medkit on the raft. The help were running around the raft. I was afraid one would kick the gun in the water. Before I could get down to it, I heard three more concussions to the north and was glad. The company boys didn't know which tree we were hiding under.

I felt the slimy logs of the raft under my feet and grabbed the gun. It was OK. But I was covered with ashes and sparks, and the right leg of my shorts had burned away. I splashed water over my shorts and legs and head. The hair on my right leg was gone, and the skin was red and blistered where the shorts had burned.

The help swarmed past me into the roots, screeching. The fur on the back of one was on fire. I pulled him out of the roots and slapped out the fire, but he bit my leg and I dropped him. He scrambled back up into the roots. "Come back!" I yelled, but none would. I was afraid the company boys in the helicopter would see the help and know for sure which tree we were under. I shook the ashes and sparks out of Sam's hair and covered him with the wet burlap sacks the help had left scattered. One sack was floating on the water. I pulled it onto the raft.

The help were still screeching in the roots. I dragged one down by the foot. "Stay here!" I yelled. But the others came down without being dragged, holding their eyes. The daylight and the fire were too bright for them. One would not stop screeching. I slapped his face and knocked him sprawling. "Be quiet!" I said. He sat up, hissing and baring his teeth, but quiet. I could not hear the helicopter.

All the help grew quiet. They stopped running around the raft and sat close to each other and slapped at the sparks that fell on their fur. Burning branches dropped on the roots and scattered us with sparks before sliding into the water. The help pulled sacks over their heads.

And I heard the helicopter.

I grabbed my gun and pulled myself back in the roots. The helicopter hovered across from the burning trees north of us. I could see two company boys

in their seats, the one closest to me talking through a
headset. I knew them. They knew Sam and me.
They fired and hit the third tree up from us, burning
the roots, then straight up the trunk to the branches.

Our turn was coming, again. The company boys
watched the trees, careful. They knew we had guns.
One kept talking through his headset. The other flew
the helicopter across from the second tree and burned
it. The heat from that fire rushed over me and blew
my hair like a wind.

I'd get one shot. Once I fired, they'd know where
we were. If I missed, they'd kill us. My right hand
was shaking, so I held up the gun with both hands to
try to keep it steady, aimed at the base of the main
rotor, and fired.

The rotor snapped off and whipped into the trees,
cutting trees in two, and the helicopter slammed into
the bayou. "It's down!" I shouted. I dropped to the
raft. The help ran out from under their sacks, screeching. "Helicopter's down!" I shouted.

The help didn't understand. They rushed up in
the roots again, thinking we were going to be burned.
I grabbed my pole and shoved the raft toward the
hole I'd cut in the roots.

The roots closest to the bayou were all on fire. I
cut them down with my gun. They fell in the water
and hissed and smoked, and one kept burning, it was
so hot. Six help dropped onto the raft and cowered
back by Sam, trying to shade their eyes. "Come
back!" I shouted at the rest of the help. "Come
now!" They wouldn't come, so I fired the gun above
their heads. They screeched and dropped onto the
raft and clung to each other. I shoved the raft through
the hole I'd cut.

The helicopter was on its side in the water, and
sinking. The door slammed open, and I heard one of

the company boys swear. The help shaded their eyes to look at the helicopter and chittered and spit at it. I poled the raft down the bayou, fast. I wanted to get around at least one bend before the company boys climbed out and inflated their emergency raft. I wanted them to wonder where I was and if I wouldn't shoot them.

And I wanted to get away. American Nicoji would rescue its boys, fast, and the rescue would hunt us: I'd wrecked a helicopter, and the company had only three. If they caught us and found out who we were for sure and didn't kill us outright, our contracts would make us pay for the damages. Sam and I could work our whole lives at their wages and not pay for that one helicopter.

I got to the first bend and looked back. One company boy lay flat on the side of the helicopter, aiming a gun. He fired, hit the logs at my feet, and burned through the lashing between two logs. I fell to the side, nearly off the raft, afraid he'd raise the beam and burn me in two. He fired again and hit the far edge of the raft, and I managed to shove the raft around the bend. The company boy kept firing into the roots above us and below us and all around us. The help screeched every time they heard a root splash in the water or saw the beam from the gun arc through the air.

They'll follow us, I thought. I kept shoving the raft down the bayou as fast as I could and got us out of gun range. Soon the only smoke I could smell was the smoke in my hair and the help fur. But the pântano was quiet, and it stayed quiet. I needed to look around. We needed to hide if the company boys were behind us in a raft or if other helicopters had already picked them up. I shoved the raft against the roots of a big tree. I was too tired to climb it, but I had to. I pulled the sacks off the help, and they hunched down on the logs, hands over their eyes. "You've got to take the rope up this tree and hold it so I can climb up," I said. "I've got to find out if we're being followed."

None moved. I grabbed a help and shoved him into the roots. He hissed at me but started climbing through the roots toward the trunk, shading his eyes. "I'm sorry, guys," I said. "But we've got to do this." Suddenly all the help swarmed into the roots and hurried up the tree trunk. They hadn't taken the rope.

"You've got to take the rope!" I shouted.

No answer. I could see only three help climbing around in the lower branches. One held onto a limb and urinated, splashing the water close to where I stood on the edge of the raft. I stepped back. "Can you see anything?" I yelled. The help looked at me, then disappeared in the branches. Damn, I thought. My leg that the help had bitten was bloody and sore. I got the alcohol from the medkit and dumped alcohol over the bite. Then I lashed the logs back together. The logs were charred and splintered.

I gave up on the help and shoved the raft back out on the bayou. The help started chittering and jumping through the branches from tree to tree, trying to get ahead of me. When they did, they swarmed down a tree trunk and clung to the roots and closed their eyes. I shoved the raft against the roots so they could jump on. Help-with-the-hurt-hand came last. He patted my cheek before swinging out of the roots. "Gone," he said. "Hel-i-op gone."

"How do you know? How can you see in the light?"

"Help hear no heliop. Pântano quiet. Quiet, Jake."

Fine, I thought. I could accept that as a true and valid observation. They could hear better than me.

"But what about rafts?" I said. "Were any rafts following us?"

The help just squinted at me. They had no answer. I decided to keep moving, to keep putting distance between us and the downed helicopter. I covered up Sam again, shoved us out on the bayou, and headed south, fast, watching the sky whenever there were breaks in the leafy canopy above us and watching behind me for another raft.

The bayou forked, one channel flowing south, the other east. Only five help had climbed under the sacks with Sam. The rest stood with me trying to watch the bayou through tiny slits between their fingers.

"This way, Jake. This way," Help-with-the-hurt-hand said, pointing east.

"The new town's in the other direction."

"Sam better this way."

"What do you mean?"

He didn't answer.

"We've got to get Sam to a doctor in the new town," I said. "And the town's south of here."

"This way, Jake. This way!" Help-with-the-hurt-hand said.

The others started chittering. "This way," they repeated, pointing east and pounding the logs. They took turns pounding Help-with-the-hurt-hand on the head, letting him know they agreed with him.

"Damn it, what's east?" I yelled, shoving my pole in the mud and guiding us toward the east fork, not the south.

"Help get Sam better. Better, Jake."

"How?"

"Then Jake give help knife. Knife, Jake."

"Bowls, Jake. Bowls."

They started chittering about all the things they wanted from me once they'd cured Sam: the chest, nicoji, the entire freeze-shack to sleep in. I stopped the raft. "You're trying to strike a bargain?" I asked. "You can make Sam better?"

"Make Sam better, Jake. Better."

"Why didn't you tell me this before?"

The help just looked at me. But I knew why. It hadn't occurred to them, till now, that Sam's life was a commodity I'd bargain for.

"Got give shirt, Jake. Shirt."

"Sure," I said. "I'll give you anything you want—ask me for the sky, ask for the moon. We'll have Christmas if you make Sam better."

The help chittered and pounded the logs, and I shoved the raft toward the east. But I didn't know if I could trust the help to really do something to make Sam better. They had tried to kill Sam once already. "I want Sam to live," I said.

"Sam live this way."

"How?"

No answer.

Sam and I had always thought the help lived south of American Nicoji's concession, so we were probably in territory familiar to the help, and I started wondering if the new company had set up some kind of jungle supply center the help knew about. I wondered if they were taking us to a place where Sam could get medicine and get better. I hoped that was it. I would have loved them for it. Sam could have used an Albert Schweitzer.

The help crawled back under sacks. One or another kept poking out his head, making sure I took the east channels when the main channel forked. "Where are we going?" I asked.

No answer. I poled us east for over an hour, and

the bayou got deeper and deeper. I had to keep the raft against one side so I could maybe touch bottom or at least snag my pole in the tree roots and shove us along. I saw no sign of a helicopter—but also no sign of anything else. I'd had it. I shoved my pole between two roots and stopped the raft. The help peeked out at me. "I won't go any further unless you tell me where we're going," I said. "What's east? Why will Sam get better if we go east?"

Still no answer. I started shoving the raft back toward a south-flowing channel. Help-with-the-hurt-hand squinted up at me. "House east," he said. "Help house east. Sam better there."

Help house? What did he mean? The place where his people lived? We'd never seen any young or old help, or any females. Sam and I had teased them about the females, but when we asked where they lived the help would only rock back and forth, pounding the logs of our raft and making vague motions in directions that took in half the pântano.

"Your people can cure Sam?" I asked.

They would not say anything else.

"That way," Help-with-the-hurt-hand said, shaking his hand impatiently toward the east.

I shoved the raft that way.

The help were natives. They'd have had to deal with lagarto poison before. So they just might be able to help Sam.

VI

We went around three bends in the bayou, and abruptly the water extended from the edge of the raft to the horizon. I had to shade my eyes from the glare of light on the water. I thought at first it was the sea, but it was a lake. The bayou had flowed into an enormous, shallow lake. I could not see the eastern shore. Hills rose up on the south, high and forested, part of the foothills of the mesão—and the mesão itself loomed over the south. We were so close.

Brown mud flats dotted the lake. They were covered with nicoji holes—millions of them. "Sam," I said. "What a time for you to get sick." We could have bought our passage home with the nicoji in that lake. We'll come back, I thought. As soon as Sam gets better and our situation with the companies straightens out.

The help all stood and squinted south. Help-with-the-hurt-hand pointed in that direction, toward the hills. I stopped the raft and listened for a helicopter. I couldn't hear one, but I didn't like going out on an open lake. The help started chittering and pointing and touching my pole. I looked at Sam. "All right," I said.

For over an hour I guided the raft around mud flats while looking for channels the raft could fit through and watching the sky. The help lay around the edges of the raft, shading their eyes with one hand and trying to grab nicoji with the other. Most nicoji had burrowed into the mud, but my help caught a few still swimming. Watching the help eat raw nicoji made me realize how hungry I was. I hadn't eaten all day.

One of the help suddenly jerked his hand out of the water and screamed. The other help crowded around him, chittering. One threw something in the water, and I could smell sulfur.

"What was it?" I asked.

The hurt help was scraping his arm on the logs and cooing. I looked in the water and saw movement— not nicoji, something longer, thinner, almost transparent. I let the raft drift and knelt to look. We were over a school of foot-long, crystal snakes with teeth and black eyes. They would curl up, then unwind, fast, in the direction they wanted to go, and drift through the water. One brushed against a nicoji that sat frozen on the mud, and curled tight around the nicoji, bit off its head, and burrowed through the neck into the body. The nicoji's heart and intestines slid down around the coils of the snake.

I stood up and smashed the snake into the mud with my pole. Then I walked to the help who'd been bitten. He wouldn't show me his arm. I had to pull it out from under him. It was bloody. He'd been bleeding on the logs, and blood had run into the water. Snakes were swarming around the raft. I wrapped the help's arm in a sack, told him not to let the blood get in the water, and shoved us toward the south shore. Snakes followed us for a long time.

As we got closer to shore, I saw a help walking on the muddy beach below the headland, not seeming to mind the sun. Was this whole world going crazy? The help would feel for nicoji holes, pull up the nicoji, touch them all over, and toss away the ones it didn't want.

Suddenly it stood up straight, listening. It had heard me shove my pole in the water and push the raft ahead. It looked out over the water, head tilted back, arms and hands held warily in front. It was female. Eight thin, sagging breasts, covered only in spots with fur, hung from her chest. "Here's one of your women," I said to my help. They squinted and shook their heads and tried to look through cracks between their fingers—then stood up and chittered and pounded the logs and slapped the water. The female ran across the beach, felt all over the rocks at the base, then suddenly climbed up the cliff and disappeared in the trees.

"Not see," Help-with-the-hurt-hand said. "She not see."

Blind? I thought. And female. That explained why light didn't bother her. But the help had a more advanced social structure than I'd imagined if they supported blind females.

I poled us onto the beach, and my help scampered off the raft and climbed into the trees and shadows. "Stay!" Help-with-the-hurt-hand called down to me. "Stay raft!" He disappeared. I tied the raft to a root,

cut down eight leafy branches, and laid them over
the raft to camouflage it. Some of the leaves were
crinkling up, turning brown. The beach was scattered with dry leaves.

I sat by Sam under the branches. He lay there,
not moving, hardly breathing, hot with fever. "We're
rich now, Sam," I said. "This lake's going to take us
home."

When I looked up, I saw three help standing in
shadows under the roots, help I'd never seen. They
squinted at Sam and me and stood very still. I did
not move. I did not want to frighten them. One
started chewing on the root I'd tied the raft to, just
above my knot. Another crowded in and started scraping his teeth across the same root, faster and faster.
They gnawed deep gashes in the root, then twisted it
till it broke off. The third help picked it up, squinted
at me, and threw it as hard as he could.

I caught it in my hands and held it. The raft
bobbed up and down on the little waves that washed
ashore from the lake, scraping east along the muddy
beach. The help disappeared in the shadows. I just
sat and held the root and watched the trees up the
headland for my help.

Only Help-with-the-hurt-hand came back, holding
leaves in front of his eyes. He stared at the camou-
flaged raft, then dropped the leaves in the water,
climbed under the branches by me, held his hands
over his eyes, and looked dejected. "Help not happy,"
he said. "Not happy."

I untied the rope from the piece of root I was
holding and threw the root on the beach. "What do
we do?" I asked. "What can we do for Sam?"

No answer.

"Should I just take Sam and try to get to the
mesão?" I asked.

"Afraid," he said. "Afraid humans take nicoji, take lake."

I looked away from him, ashamed. They had reason to be afraid. They had reason to be afraid of me. The help who had worked with Sam and me had offered to help Sam, had brought us to where their people lived—and I had made plans, without thinking of consequences to the help, to harvest the nicoji they depended on. Who did I think I was?

"Got lot help eat nicoji, Jake. Lot help."

I looked at him, and suddenly some things started to make sense. "You've been guiding us away from this lake, haven't you—all of you, all the help."

He said nothing.

"You came out to work with us to make sure we didn't find this lake, and that's why the other help are so mad: you brought us here and we have seen it."

He started to crawl away, but I pulled him back. "I'm not mad," I said. "You did the right thing."

What else could they have done? Once they learned what we had come for, what else could they have done?

He squinted up at me. I had thought of him and all the help as innocents who sometimes did good work for a few nicoji and an occasional trinket. But all along, they had been controlling us. I rubbed the top of his head. "It wouldn't have worked forever, you know."

Somebody would have found the lake, eventually.

"Work long time, Jake. Keep you away lot long time."

I smiled. He kept squinting up at me.

"We've still got to help Sam," I said.

He reached under the sacks and touched Sam's chest, feeling for his heartbeat. "Stay," he said, finally. "Stay raft."

I grabbed his arm before he could leave. "Tell them Sam is dying." I didn't know if it would help. I didn't know if they would care. It was a human appeal. Help-with-the-hurt-hand hurried across the beach, wormed his way through the tangled roots, and disappeared. I heard chittering under the roots, then quiet.

It was late afternoon when he came back with seven help who had worked with Sam and me. "Sam," he said. "Bring Sam."

I wondered how he'd convinced the others to help Sam, but I didn't take time to ask. I strapped my gun to my waist, grabbed the rope, and tied it to three roots, hoping the help wouldn't gnaw them all off and let the raft drift away. "Will the raft be safe?" I asked.

The help pulled the sacks off Sam and tugged at him. They paid no attention to me or my question. I hefted Sam over my left shoulder and staggered onto the muddy, slippery beach. "Where to?" I asked.

The help ran ahead of me and showed me a narrow path up the cliff. Halfway up, a stick hit my head. I looked up and saw help crouched along the cliff edge throwing leaves and sticks and rocks at us. I shoved Sam against the rock and hung onto him. My help rushed up the path, chittering and waving their arms, and the other help disappeared. I couldn't see any of them when we got to the top.

I carried Sam inland along a trail under the trees. They had me lay him on the bank of a clear stream that bubbled out of the rock, forming a series of pools before it flowed off. The help waded into the pools and tore grass out of the water and heaped it up on shore. I pulled Sam onto their piles when they were done. The grass was cool and wet.

The help ran off and soon came back with handfuls of wilted, red-veined leaves. They sat in a circle around Sam and chewed the leaves.

"What are the leaves for?" I asked.

But none of the help could talk. Their mouths were full. After a time, Help-with-the-hurt-hand leaned forward toward Sam, slowly, as if he were going to kiss him. I got up to shove him away, but the other help pulled me back. Help-with-the-hurt-hand touched his lips to Sam's, and I could see his cheeks working.

He was spitting the juice of the chewed leaves into Sam's mouth.

"Stop that!" I yelled. Sam could get diseases from help spit. I tried to crawl up and knock Help-with-the-hurt-hand away from Sam, but the others clung to me and held me back. One pulled on my shoulders so hard he spit the juice out of his mouth. It ran down my arm, warm and red.

Help-with-the-hurt-hand sat back, pulled a wad of leaf pulp from his mouth and held it, spit three times in the grass, then wiped his mouth with the back of his hand. "Jake want Sam live?" he asked. "Want live?"

"Yes, but—"

Help-with-the-hurt-hand pulled one of the help off my back and shoved him toward Sam's head. A trickle of red juice had run from Sam's mouth to his ear. The second help grabbed Sam's head, put his lips to Sam's, and started spitting juice in Sam's mouth.

"You don't have to spit in Sam's mouth," I said. "I can get pans and bowls from the raft and make tea."

"Not work," Help-with-the-hurt-hand said. "Not work. Help spit make leaves work."

I thought about that. Chemicals in the help spit *could* react with chemicals in the leaves to create a compound that counteracted lagarto poison. I didn't know what to do. Help-with-the-hurt-hand crawled to Sam's legs, tore off a bandage, and rubbed his chewed leaf pulp over the wound where the lagarto tongue had punctured the skin. He started taking off the other bandages, and I helped him. The skin on Sam's leg was purple around the puncture marks, then white—blanched—around the purple.

Infected.

If only I could have found the antibiotics from the medkit.

A third help crawled off my back and spit juice in Sam's mouth while the second rubbed leaf pulp on Sam's leg.

"Agree now?" Help-with-the-hurt-hand asked. "Jake agree good spit Sam?"

"Maybe," I said.

Sam never moved till the fourth help spit juice in his mouth. He coughed and sputtered, and I thought he opened his eyes. Two help cooed and put their hands over Sam's heart.

"What's it doing to him?" I asked.

Help-with-the-hurt-hand threw me a leaf. I picked it up. It didn't look healthy, and I wondered if blighted leaves could have the effect on Sam the help were hoping for. I put the leaf in my mouth. It tasted bitter, salty, and it numbed my mouth and tongue and throat. Help-with-the-hurt-hand touched my throat. "Not swallow," he said.

Great, I thought, since I'd already swallowed some juice. I spit the leaf pulp into my hand and rubbed it over one of the puncture wounds on Sam's leg. I didn't know if it would do any good. Human spit probably couldn't react with the leaves in the right way. My heart started beating fast—the leaves had some kind of natural stimulant—and my stomach started contracting around the juice I'd swallowed. I closed my eyes and had to fight not to throw up. I wondered how Sam could stand not throwing up.

The fifth help was spitting juice into Sam's mouth— When Sam leaned over and heaved black vomit. The help scattered. Sam dropped back and held his left arm over his eyes—the first time he'd moved like that on his own in a day and a half. "Sam!" I said.

He looked at me. The help scampered back, and one leaned down to Sam's lips. Sam tried to push him away, but the others held his arms and head while the help spit juice in his mouth.

"How much does he have to take?" I asked.

My help didn't even look up. I put another leaf in my mouth and started to chew it, but something hit the pond next to me and splashed water in my face. I wiped my eyes and looked across the pond. One help stood there in the twilight, the blind female. She had a stick she kept slapping on the water. Three of my help went and guided her around the water to Sam.

She'd chewed a mouthful of red-veined leaves. Her cheeks bulged with spit and leaf pulp. She held clumps of the leaves in her left hand and kept smelling them. Her hair was matted and dirty, and she stank, but she'd come to help Sam when none of the other wild help would. I liked her for it. Not even all the help who had worked with Sam and me had come. Help-with-the-hurt-hand took the stick and leaves from her hands, made her kneel by Sam's head, and pushed her face down to Sam's.

I spit the juice from my mouth, pulled out the leaf pulp, and rubbed it on Sam's leg. The pulp made my fingers numb.

The help spit juice in Sam's mouth till he'd thrown up six or seven times, till his vomit stopped coming up black and only came up red like the juice.

Sam was awake. His eyes were open and his face was white, not red. The help dragged him into one of the pools. I knelt next to it and took hold of his wrist to feel his pulse. It was beating steadily. "You OK?" I asked.

"You let them do this to me, didn't you?" he said.

"You were dying."

He raised up out of the pool and threw up on the grass. He probably thought he'd still die, except that now he'd do it in conscious misery. When he leaned back, I felt his forehead. "They broke your fever," I said.

Sam went to sleep once we got him out of the pool. I decided to go down to the raft and get the alcohol out of the medkit. It might help Sam's leg. And I could boil water and wrap the leg in hot packs to maybe kill some of the infection and bring down the swelling.

"I've got to get the medkit," I told the help. They were all sitting around me and Sam. It was dark under the trees, and quiet. It would soon be night. The help didn't say anything.

"You'll watch Sam?" I asked.

"Help watch," Help-with-the-hurt-hand said. "Help watch Sam."

The blind female suddenly stood up, cupped her hands over her ears, and ran away into the shadows. Help-with-the-hurt-hand stood and pointed toward the lake.

And I heard the distant thumping of helicopter rotors.

Fool, I thought. I've been a fool. I should have dragged the raft into the trees.

I ran down the trail to the cliff. The raft was bobbing in plain sight on the lake twelve feet from shore—the other help had pulled off the branches, thrown them on the water, chewed through the roots I'd tied the raft to, and let the raft drift out on the lake. I could see help tracks on the beach. The tide hadn't come in yet. I looked for the helicopter and saw it, black over trees across the lake, the last light glinting off the metal. Maybe they won't see the raft, I thought. It's small. I crouched in the underbrush, thick near the cliff where the trees cast less shade. The helicopter flew back and forth over the treetops for a time but suddenly struck out straight across the lake toward the raft. I crawled back under the trees, unstrapped my gun, turned it on, and listened to it hum.

The helicopter hovered over the raft: American Nicoji 0109-1. It flew out of sight across the headland, then back over the trees to hover above the raft again. A company boy dropped a ladder and started climbing down. I knew him. He was the guy whose nose I'd broken in the fight before the doctor implanted the locators. I raised my gun and aimed it at his head. I could have killed him. I raised the gun a little higher and aimed it at the base of the rotors—one shot and I could have brought down the helicopter and picked off the company boys as they got the doors open or broke the windows and swam out of the wreck.

I did nothing.

The company boy jumped down on the raft, opened the chest, and threw the bowls, the medkit, and Sam's *Pilgrim's Progress* out of it. Something touched my hand. I spun around. It was one of my help. "Go back," I hissed. "Get!" If the company boys saw the help they'd maybe start shooting. The help scampered back and stared at me wide-eyed. "These men burn trees!" I hissed. The help blinked and ran off through the shadows, remembering what had happened earlier in the day.

When I looked back, another company boy had climbed down to the raft. He and the first were carefully putting something in the chest. They gingerly closed the lid. The new guy strapped Sam's gun to his waist, and they hurried up the ladder and pulled the ladder in after them.

They'd left a bomb for Sam and me. The company set movement-sensitive bombs in the bayous around the company town to kill lagarto trying to get to the garbage dump. They had to set new bombs every two or three nights, so many lagarto tried to get to the dump to eat our garbage. The explosions would rock the town, gouge out deep holes in the bayous, disintegrate whole sections of forest.

And they'd put a bomb in our chest.

One of the company boys came back and stood in the helicopter doorway and pointed a remote down at the chest to activate the bomb. Then he slammed the door, and they flew out of sight to the north, back toward the company town.

I watched the helicopter fly away and wondered if I could wade out to the raft, pick up the medkit, and get back to shore without dying. Sam needed the alcohol. We both needed the stuff they'd scattered. But what would Sam do if I got killed? He'd have to build a new raft, and I didn't know when he'd feel well enough to do that. In the meantime, who'd take care of him? The help—when most help didn't want him? What would they feed him—grubs, raw nicoji? Sam would die from the diet, if not from the lagarto poison.

I strapped my gun to my side, climbed down the cliff, and stood on the shore with my toes in the water, squishing mud through them. A breeze was blowing off the sea, and it made me cold all over. The medkit lay on the near edge of the raft, ten steps out. I could pick it up and walk back and decide what to do after that.

I took one step in the water and watched the ripples fan out from my leg. You're a fool, I thought. This isn't worth it. You can get along without water-purification tablets and alcohol. The new company town is only a day away. I took another step. Easy, I thought. One at a time. The nets were piled in the middle of the raft. We'd need those. We couldn't pole into the company town completely destitute. I didn't want to have to buy everything new and start out owing a lot of money. Another step, then another. Six more, I thought. A little wave washed in. I stopped and watched it lift up the far end of the raft, come out under the near end, and wash past my legs to the shore. When it flowed back out, it pulled away some of the mud under my feet. I sank down. A nicoji squirmed under my right foot. I took another step, and another, careful not to disturb the water more than the wave had. Another step. I could see one of our lights underneath Sam's red shirt next to the medkit. We'd need a light. I took three more steps and was at the raft. I looked at a burlap sack—made sure nothing was on it that could drop and set off the bomb—and picked it up, shook it open. I set the medkit in the bottom of the sack. I picked up the light and Sam's red shirt and shoved them in the sack. My picture of Loryn was under Sam's shirt, still wrapped in plastic. I dropped it in the sack. The bowls, I thought. We'd need bowls to dissolve water-purification tablets in. I picked up three bowls, one at a time, and put them in the sack. Each bowl was chipped now, after being thrown on the logs. Pink clay showed through the brown glaze. Enough, I thought, I've got enough. Then I saw Sam's *Pilgrim's Progress,* closer to the chest. It was his only book. I took two steps around the edge of the raft, reached for the book, grabbed the front cover, pulled up the book, and shoved it in the sack. That's it, I thought. That's all I'm putting in the sack.

I left the can of liquid nitrogen, threw the nets and the burlap sacks on the beach, took the firebox and the mesh grill and my sack of stuff, turned around, and started for shore. I'll carry what I've got in my hands to the top of the cliff, then come back to the beach for the sacks and nets, I thought—

When I heard rushing water behind me.

The tide.

I looked back at a wave four feet high flowing over the lake from all the seaward bayous. I ran. I got to the shore, dropped the grill and the firebox, and started climbing. It's going to hit the raft, I thought. The wave's going to hit the raft. I reached the hilltop and still had the sack. Fool, I thought. Drop it! But I didn't drop it. I turned to look back, once.

The wave splashed over the raft and lifted it up, shoved it toward shore.

And the bomb exploded.

The logs of the raft blew apart, and there were leaves and mud on my face and chest and something salty in my mouth. I was lying on my back. I spat blood and stood up. The entire side of the cliff was on fire. Even the water burned where the raft had been.

The flames would bring back the helicopter. I grabbed the sack and ran. "Sam!" I shouted. "Sam!" I didn't know why I was shouting. Sam couldn't get up and run. I could only drag him somewhere and hide.

But Sam wasn't in the clearing. "Sam!" I yelled. What had happened?

I ran across the clearing to the other side. "Sam!" I kept yelling.

It was dark now, night. I couldn't see. I stopped to listen, and above the roar of the fire I heard the helicopter. I didn't know where Sam was, but I had to hide. I ran under the trees, and something plucked at my legs. I rolled to the ground and pulled out my gun.

"Not shoot! Not shoot, Jake!"

It was one of my help. He tugged on my arm. "Come, Jake. Come." I grabbed the sack, and the help took hold of my hand and led me deeper into the forest. The land sloped down. The help dropped my hand and disappeared. "Where are you?" I whispered. The helicopter flew over the headland, shining lights through the trees. I crouched down, and the help poked his head out of the ground.

"Hole," he said, and he pulled on my arm. "Hole." I shoved my sack ahead of me and crawled in the hole, into a cave.

The ceiling was so low I couldn't sit up. I had to lie on my stomach. The cave smelled musty, like the help. I hoped just the help who had worked with Sam and me were in there, but as my eyes adjusted to the dark I could see pair after pair of silvery help eyes looking at me, rarely blinking. All the help were in this cave. I could hear them breathe. I watched their eyes and tried not to breathe hard.

Something soft and warm splattered over my forehead. I wiped it off: help dung. More hit my neck. "Bastards!" I shouted.

"Jake!" Sam shouted back.

The help started chittering when they heard our voices. Dung hit my legs. All I could see were gleaming help eyes.

"Get me out of here, Jake."

I felt around the cave floor for my sack and found
it kicked against the far wall. I pulled out the light,
turned it on, and shined it around the cave. The help
screeched and rushed into corners. The cave was
weird: human junk was heaped in piles in it—wires,
plastic sacks, empty tin cans. The help had been
packing off our garbage and stealing from us and
storing the loot here. Sam was leaning against the
south wall. He was covered with dung. I crawled to
him and shoved one of the help aside. It hissed and
tried to bite my arm, so I shined my light in its face
and made it cower back. "How did you get here,
Sam?" I asked.

"Our help dragged me, but we can't stay. The wild
help were working themselves up to maybe tear out
my throat."

"They blew up the raft, Sam. Company boys blew
up the raft. They meant to kill us."

The help were chittering and hissing. One tried to
grab the light from my hand. "Light," it said. "Stop
light. Not talk. Not talk scare help."

It was Help-with-the-hurt-hand. When the other
help heard him speaking English they hissed at him
and tried to pinch him through his fur. Help dung
splattered across the back of my neck. "We'll leave!"
I shouted. "Just let us go."

The helicopter passed over. When the help heard
it, they hissed and threw sticks and rocks at Sam and
me, not just dung. I threw the sack out of the cave,
grabbed Sam's arms, and dragged him out, thinking
we could hide under the trees, somehow.

None of the help followed. I kept thinking that till
I could build a new raft Sam and I were stranded
with the help and what was that going to be like?

We sat in shadows for nearly an hour, listening,
but never heard the helicopter again. I helped Sam

to the pools, and we tried to wash off the dung. We needed soap. I kept wishing I'd carried the soap away with me from the raft. Sam and I still smelled like help dung when we gave up and collapsed under the trees.

Sam was exhausted. He went to sleep as soon as he lay down. I tried to keep watch and managed to stay awake for some time, listening for the helicopter or the help. I heard the hush after the fire went out on the cliff and a wind come up that rolled waves against the shore. I turned off my gun.

And someone whispered my name. I turned the gun back on.

"Jake," the whisper came again, and I realized it was a woman's voice.

The moon had risen, and in its red light I could see piles of junk stacked under the trees: old pans, empty liquid nitrogen cans, the complete motor from a rusted freezer.

"Jake?" I heard the voice again. It was the voice of the girl with red slippers.

I looked around. "Where are you? I can't see you," I whispered.

"What are you going to do, Jake?" she asked.

I turned off my gun, thinking I was scaring her. "Come out," I said.

When she answered me, her voice seemed far away. "What are you going to do?" she called.

"Come back!" I said. But all I could hear was the wind and the waves on the shore.

I opened my eyes. No girl from Kansas stood in the shadows. I took the light and the picture of Loryn out of the sack and sat there looking at Loryn.

VII

"Jake! Jake!"

I sat up and wondered if I was dreaming again, but I hurt in so many places I knew I was awake. I shook my head and tried to see. It was still dark, night. Red moonlight made patches on the ground here and there like islands on a map of some black sea.

"Jake!"

"Here," I shouted.

It was Help-with-the-hurt-hand. He walked out of the shadows, holding his hands over his eyes and watching me through slits between his fingers as if it were daylight. "Leave, Jake," he said. "Take Sam. Take raft. Go new house."

"The raft is gone," I said. "Company boys blew it up."

He sat down when I said that. Sam rolled over and kept sleeping.

"I have to build a new raft," I said. "That will take time."

"Help not happy. Not happy you here."

"I know."

"Help not happy, Jake."

I scraped a gob of dried help dung off my shoulder. "What do you want me to do?"

He flinched when I said that. I hadn't shouted, but my tone hurt him.

"We're stranded here," I said. "Sam's not well enough to help me build a new raft. I've got to do it alone."

"Help not happy, Jake. Not happy."

"What will they do?"

He said nothing.

"Will they try to hurt Sam and me?"

Nothing again.

"Answer me!"

"Help not happy."

"What does that mean?"

He stood up and started to walk away. I grabbed his arm, tight. He turned and hissed at me and almost bit my hand, but he didn't bite it. His arm was wet—bloody. I let go and rubbed my hand clean on the grass.

"What happened?" I asked.

He was shaking his arm. "Help pinch," he said. "Other help pinch."

"Why?"

"Talk English Sam. Talk English Jake."

I just looked at him. The other help had pinched him till he bled because he spoke English to Sam and me. English must have made him seem like us—alien. "I've got alcohol," I said. "I saved the medkit from the raft."

But the sack with everything I'd saved was gone. My gun was gone. I jumped up and started kicking through the grass, but everything was gone. "Where's the sack?" I shouted. "Where's my gun?"

Help-with-the-hurt-hand crawled away into the shadows. He chittered something, then was quiet. I saw him climbing a tree.

"Where's our stuff?" I shouted.

He kept climbing. I threw a stick at him, and it slammed into the tree trunk. "Bring back our stuff!"

"Help fix Sam, Jake. Fix Sam. Help got take bowls, got take sacks, got take—"

I threw another stick at him, and he shut up.

"What's wrong?" Sam asked, groggy.

"I bargained away everything we owned for your life," I said. I'd forgotten that. I'd forgotten I promised the help the sky and the moon when they offered to cure Sam. I kept kicking through the grass, thinking maybe they'd missed something. Missed the gun. "I have to get back the gun!" I yelled at Help-with-the-hurt-hand, but he didn't answer. I couldn't see him in the tree.

"What will they do with a gun?" Sam asked.

"Kill each other, I hope—no, that's too good for them: cut off each other's feet so they have to crawl through mud trying to catch some dirty, stinking bug to eat—"

"Jake! Jake, got bargain," Help-with-the-hurt-hand whined from up in the tree.

"Get back our stuff. You need the alcohol. I need my gun."

"Why does he need alcohol?" Sam asked.

I explained what the other help had done to him.

"Sting," Help-with-the-hurt-hand said. "Sting."

"What stings?" I asked.

"The alcohol," Sam said.

"It's supposed to," I said. "We've got to disinfect your arm."

"Help not disinfect before humans, not disinfect, Jake."

I looked at the tree and could see Help-with-the-hurt-hand hanging onto the trunk. He jumped down and crouched in the shadows, looking at me.

"Yes, and I'll bet a lot of you died," I said.

Sam started rubbing his leg. I kept kicking through the grass but found nothing. Everything was gone. The help had left us nothing but the scraps of shorts we wore. I hated to think of the help crawling around Sam and me—robbing us—while we slept. We were crazy to have slept on the ground like that. I was crazy to have gone to sleep.

Help dung splattered across my left eye. I wiped it away and flicked it to the ground. Help-with-the-hurt-hand was gone. At first I thought he'd thrown the dung. But more hit Sam and me—then sticks, leaves, and rocks. One small rock slammed into my forehead. Sam tried to stand, but he couldn't put weight on his leg. Blood ran from my forehead into my eyes. I wiped it away, pulled Sam up and got him into the clearing by the pools. I grabbed sticks to fight with in case the help came after us, but none came. The help stayed in the trees and kept throwing rocks, dung, and sticks. Most landed short. Sam and I were smeared with dung again, and my face was wet with blood from the cut on my forehead. Sam still had his pocketknife in the pocket of his shorts. I borrowed it and sharpened a good stick into a spear.

Suddenly the help stopped throwing things. The forest was quiet.

"We've got to get out of here," Sam said.

I threw down my sticks, knelt by the pool, and washed off my face. "Let's go," I said.

I pulled Sam up, hung onto him to help him walk,

took my spear and set out around the pools into the trees across the clearing.

We got to the cliff over the lake. The fire had burned the cliff down to dirt and rock. Some rocks we stepped on were still hot. I looked at what the fire had done and realized I was a fool to have gone after gear on the raft, especially since the help took it anyway.

"Here's my book," Sam said.

"Where?"

Sam picked up a page torn from his *Pilgrim's Progress*. I looked over the cliff and saw the other pages scattered on the rocks. Sam let go of his page, and we watched it flutter back and forth till it caught on a ledge. "I've got to sit down," Sam said.

We sat on the edge of the cliff. Neither of us said anything about the book. I wondered what the help had done with my picture of Loryn.

Sam started rubbing his leg. He needed antibiotics. I looked away from him. He needed more than just antibiotics, of course. So did I. For one thing, we were both starving. I hadn't eaten anything the day before, and I knew Sam needed food. He also needed rest and all kinds of medical attention. My own stomach hurt from all the throwing up I'd done; my leg hurt where the help had bit me and where my skin had blistered after my shorts burned away; my wrist was sore where I'd cut out the locator, and it had bled in the night—I'd bumped it against something. The skin on my legs and feet was peeling away wherever the froth had touched it, and it stung. I wanted a hot shower, plenty of soap to get the smell of help dung off me, a competent doctor, and rest—I could have slept all the coming day. I didn't want to have to catch my own food because I worked for a company that forced me to live off the land as much as possible, cook the food myself if I could start a fire, then try to build a raft without a gun to cut down trees or notch logs with—while taking care of Sam, watching for the help, and hiding from helicopters. I didn't know if I could do it.

Sam's head slumped down on his chest. He was going to sleep. I held onto him so he wouldn't fall over the edge and watched the lake. It was black in the red moonlight, and the tips of the waves were touched with red. A gentle wind moved over the water and blew my hair. It dried the blood on my face.

The leaves in all the trees started to rustle in that wind. Pages from Sam's book blew off the rocks and ledges and settled onto the water. I sat there and let the wind blow on my face and thought of the two guys I knew who'd gone to college and on to safe jobs in corporate arcologies in Boise or Helena—maybe even making enough to once a year eat two or three of the nicoji we sent back. Here Sam and I sat, risking our lives to look at another corporation's operation on the chance that it would be so much better than what we already had we'd want them to buy our contracts.

I dropped a stone over the cliff and listened to it clatter on the rocks below. Lose hope, I thought. That's it. Lose hope and see where you'll end up. The breeze gusted against Sam and me. I took a deep breath of the cool air—and saw the logs. Three logs from our raft were floating near shore.

"Look at the *logs*," I said to Sam.

He tried to open his eyes. "What logs?" he asked.

"Those, on the lake."

I had to get them. I could use them as the framework for a new raft. Of course, I couldn't build the raft on the lake. The company might send helicopters looking, making sure. I didn't want to give them reason to keep looking. The lake curved south, then west. East, then, was the direction I'd go. I'd drag the logs east to a bayou, build the raft away from the lake, then float it south to the mesão.

Before I stood up, the tide started out. I heard the exact moment it turned, as if with a sudden intake of breath the sea started sucking water off the land. The logs began drifting out. I stood up and pulled Sam back from the edge. "I've got to go get those logs," I said.

Then I heard chittering by the water. Eight help had climbed down to the base of the cliff and were poking their hands in mud along the shore, trying to pull up nicoji. As the water receded, the help slogged farther and farther out, shaking the mud off their hands. I could tell from the high-pitched tone of their chittering that something was wrong. Good, I thought. I didn't mind if the help were hungry and couldn't catch any nicoji. One help ran back to the rock, scraped mud from its legs and hands, then hurried up into the trees where I heard more chittering. Chittering spread through all the trees around us. One help, far back toward the pools, started wailing. The others grew quiet. All I could hear was that one help wailing. Had a help died?

"The help are all around us," Sam said.

I stood and pulled Sam up. I couldn't leave him on the cliff for the help to maybe push off. "I've got to take you down with me."

I hurried him along the cliff edge, looking for the trail down, watching the trees. I could still hear only that one help wailing, but I knew the other help were in the trees.

I found the trail.

"You carried me up that?" Sam asked.

It looked doubtful even to me—and I knew I'd done it. I was glad I wouldn't have to carry Sam down this time. If I helped him, he could walk. I pulled down a vine, tied it around Sam, and we started down. The rock was hot under our feet. We were careful not to step in the ashes: we didn't want to blister our feet on live coals covered with ash. We already hurt in enough places. The help down in the mud looked at us and hissed and crowded together. Fine, I thought. Just as long as they stay away. I held my spear tight.

The shore was muddy and slimy. I handed Sam my spear, left him sitting on a rock, picking up pages from his book, and ran out into the mud and water after the logs.

Froth covered my legs almost at once. I knew then what worried the help. I tried to shove it away but just got it on my hands, and I couldn't keep it away. The froth was agony on my skin. I wanted to go back—get out of the water—but I had to get the logs. I waded out till water was past my belly, grabbed the nearest log, dragged it to shore, and climbed up on the rocks by Sam. I was shaking. "It's the froth," I said. "It's here, on the water."

"Did it follow us?"

"No." There was too much of it. In the growing light, I could see that the froth covered the lake.

This was a plague.

"I've got to get the other logs," I said.

"Leave them."

"And build the new raft out of what?"

Sam shook his head, then looked at me. "Tie the vine around one of the logs and throw me the other end. I'll pull it in while you bring the other."

I didn't know if he had the strength, but it was

worth trying. Sam untied the vine from around his stomach. I took the vine and waded back out. The logs had drifted farther away, and I had to wade out chest-deep. I closed my eyes while I tied the vine to the log—I didn't want to splash froth in my eyes— shoved the log back toward shore, and threw the vine to Sam. It fell short, on mud below the rock. Sam limped down to it and started pulling in the log. I waded to the other log, dragged it to shore, and helped Sam finish pulling in his. I had froth all over my skin. Sam got back on the rocks and started scraping mud off his feet. I couldn't get the froth off my skin. "It's all over me!" I said.

"It's sticking to your skin."

"It's eating my skin."

Sam used pages from his book to try to rub the froth off my skin but that just smeared it, so he scraped up dirt and ash and rubbed it on my legs. The dirt was burned dry by the fire. It rubbed off the froth. We started rubbing dirt all over my chest, back, and legs. Sam rubbed dirt over his muddy feet while I got the froth off my arms.

Three help started edging warily toward us, holding their hands in front of their eyes. I grabbed the spear. "Keep back!" I shouted.

"Jake?" one asked. "Jake?"

It was three of our help. I dropped the spear. They hurried up by Sam and started scraping mud from their feet. One grabbed my legs. I winced at the touch of his hands. "Not walk mud," he said. "Not walk."

"I know," I said. I pulled his hands off my legs and held them away from me.

"Not eat nicoji," one said. "Not eat nicoji now."

That's when I first wondered what the froth might be doing to the nicoji. I could see froth oozing into the mud like it had the day before. The nicoji had already burrowed down. "It's eating the nicoji, isn't it?" I said. The help started chittering and pointing.

I had to know. I waded back into the mud and shoved my hand down nicoji holes but couldn't feel any nicoji, so I scooped the mud aside, trying to find where they'd crawled to. I dug up two nicoji and held them in the light. They looked fine. Then I saw a nicoji farther out on mud where more froth had oozed down. It had crawled back up from its hole—into the light and air, things nicoji don't like. Another nicoji crawled up a little farther out. I dropped the nicoji in my hands, hurried out to the others—

But didn't pick them up. Their bodies were red with blood. One was dragging its intestines behind it across the mud. It soon stopped and lay gasping. The froth had eaten through its delicate skin. I crouched down and saw froth bubbling in the nicoii's intestines.

"Jake!" the help called. "Come back, Jake!" All three of them were still chittering and running up and down the muddy beach. I walked back to the rock and rubbed the mud off my legs and feet. The help cooed and tried to touch my skin. I swatted their hands away.

"It's killing the nicoji?" Sam asked.

"Here. I wonder how far it will spread."

"If far enough, maybe they'll send us home."

I doubted that. We had contracts, and we had debts. If the nicoji market collapsed because of a plague, the company would just send us to another world to do some other kind of work.

The logs were covered with froth. But as the light grew, the froth oozed down the sides and disappeared into the mud. All the logs were charred with fire. One was badly splintered.

The vine was saturated with froth. I pulled a new

one out of a tree down the shore, tied it to the logs one at a time, and pulled them each up the trail to the cliff top. The help tried to push the last one along from behind, then disappeared in the trees when we got to the top. I could still hear that one help wailing, and I wished it would shut up.

When I went back for Sam, he was asleep. "Let's go," I said, shaking him awake. A page from his book stuck to the bottom of his right foot, but it scraped off on the rock as he stumbled upwards. I got him to the top, gave him my spear and tied him to a tree so the help wouldn't throw him over the edge, lashed the logs together, and pulled them a hundred yards east through the trees away from the cliff. I turned to go back for Sam and saw, in the tree above me, a help wearing Sam's red shirt.

"Drop that shirt!" I shouted.

The help just squinted at me, then quietly climbed around to the north side of the tree where I couldn't see him.

I picked up a rock and threw it into the branches. The rock hit the trunk. The branches immediately started to rustle, and I could see that the tree was filled with help. I picked up another rock and held it, tight, in my right hand and backed toward Sam.

I never thought I'd be afraid of the help.

"Sam," I yelled. "Wake up."

I didn't turn to see if he were awake or not. The help were moving toward me through the trees, keeping to the shadows, coming slowly. I kept wishing I hadn't thrown that rock. Never drill for oil, the Bhutanese said, meaning that if no one noticed you, you might get to live in peace. One help threw a stick at my feet. It didn't hit. Their aim wasn't as good in the daylight. I couldn't see our help in the trees. "Sam and I are leaving," I shouted anyway, not knowing if even one of them could understand me. "You'll never see us again. Just let us go."

The sound of my voice infuriated them. They started throwing rocks and sticks. Dung splattered into my hair. I turned and ran back to Sam. The help swarmed through the trees after me, throwing everything they could grab. I stood in front of Sam's head to shield him.

But the help weren't throwing things just at Sam and me. The blind female was on the ground, and they were pelting *her* with dung and sticks. She was stumbling around, trying to get away—and headed for the cliff.

"No!" I shouted. "Stop!"

I ran and pulled her back from the cliff. She bit my arm—but let go at once—shocked, it seemed, to have tasted human blood, to have had a human arm in her mouth. I dragged her back by Sam. She whimpered and cowered down by Sam and held her hands over her head.

And the attack stopped. The help were still in the trees, watching. I untied Sam from the tree, pulled him to his feet, and hung onto him to help him walk. "Let's go!" I said. We started to walk away, but the blind female grabbed my right leg and hung on. I kicked my leg out of her hands, so she grabbed the left one.

"Good grief," I said. I leaned Sam against a tree, pulled the help's hands off my leg, dragged her away from us, and let her fall in the grass. She lay there and did not move. I walked back to Sam. The help in the trees started throwing sticks down on the blind female, one stick at a time. She did not move when they hit her.

"We can't leave her," I said.

"What will we do with her?" Sam asked.

I didn't know.

"She's a mess," Sam said.

But she'd tried to help Sam. She'd chewed up leaves and spit juice in his mouth when he needed it. Maybe it was our turn to do her a favor. She obviously hadn't wanted to stay here alone while the other help were angry with her. I walked over to her and picked her up. "We'll carry her away from these help, give them time to calm down," I told Sam.

I carried her and the spear and half dragged Sam into the trees east past the logs. The help didn't follow. I went back for the logs, dragged them past Sam and the blind female, then took Sam, the female, and the spear past the logs, and so on. By noon I'd gotten us far away from the lake and, I hoped, the help.

VIII

We couldn't talk to the blind female. I wanted to ask her why the help had attacked her and if she thought they'd attack her again, but I couldn't speak her language and she couldn't understand English. I didn't want to leave her alone if she were in danger, so I kept carrying her along, thinking she'd eventually decide herself that she'd gone far enough with us. She was cut and bloody and bruised. Every time I picked her up, she'd put her arms around my neck and hang on tight, and when I set her down she'd crouch close to Sam and never move.

At noon we found a stream. The water looked clean, and we all drank it. Sam and I tried to wash off the blood, dung, and sweat, but the blind female wouldn't. I sat the female on the logs so she'd have something to hang onto that she'd understand, then splashed water over her and tried to scrub the dung off her fur so every time I picked her up I wouldn't smear more of it on me. She clung to the logs and howled.

"How will you dry her?" Sam asked.

I set her in a patch of sunlight. The light couldn't hurt her blind eyes—she didn't even squint them shut. She was wet and shivering, and she sat still in the warmth. Her ears pricked up, and she jerked her head from side to side at the least sound, not knowing what to expect next.

"I'm hungry," Sam said.

"That's an improvement."

He pulled up some grass and smelled it.

"I'll see what I can find," I said. I took my spear and went looking for something—anything—to eat. I would have tried lagarto steak if I'd had a gun and had seen a lagarto to kill. It wasn't the season for gagga berries, but I looked for gagga trees, thinking I might find old berries on the trunk, dried like raisins.

Something dropped to the ground behind me. I spun around. It was Help-with-the-hurt-hand. He stayed in the shadows. I crouched down in front of him. "Are the other help following us?" I asked.

"Not follow. Not follow now, Jake."

"But they might later?"

He said nothing.

"Why did you follow us?"

He backed further into the shadows and said nothing. I wondered if he had a guilty conscience. I wondered if he cared about what happened to Sam and me even though we couldn't give him anything anymore. I wanted answers. "Why did the other help attack the blind female?"

"Not got food. Not got food blind female."

"What?"

"Got froth, Jake. Froth."

"So move away from it. Sam and I have never seen it anywhere else in the pântano."

He squinted up at me. "Not time," he said. "Sam and Jake not see froth not time froth."

So the froth came in cycles?

"Sam and Jake see froth now, see lot froth. Cover pântano."

"Surely the froth won't spread over the whole pântano."

He put his hands over his eyes and looked at me through slits between his fingers. "Learn live trees. Sam and Jake learn live trees—run tree to tree get away froth."

I almost started arguing with him about how Sam and I could never run from tree to tree, but that wasn't the point. "You've seen this happen before?" I asked.

He pounded his chest. "Nicoji gone. Nicoji all gone. Help eat leaves, eat grass, stomachs hurt."

"How long?"

"Long time, Jake. Long time."

"What does that mean?"

"Little help grow big, Jake. Grow lot big—have babies."

"I don't know how long it takes you to grow up."

"Lot time, Jake. Got be hungry lot long time. Not got food old help. Not got food sick help. Not got nicoji long time."

Famine. He was describing a famine. The Brazis had first come up eight years before, so nobody had been on this planet long enough to learn its cycles. We'd learn them now.

"The other help drove away the blind female because it might be hard to find food for her?" I asked.

"Not got food, Jake. Not *got* food."

Survival of the fittest among hunter-gatherers. I was glad we'd learned agriculture on Earth. "Who else will they drive away?" I asked.

He stared at me through slits between his fingers. "Who?"

Nothing.

I kept looking at him, hard. "Did they drive *you* away?"

He moved his fingers together and closed the slits he'd been squinting out of.

It was easy for me to hate the help, then. But I'd never lived through a famine. It still happened on Earth. I'd seen it in pictures. People starved in California, the Dakotas, Africa. In Idaho we'd always had at least potatoes to eat. If he was right, we were through harvesting nicoji. "What can we eat, today?" I asked.

He led me around under the trees, trying to look up at the leaves, but the light was too bright for him. He could only peek out from between his fingers now and then. Still, he found what he was looking for, probably by smell. "Eat leaves," he said, stopping by a tree covered with ants. "Eat leaves."

The tree smelled oddly familiar. The nearest leaves grew on branches twenty feet up. Something had already been eating them—four branches were stripped of leaves. Ants stopped on the trunk and waved their heads at me, snapping their two sets of pincers together. They started crawling over my feet. I jumped back and brushed them off. "What do you do with the ants?"

"Eat, Jake. Eat." Help-with-the-hurt-hand plucked at his fur and put his fingers to his mouth as if he were pulling off ants and eating them.

"No thanks," I said.

He ran over to me, plucked an ant out of my leg hairs, and shoved it in his mouth. "Eat, Jake! Ants crawl hair, eat ants."

"No," I said. "I can't. Look at me! I don't have enough hair on my skin. Ants would eat me before I could eat them. They just crawl over your fur—they can't bite you."

He squinted at me as if he hadn't seen my skin before. Suddenly he climbed the tree, jerked a branch back and forth till it broke off, then threw it down at my feet.

The branch swarmed with mad ants. The smell was stronger with the leaves that close, and I suddenly recognized it. "Jamaican sausage!"

Help-with-the-hurt-hand climbed down the tree and sat in shadows plucking ants from his fur and eating them. He wouldn't look at me or say anything.

The smaller leaves at the tip weren't covered with as many ants. I pulled off a leaf and smelled it: Jamaican sausage. "I don't believe this," I said. The leaf was heavy and maybe a quarter of an inch thick. I brushed off the ants and took a bite. It tasted like Jamaican sausage, except sweeter—

An ant bit my tongue. I spit it out. The leaf was honeycombed with ant trails—the ants lived in the leaves. I spit again. My tongue throbbed. Great, I thought. I pulled the leaf apart and dropped it: ant trails led to the middle and a clutch of larvae. The workers went mad and tried to carry the larvae to safety but got lost in the grass. "Sam and I can't eat these leaves," I said.

Help-with-the-hurt-hand didn't answer. I looked at him. He was chewing on a thick leaf from the base of the limb and relishing the ants. "Eat, Jake," he said. "Eat leaf now. Other help come eat all leaves. Tree die. Tree die soon, Jake."

It *was* all we had. I picked up the tip of the branch. "I'll pull this back to Sam," I said.

Help-with-the-hurt-hand squinted at me and kept chewing his leaf.

I hoped to lose some ants while I dragged the branch through the grass but only made the ants mad. I had to keep dropping the limb and brushing ants from my hands. I got ant bites all over my hands. When I reached the stream, I threw the limb in the water, thinking the ants would drown, but that only made the ants wet and mad. Then I had an idea. I dragged one end of the branch onto the bank and left the rest of it in the water: given time, the ants would either drown or climb off the branch.

"Jake," Sam called.

I walked over to him.

"Look at this," he said. He held up a grass net two feet square. Mud was caked on it, so it wasn't new—he hadn't made it.

"I pulled it out of the mud by the stream," Sam said.

The help had made it.

"They've been learning," Sam said.

"But the idea didn't take," I said. "This morning the help were catching nicoji with their hands, in the mud." They should have been catching nicoji with nets, at night, before the tide turned and the nicoji burrowed down. Still, the net was an accomplishment. We'd seen the help use only simple tools— sticks to poke down ant holes, leaves to hold over their eyes against the light. Our help had watched Sam and me mend nets and weave grass mats to sleep on, and we'd tried to teach them to do those things for us, but they either couldn't—or wouldn't. Wouldn't was more likely. A help had obviously learned how to weave a net, somewhere. I handed it back to Sam and walked down to the branch.

Drowning ants were floating away from it in a long line. I swished the branch through the water, dragged it up to Sam, picked a leaf and handed it to him. "It doesn't taste bad," I said.

Sam smelled the leaf and looked at me.

"I ran into some Rastafarians," I said.

"These are leaves!" Sam said. "How do they smell like this?"

He took a bite.

"Watch for the ants," I said. I handed leaves to the blind female, then picked one for me and started taking little bites around the edge.

"Imagine the fortune these leaves would bring back home," Sam said. He ate one leaf, then lay back and closed his eyes.

I looked at him and realized what I'd missed most while he'd been sick. "Talk to me, Sam," I said.

He opened one eye. "What do you want to talk about?"

"Anything. Just talk to me."

But he couldn't keep his eyes open, and he went to sleep. I let him sleep for a while, then got up to pull the logs east through the trees.

Help-with-the-hurt-hand walked out of the shadows. "Where build raft, Jake? Where?"

I pointed east.

"Got lake that way, Jake. Lake."

I hoped he meant a new lake, not an extension of the one we'd been on yesterday or we'd have trouble with the froth. I pulled the logs into the forest, following the stream, then came back for Sam and the help. I got them deep into the forest, under growing shadows. Sam said little and was breathing

hard. I hoped I wasn't pushing him too far. He
needed rest, but he also needed a doctor. So I kept
him going. We took three long rests in the afternoon. But by night, he was definitely worse.

"I've got to rest, Jake," he said.

I let go of him, and he fell to the ground.

"I'm fine," he mumbled. "I'll get up in a minute—"

But he went to sleep, that fast. I sat down next to
him. The moon was rising, and its red light glim-
mered down around us through the leaves. The forest was very quiet. I felt nervous being in it, on the
ground, without a gun. "How far is the lake?" I
asked Help-with-the-hurt-hand.

He disappeared into the trees and soon came back.
"Not far, Jake. Not far," he said.

I didn't know whether to wake Sam and try to take
him to the lake or whether to spend the night where
we were. But I was hungry, and Sam needed more
to eat than one leaf. I could probably catch nicoji in
the lake. "Sam," I said.

He didn't move.

"Sam."

"Huh?"

"Do you want to sleep here, or do you want to go
to the lake and eat nicoji? It's not far."

He opened his eyes and looked at me. "I'm hungry," he said.

I helped him up, and we made it to the lake. He
dropped into the grass on shore and went to sleep
again. I looked at the water. It was black in the
moonlight. Only the tips of the gentle waves that
washed ashore were etched in red. The froth hadn't
come here yet, and there were nicoji in the water. I
could see the water boiling. The help waded out to
catch nicoji, and I waded out after them. Mud

squished up between my toes, wet and cool. Nicoji
brushed against my legs. I reached down, and nicoji
swam against my hands and between my fingers. I
could lift handfuls of nicoji out of the water. I carried
six nicoji to shore, broke their little necks so they
wouldn't try to crawl back down to the lake, then
went out for more. Eventually I caught twenty-seven
nicoji. We'll have a good supper, I thought. The
nicoji were young, and I didn't even need a knife to
gut them. I could just poke a finger under the delicate skin over their abdomens and slide out the
intestines, then rinse them off in the lake. The help
stood in the water, shoving nicoji in their mouths.

I found dry sticks under the trees and rubbed two
together to start a fire, but it didn't work. I didn't
even get smoke. I looked at Sam, and he was awake,
watching me. "I flunked Boy Scouts, you know," I
said.

"You didn't flunk—they expelled you, and not because you couldn't start a fire with sticks."

I'd started a fire with matches and burned down
the scoutmaster's tent. I smiled and kept rubbing the
sticks together, fast, but nothing happened.

"I'm no help to you, Jake. And I can't stay awake."

"It's OK." I gave up and threw the sticks out on
the water.

"How will we eat the nicoji?" Sam asked.

I carried them up to Sam and handed him one. He
bit into it, raw. I did the same. The meat was slippery in my mouth, then chewy. Raw nicoji didn't
taste as good as cooked.

The help came and sat behind Sam. They closed their
eyes and held their stomachs and looked tired. But
after a minute, I saw Help-with-the-hurt-hand watching Sam and me out of one eye. I'd picked at three
nicoji and dropped the scraps in the grass in front of
me. I tossed them to Help-with-the-hurt-hand, and he

ate them. The blind female heard them land and felt quickly through the grass, but didn't get any scraps. "Let the female have this one," Sam told Help-with-the-hurt-hand, and he threw a half-eaten nicoji into the grass in front of her. She heard it land and snatched it up and stuffed it in her mouth.

"What do you call her?" I asked Help-with-the-hurt-hand.

He stopped chewing and looked at me. I suddenly realized I didn't know the names of any of the help. How could I have gone this long and only called them by nicknames? "What is *your* name?" I asked.

Help-with-the-hurt-hand chittered at the blind female. She crawled away from us.

"Do you have names?" I asked. "Do you know what I mean? I'm Jake. This is Sam. What do you call each other?"

"Maybe they're superstitious," Sam said. "Maybe they think we'd gain power over them if we knew their names."

"We should have been finding out things like this all along," I said. The Brazis had told us you couldn't pronounce help names so not to bother with them. They were probably right, but I wanted to try, now, tonight.

The blind female started chittering from the shadows where we couldn't see her—"Chiddiditha, Chiddiditha, Chiddiditha"—over and over again.

"What is she saying?" I asked Help-with-the-hurt-hand.

"Name," he said. "Name Chiddiditha. She Chiddiditha."

"Chiddiditha," I said.

She chittered excitedly when I said it, and I could hear her pounding the ground.

Sam said it, too. "We can pronounce it," he said.

"What's your name?" I asked Help-with-the-hurt-
hand, again.

He said nothing.

"Do you have one?" Sam asked.

He stood and walked around us twice, then stopped
and looked at Sam and me. "Midekena, Sam. Midekena,
Jake."

"Midekena," I said.

"Midekena," he said.

"Does it mean anything?" I asked.

He scratched his head, then looked at me. His
eyes glowed silver in the dark. "Sun rising east over
pântano," he said.

"That's a good name," I said, though I thought the
meaning didn't sound very masculine.

"Midekena?" Sam said. "We'll have to shorten
that. How's Kena?"

"Kena?" I said. "I like it."

Kena wrinkled his nose. "Kena," he said, as if
tasting it. "Kena."

"Ditha for the female," Sam said.

"Sa-am," Ditha said. "Sa-am."

Sam and I laughed. She crawled back to us, and
Sam patted her head. Kena tried to get her to say
Jake. He tried for a long time, but she could never
say it right.

I held my spear and tried to stay awake all night,
but I couldn't. I kept falling asleep.

"Help watch," Kena said. "Watch Jake and Sam.
Sleep, Jake."

"OK," I said.

Before I went to sleep, I could still hear him
whispering "Jake, Jake" to Ditha.

"Jack," she'd whisper back.

"Jake," he'd say.

"Jig."

"Jake. Jake."

"Gake."

"Jake," I heard a soft, female, *human* voice say, a voice with a Kansas accent, and I knew I was dreaming then.

I woke before dawn when a rain started. It was a cold, hard rain that beat the surface of the lake. I got Sam up and helped him under the trees. We sat there, cold, while the rain dripped on us through the leaves. The help came and sat by us. Ditha smelled Sam, then me. "Jay-kee," she said. "Jay-kee."

"Very good," I said. Help names had so many syllables, maybe human one-syllable names seemed poor to her, and she had to give me at least two. She sat down between Sam and me and held her head. Kena was holding his head, too, and sometimes rubbing his hands over it. "Do you have headaches?" I asked.

"Got pain, Jake. Pain."

I thought of the medkit the help had stolen, but Sam and I had taken all the aspirin so I couldn't have given the help any even if we still had it. I hoped the help weren't getting sick now. We all sat huddled together in the cold.

The rain lifted by morning, and the clouds were gone from the sky. It turned into a beautiful day, warm and clear. After the tide went out, the lake was narrow and shallow, dotted with brown mud flats. A muddy beach sloped gradually seventy feet down to the lake, wide enough to accommodate the tide. The lake stretched south, and at its southern edge, only a mile away, the cliffs of the mesão rose up out of the pântano, sheer and green with trees. It towered a

thousand feet above us. On the south side of it was
the new company town.

I helped Sam onto the grass by the beach, in the
sun. Kena was jumping from tree to tree, squinting,
sniffing the air. Ditha sat on the beach, holding her
head and sniffing the air, too. Kena came down and
shook water from his fur.

"What's wrong?" I asked.

"Got build new raft, Jake. Got build new raft
now."

"Sure I do, but what's wrong?"

"Got lot logs here! Logs here, Jake." He scampered away, skirting the edge of the muddy beach,
motioning for me to follow.

"What's got into them?" I wondered aloud.

Sam shook his head. He was rubbing his leg. I ran
off around the mud flat after Kena.

"Jake! Jake!" he shouted. "Got log here."

He was jumping back and forth over a stick only as
thick as my arm.

"That's no log," I said. "Logs are big—this big
around." I held out my arms in a wide circle.

He started jumping on a stick half buried in mud.

"No," I said. "Think of the logs I dragged here
from the old raft. Help me find logs like those."

"Got use sticks," Kena said. "Got use lot sticks."
He grabbed two muddy sticks and put one on top of
the other. He was in a terrible hurry for some reason.

"What's wrong?" I asked again, but he wouldn't
say. I looked up and down the beach. "There's a
log," I said. I ran through the mud to a log wedged
between two trees. It was two feet thick and sixteen
feet long. "Three or four more like this, and we'll
build a raft."

Kena ran to the far end of the log and started

breaking off little roots. It wasn't like him to work like this.

"What are you anxious about?" I asked.

"Got build raft, Jake. Got build raft fast."

I couldn't get him to say more than that.

By noon I'd found and dragged five logs up on the beach by Sam and sat down to rest, sweaty, tired, and hungry. The air was still and hot. It seemed thick, wet. Sam had hobbled around through the trees and managed to pull down vines and saw them off with his pocketknife. He crawled up to me, dragging vines.

"It's a storm," Sam said. "The help are afraid a storm is coming."

"We can still get to the mesão today. If the rain's too bad, we'll stop and build a hut—"

"I think it's a hurricane."

Ditha was pulling a vine through her hands, sniffing the air. Kena was in the trees squinting south toward the sea, holding his head.

"It's got all the signs," Sam said. "Muggy heat; still air; the help are worried. This isn't just a rainstorm coming in."

I stood up. "What do you see?" I yelled at Kena.

He chittered something and kept squinting south.

"What do you see?" I yelled again. "Speak English!"

On Earth, where tides are normally four or five feet high, hurricanes cause tidal surges of thirty-nine feet. Here, where tides are twenty feet high, the surge could possibly top 200 feet.

Kena suddenly rushed down from the tree. "Build raft fast, Jake. Fast!" He started dragging a log down by the lake. Every so often he'd stop to hold his head, then he'd grab the log and drag it a little farther.

"Is it a storm?" I asked.

He just kept jerking the log toward the lake.

"Will there be rain?"

"Got lot rain, Jake. Lot rain."

"Will there be a big wind?"

"Got lot big wind, Jake. Big wind snap trees."

We were getting a hurricane.

I grabbed one of the logs from the old raft and dragged it down by Kena's. The water was rising in the lake, hours before the tide. I hurried to lay out the logs in order, and the logs looked crazy. One was nearly twenty feet long and another only eight. It was going to be an odd raft. I put the good logs from our old raft on the outer edges and the badly splintered log on the inside with the others I'd found. I saved some of the best logs for crosspieces.

I started lashing the logs together on the end near the lake. Sam and Kena did what they could to help—holding knots together while I cinched them up, cleaning mud off the logs. Suddenly Kena grabbed my legs. I tried to pry him loose, but stopped.

We could hear the other help chittering in the trees. I stood, holding my spear, to watch. Kena and Ditha cowered down by Sam. The help swarmed into the trees across the beach from us. One help still wore Sam's red shirt. A female had plastic wires wrapped around her arms. Another had tin cans pulled over her wrists and ankles. They chittered and squinted at us, and one threw a stick that hit the raft.

Then I saw a help carrying my gun.

"Give me the gun," I said.

All the help grew quiet after I'd spoken.

I pulled Kena up. "Tell him to give back my gun."

"Not give, Jake. He not—"

"Tell him."

Kena chittered and waved his arms and pounded the logs, then ducked back down. The help with the gun just pointed it at my chest. I didn't move. "Give it back," I said with as much authority as I could muster. If he'd learned how to turn on the gun and pull the trigger—

He pulled the trigger, and nothing happened. He pulled the trigger again and again, pounded the gun against the branch he was sitting on, and pulled the trigger.

Nothing happened.

"Get down, Jake!" Sam said.

I threw my spear at the help's legs, hoping he'd drop the gun and rush up in the tree, but he didn't. My spear missed him, and he spit at me. All the help started chittering and spitting, but they moved on, swarming south through trees along the western edge of the lake.

"That bastard!" I said. I ran and pulled my spear out of the grass where it had fallen.

"Where are they going?" Sam asked Kena.

Kena pointed at the mesão. "Help not got time," he said. "Not got time."

"Is the storm that close?" I asked.

"Got build raft, Jake. Got build raft."

I finished lashing the raft together and dragged it down to the water.

"Got lot humans," Kena said, shaking his arms at the mesão. "Got lot humans."

"What?"

"Lot humans scare help. Help not got time, now. Not got time."

"You're scared of the humans on the mesão?" Sam asked.

"Not scared! Help scared. Other help scared."

"Why?" Sam asked.

"Humans live mesão. Help hide storm mesão. Help not got place hide, Sam. Not got place."

So the new company had scared the help from going to where they waited out hurricanes.

"Help wait pântano too long. Wait too long go mesão. Got lot humans scare. Lot humans."

"They're going now," I said. "Maybe they'll make it."

I found a pole and took the raft out alone to test it. The water was already at full tide, hours early: the front of the tidal surge ahead of a hurricane. The raft was unwieldy, but it floated. Having Sam and the help on board would help balance it.

Something bumped the raft. I stood very still. It bumped the raft again, harder. I put down my pole and picked up my spear, ready to stab whatever was under the raft. I wasn't far from shore. Sam and the help stood there waiting for me. Damn, I thought. I had to get back. I didn't know what was under the raft, but I had to get back. The tidal surge would drown Sam and the help.

I saw nothing in the water. I saw nothing in the water at all.

Then something west of me bellowed, on the land, deep and huge. Whatever was testing the raft scraped away along the bottom of it. I could see something dark swim away to the east.

Another bellow came, closer this time. The tops of trees west of me were moving as something slammed through them toward the lake. I took my pole and shoved the raft to shore. Sam and the help were gone—hiding in the trees.

I pulled the raft up on the grass and ran. The sky went dark. It can't be that big, I thought, and it wasn't. Clouds were scudding across the sky. A sudden wind pressed down the tops of all the trees.

We had to get to the mesão.

I crouched in shadows in the growing darkness and watched something huge and black plunge into the lake, wallow across to the eastern side, and slam away through the trees to the south, heading for the mesão.

"Let's go, Sam!" I yelled. "Where are you?"

"Here!"

I got him up and onto the beach. Kena ran along behind us pulling Ditha. Water was rising over the grass. I shoved the raft out on the water and got Sam and the help on it. I shoved the raft farther out, jumped on, and started poling it south. My pole was barely long enough to touch bottom.

"Get closer to shore," Sam yelled. "It won't be so deep there."

I guided the raft closer to the west shore, and my pole could touch bottom. We had a mile to go. The wind gusted around us and whipped the trees back and forth. I'd gotten us halfway to the mesão when we saw the other help in the trees, chittering and screeching, trying to hang on.

I shoved the raft away from shore so the help couldn't throw dung on us, but suddenly the help wearing Sam's red shirt fell in the water. He screamed and sank out of sight. The other help screamed and chittered. Some tried to reach down to the water, from twenty feet up. I couldn't let him drown, even if he had stolen Sam's shirt. I shoved the raft to the spot where he'd fallen in the water, but I couldn't see him.

"Where is he?" I yelled. I was looking at the water, trying to see the help. Suddenly he grabbed my pole and almost pulled it out of my hands. I held it tight, and he climbed up and over the side of the raft and rushed to Kena and Ditha. They held onto him and chittered and chittered.

I looked at the help in the branches. They'd never live through the storm, not there. They'd drown in the tidal surge. I decided I couldn't let them die, either. Not if I could help them. I shoved the raft against the roots. "Kena," I shouted above the wind. "Tell your people to get down on this raft and I'll take them to the mesão."

"No, Jake!" he shouted back. "No!"

"Go!" I yelled.

He ran across the raft—trying to keep his balance—and pulled himself into the roots. "Help pinch, Jake. Help pinch!" he yelled.

"Jump back down and we'll leave them if they try to hurt you," I said.

He climbed up the tree and disappeared in the branches. The wind got worse. "We've got to go!" I yelled. "Come now!"

The help came. Forty or fifty swarmed down onto the raft. They held onto Ditha and Kena and each other. Help clung to the entire length of the twenty-foot log I'd lashed to the raft. I shoved the raft back out on the lake, headed for the mesão, and poled us nearly there. We were so close I could see individual trees along the base of the mesão. The mesão loomed dark and huge above us.

But the wind was getting worse. Branches slammed into the water. Waves started rolling in, surging through all the trees and over the lake. We breasted two of them, but a third came out of the trees west of us, eight feet high. "Hang on!" I shouted.

I tucked my pole between my legs, dug my fingers between two logs, and the wave surged over the raft. We boiled out of the back, and the help were in the

water. I shoved my pole toward one. She grabbed it,
and I got her on the raft, but she wouldn't let go so I
could put out the pole for the others. I slapped her
head to make her let go, and Kena pulled her down
and held onto her. Some help had swum to the raft
on their own. Some had gone down and didn't come
up. I shoved the raft toward the mesão.

It was so close. Another wave rushed over us and
slammed us against the trees on the east shore of the
lake. I shoved the pole against the tree trunks and
pushed us back out. Then the water surged beneath
us and slammed us into the trees at the base of the
mesão.

The help swarmed into the trees. Only Sam and
Ditha and I were left on the raft. I tried to shove the
raft farther back among the trees, against the rock.
The water surged again and slammed us up in the
branches. When it went down, we were left on rock.

I grabbed Sam and Ditha and pulled them on the
rock. The water surged over us and slammed us into
rock higher up. We were cut and bleeding, stunned.
Sam pulled me up, and we got a little higher and
hung onto a tree while the water surged over our
heads. Ditha had her arms clenched around Sam's
neck, and she screamed and screamed every time
the water dropped away from us.

Then we were above it. The water surged and did
not cover our heads. "Run!" I yelled.

But I was the only one who could run. I grabbed
Ditha and put her arms around my neck and pulled
Sam up.

"Jake! Jake!"

It was Kena, shouting from somewhere above us,
faint in all the wind.

"Run, Jake! Run, Sam!"

We climbed as fast as we could, and the hurricane

hit. The wind and rain knocked us to the ground, and I couldn't breathe. The tidal surge hit—but we were above it. It boiled along below us, a wall of water plunging across the pântano a hundred feet above trees a hundred feet tall. Then it went black, and I couldn't see.

Branches slammed to the ground all around us. One hit Sam in the stomach, and he doubled over and vomited. I helped him up, and we kept climbing. I had to hold a hand in front of my nose to breathe.

Hands grabbed my legs and hung on.

It was Kena. He was crouched in the entrance to a cave. I shoved Ditha and Sam ahead of me and crawled in. Help hands pulled me down and held onto me. Help were all around me, chittering, holding their heads, trying to knead water out of their fur. The cave was damp and cold and stank of wet help, but I could breathe and we were out of the storm.

We sat huddled together for hours while the hurricane raged outside. When the eye passed over, no one left the cave. Kena grabbed my arm as if to hold me back. "Got more storm, Jake. More storm."

It was suddenly very quiet. The help stared at the entrance of the cave. One bright star gleamed there in the night sky. But it wasn't a star. It was too bright for that. It was the station. Clouds scudded across it, and it only blinked through now and then.

Kena slowly lifted his hand and touched my face so I would look at him. "Storm look help. Look Sam and Jake!" he hissed.

The other help stared at him wide-eyed and tried to shush him.

"Storm too big come here, Jake. Storm not come in here."

But it came back, outside. I went to sleep, huddled with the help, listening to the wind howl.

When it was light outside, I left the cave. I couldn't see through the mangled trees and had to climb high up the side of the mesão before I could look out. The pântano was awash with water, and as far as I could see the trees were flattened.

I felt like Noah looking down from Ararat on a ruined world.

IX

Sam's fever was back. When I crawled in the cave after seeing the pântano he asked me for water and he sounded so bad I felt his forehead and knew his fever was back. "Kena," I said.

None of the help stirred.

"Kena, I need the plant you chewed up and spit in Sam's mouth."

No answer. I tried to see which help was Kena, but the cave was dark and I couldn't tell. I shook the nearest help—it was wet with sweat, and hot. I touched all the help around me, and they were all hot. None moved. I felt my own forehead, but I was fine.

"Kena!" I said. I started turning the help over one by one, looking at their faces, wishing I had a light. I pulled back two of the helps' eyelids, and their eyeballs rolled down towards their noses.

"Jay-kee, Jay-kee."

"Kena, where are you?" I couldn't tell from the sound.

"Jay-kee."

I saw the gleam from one pair of open help eyes not looking at me, and I recognized the voice. "Ditha."

I crawled to her and touched her face. She was wet with sweat, and she stank. I wiped my hand on my shorts. "What's wrong with you?" I asked, but she couldn't understand me. She took hold of my arm and seemed to want me to stay close to her, but I couldn't. I kept turning over the help and found Kena. He was farther back in the cave and sick like the others and not moving. He shivered when I touched him, so I shook him hard, thinking he might come out of it. "What's wrong?" I asked. "Why are all of you sick?"

He didn't answer. But he opened his eyes and looked at me. I wondered if he didn't know the words in English to tell me what was wrong. "What can I do?" I asked. "What do you need? Do you need the plant you chewed for Sam? Where can I find it?"

He didn't answer. He just kept looking at me.

So I decided on water. Sam wanted water. I'd bring the help some, too, and maybe when I was looking for water I'd find the plant. I started to crawl away, but Kena grabbed my arm—in a strong grip. I didn't think he'd be so strong when he was sick.

"Help not able work, Jake," he said.

"Huh?"

"Not able work."

He blinked his eyes, then closed them but hung onto my arm. What was he trying to tell me? Of course he couldn't work. No one expected him or any of the help to work when they were sick. But suddenly I looked at him and realized what he was saying. He didn't have anything to bargain with—he couldn't do anything for me and had nothing to give me. He didn't expect me to help him if he couldn't pay. I shook off his hand. "You have a lot to learn, Kena," I said, and I crawled out after the water.

The soft light filtering down through the trees left standing made me squint. I shoved aside a clump of branches, climbed over a fallen tree, and tried to make my way straight across the side of the mesão: if I were going to find water, I'd find it running down the middle of a gully or ravine.

But after walking for five or ten minutes I hadn't found any water. I stopped to listen for it, and the world was suddenly silent. I'd been making the only noise. The pântano and the mesão were absolutely still. I listened for any noise—an insect droning, wind in the leaves, anything—but heard only my own breathing. The pântano was usually quiet after just a rainstorm, but not this quiet. The hurricane had brought an enormous calm.

It made me think of a Gregg Thorsen movie I'd seen. In it, Gregg tried to save a planetary-survey team trapped in a forest haunted by a demon that came up under the men to chew and claw its way through their feet and legs and bellies to their hearts, and every time, just before the demon tore some man apart, the forest would become absolutely still and all the men would know one of them was about to die. I hadn't thought of that movie in two years.

When I'd first come up, the noise of the pântano kept me awake at night, followed me into buildings, became a constant companion. Once I climbed a tree and shouted "Shut up! Shut up! Shut up!"—and for a few seconds the noise died away and I heard only the wind.

Now I wanted the noise back. I wanted to hear if it

would sound the same and if I would know what I was hearing. Somehow I felt I wouldn't, felt the world had changed after all this, though it left me the same tired and hungry Jake. How was I going to fit into a new world, and what was it going to be?

Then I heard water trickling over rock. I pushed through the brush and found a tiny stream choked with leaves. I could fit my hand over the breadth of it. The natural drainage from the top of the mesão must have been in some other direction, down some other gully. We weren't getting much. I cupped my hands and let them fill with water. It was clear and cold, and I drank it. I didn't bother to walk twenty feet upstream looking for some dead animal in the water—I'd always thought that Boy Scout rule stupid: if you walked twenty feet up a stream, a dead animal could be twenty feet beyond that. So what were you supposed to do, follow every stream to its source before taking a drink?

I looked around for something to carry water in to Sam and the help. I couldn't see fruit to hollow out, or bowl-shaped rocks, or shells. So I picked up leaves from a fallen tree, cupped them in my hands, and filled them with water. By the time I got back to the cave, most of the water had leaked out. I took what was left to Sam.

"Water," I whispered. Sam tried to sit up, shaking, and I poured the water into his mouth. Most ran down his chin. He sank back on the dirt.

"I'll get more," I said.

"Let's get to the town," he said. "To a doctor."

I threw the leaves on the cave floor and wished I had a doctor for Sam then, not hours later in a town I still had to find. If I'd been wearing magic red shoes I'd have wished us immediately to the new company town where I could turn Sam over to someone with the knowledge, supplies, and equipment to make him better. "I'll get Kena some water," I said. "Then we'll go."

It was all I knew to do for the help. I managed to carry more water back in the leaves that second time. I gave Ditha some, then crawled to Kena and gave him the rest.

"Don't go, Jake," he said. "Don't go."

I put the wet leaves on his forehead. "I have to," I said. "I have to get Sam to a doctor."

Kena closed his eyes and opened his mouth to breathe but hung onto my arm.

"I'll come back. I'll get Sam to the town and see if the doctors there know how to help you, but even if they don't I'll come back. Maybe we can think of something to do."

Kena didn't say anything. He let go of my arm. I pulled Sam out of the cave and started dragging him up the gully. I'd find at least a spaceport on top of the mesão and hoped the town would be easy to find after that.

The air was utterly still on top. I heard what I thought was wind, but I couldn't feel it, and I realized that even as high up as we were I was hearing the water in the pântano rush out to sea.

Sam couldn't sit or lie down, his leg hurt so bad, so I leaned him against a tree to rest while I dragged a big branch around and pointed it at the mouth of the gully we'd climbed out of, put two more branches on either side of it at fifteen degree angles—made an arrow. I had to leave a trail so I could come back to the help. Leaving trails was one part of Boy Scout lore I did believe.

"What's in the leaves?" Sam asked.

I looked up and saw clear, round bubbles darting

in and out among the leaves of all the trees around us. The leaves were turning brown and dry. The bubbles had an oily sheen that shimmered red and white, green and orange. We watched them for a long time. One as wide as my palm floated slowly down from the leaves and stopped, bobbing, in front of my face. It had four black eyes spaced evenly around its lower hemisphere and a tiny, round mouth below one of the eyes. I could see its brain, heart, and lungs in sacs above the eyes.

I'd never seen or heard of anything like them.

"What's going on?" Sam asked. "Where are new animals coming from?"

"Maybe they're native here," I said. It was possible. Species on Earth had limited ranges—these could be native to just the top of the mesão.

The bubble darted onto my neck and bit me. I couldn't brush it off—I had to pull on it, and it popped open. Warm liquid ran down my chest and stank of rotten eggs—sulfur. I threw the quivering, membranous sac of organs to the ground. My neck was bleeding. "Is its head stuck in my neck?" I asked Sam.

"I can't tell," Sam said.

I wiped away the blood and couldn't feel anything in the bite. "Let's go," I said. I got Sam up and away from there.

Hours later, we rolled down a hill and slammed up on top of flat rock. I hadn't seen the land drop away—one step I was helping Sam over knocked-down trees, the next we were falling. Sam lay on his back, holding his leg, his face white with pain. The rock was grey, flat, smooth. Water puddled on it, and it was covered with dirt and fallen trees, leaves, and branches—

It was a concrete runway.

I shook Sam's shoulder. "We've found the space-port," I said.

Sam turned his head to look up the runway, but he winced and closed his eyes. I sat up. The runway was covered with debris. I couldn't understand why the new company hadn't cleared it off—a spaceport runway would be the first thing you'd attend to after a hurricane, I thought. On the far end stood a metal building, one wall bashed in by fallen trees.

"Building ahead, Sam," I said. "Let's go."

I helped him up and hung onto him, and we limped down the runway, around fallen trees, through puddles of water. I kept staring at the building, watching it get closer. A row of boarded windows faced the runway. Half of the roof had blown off.

The door was locked. I knocked and got no answer. I knocked again. Sam looked at me. I leaned him against the building. "Can you stand here on your own?" I asked.

He nodded.

"I want to look for food and water, maybe a phone."

He nodded again.

I stepped back in front of the door, kicked it open, and walked in. Muddy rainwater covered all the chairs and desks, walls and floors. Leaves and branches were everywhere, and something dead stank. I couldn't see anything that looked human on the floor, so I walked in. Against the far wall, under hanging plywood knocked down from the roof, stood a Coke machine. I stumbled over a broken chair and fell on the cement floor, but got to the machine. I put my palm on the hand plate, but it didn't light up. No power. I beat on the machine, but nothing came out. Cans rattled inside it. I was so thirsty I stood shaking in front of the machine, trying to think of a way to get it open, wondering what a Coke would taste like after two years without it.

I looked at the chair I'd fallen over. It had metal legs. I slammed it against the cement till one leg broke partly away, then I twisted the leg back and forth till it snapped off. I pryed and pounded and beat on the door of the Coke machine till I could wrench it open.

Eighteen cans of Coke sat in the racks, warm, wet from rainwater or maybe condensation as the Coke had cooled. I wiped off one can, opened it, and drank it, threw the can on the floor. I grabbed two more cans and carried them outside, opened one for Sam and gave it to him, opened the other for me and leaned back against the wall with Sam to drink.

"Trouble?" Sam asked.

He'd heard me beating on the Coke machine. "Nothing I couldn't handle," I said.

Sam finished his Coke and wiped his mouth. I took his empty can and threw it back in the building. "Place is already a mess," I said. I walked back in for some more Coke. "We've got thirteen to go, after these," I told Sam.

It tasted great.

But there was no phone, no food.

The doors had blown in on the far end of the building. I walked over to look out and could see the sea. I hadn't realized we were that close to the edge of the mesão—we'd walked across it. A debris covered road led away from the building and over the edge. We could follow it down to the town. I went back for Sam, helped him around the building, and we stood and looked at the water stretching away to the horizon and the setting sun.

"I saw the ocean once on Earth," I said.

"I remember when your family took that trip," Sam said.

My parents had taken me to California when I was a kid. I'd wanted to take Sam, but Sam's parents wouldn't let him go—wanted to take their own trip to the coast someday, but they never did. Mom was afraid to let me out of the car, into the crowds of people on the beach, so I could only look at the ocean through the car windows.

I looked at the sea now and felt dizzy. I wanted to sit down, but Sam couldn't and he couldn't stand there alone, so I hung onto him and held myself still so I wouldn't fall over. After a minute, I realized why I felt odd: I wasn't moving. I wasn't bobbing up and down on a raft or trying to drag Sam up the side of the mesão or over fallen trees. I was standing still on stone, and I was used to being on a raft with its constant motion—had at least gotten used to standing up, sitting down, or sleeping while everything under me moved.

I wanted solid ground to feel right again.

Before we got to the town it grew dark and we could see, far below, one light. Smoke and the smell of cooking meat drifted up to us: ham, beef maybe. I wanted to run to the meat—around all the hairpin turns of the road—but we couldn't, at least Sam couldn't. We had to take it slow, take our time crawling over fallen trees and branches and slipping in the mud, watching that one light get closer and closer. Soon I could tell it was a bonfire, not an electric light at all.

We passed the dark silhouette of a building, then another: both of corrugated metal, tiny, flimsy. Probably workers' barracks.

"New town," I said to Sam.

He opened his eyes, looked around, didn't say anything. The storm had blown down the next five buildings. One must have been a general-goods store because splintered timber and glass and torn clothes and plastic buckets were scattered in the street. Something dead stank under the debris, but the smell of cooking meat was stronger. We rounded a bend and could see the fire down from us.

Somebody'd cleared a path along the cement steps and narrow platforms that began now in front of buildings built one below the other on both sides of the road. The mesão was too steep for sidewalks. We started down the steps. The buildings were dark and bashed in by the storm, but they looked like they had always been dark and cramped, thrown up by people who'd come to take, not settle. Maybe it was damage from the storm, and the night, but the town seemed impermanent to me, a disappointment. I don't know what I'd hoped for, but one thing was clear: even before the hurricane, Raimundo's great new town had been a dump.

The bonfire burned in front of the last building, below a turned-off neon sign. Twenty or thirty men were crowded around the fire, roasting and eating meat. I dragged Sam into the light.

"Hey! Olha aqui—Jake, Sam!" Somebody rushed up and hugged me.

"You came for the party I promised."

It was Raimundo. He hugged Sam. The other guys crowded around us, chewing on beef steaks, their faces covered with grease and blood—but all smiles. Most had dirty bandages around their wrists. These were our guys. I knew them.

"Give us some meat," I said. I should have asked for a doctor first, but I thought maybe we could get some meat and eat it on the way.

"There's lots of cow meat," Raimundo said. "But you'll have to cook it."

Cook it, I thought. I wanted someone to hand me cooked meat.

"What happened to Sam?"

"Lagarto bite. Where's the doctor?"

No one said anything.

"Isn't there a doctor?"

"Evacuated to their station before the storm," Raimundo said. His teeth were no better. "They have a hospital down the road. Some guys fixed themselves up in there."

I pulled Sam's arm back around my shoulders and started down the road. Since I had to cook the meat, I decided to take care of Sam first. "I'll be back for the meat," I said.

"I can eat," Sam said. "Let's get some food."

I couldn't help but smile. "OK," I said. Raimundo slapped my shoulder and walked with us toward the fire. The other Brazis started pounding our shoulders, but Manoel pulled Raimundo aside and whispered something to him in Portuguese. Raimundo nodded and walked back up to me. "Guys who went AWOL years ago and ran off into the pântano came here, thinking the new company would take them offworld," he said. "They're wild. Stay away from them."

"What do you mean *thinking* the new company—"

"Get food, Jake."

"Raimundo—"

He pointed to a freezer they'd dragged into the street. It was half full of beef and ham. "Got to eat it before it rots," some guy said. "Thawed after the storm."

I leaned Sam against the freezer, and Raimundo handed me two sticks. I shoved steaks on them and went to the fire to roast the meat. The meat flopped down around both sides of the sticks. It wouldn't cook evenly but I didn't care. We could eat off the cooked parts, then cook the rest.

"Who's left after Jake and Sam?" somebody shouted.

Cliff Morgan was standing by the fire, looking at a list. "Only fifteen guys still out there," he shouted back.

Everybody cheered and clapped.

"Fifteen guys?" I asked Cliff.

"Practically everybody came to the new town. American Nicoji was left with no workers. Most deserted."

That's why they'd fired on us in the pântano—make a few examples, scare back the rest. They couldn't let the new company get all the trained workers. Besides, American Nicoji would lose a lot of money if everybody deserted—it was expensive bringing guys off Earth to the new worlds.

"Loryn still waiting for you?" Cliff asked. His girl had written him off when we were just two weeks out—while we were still on the ship.

"She's waiting," I said. At least, I hoped she was. I suddenly felt sorry for her. She'd had a long wait, and it wasn't over.

The neon light started flashing—twenty times faster than it should have—and everybody cheered again. It was like we were under a red strobe light. Guys started jumping up and down, waving their arms and steak bones. I laughed and looked back at Sam—and saw the wild guys. It had to be them. There were twelve or thirteen of them. They all had beards, were dirtier than we were and acted like they didn't care, and they didn't say a word. They walked up through the flashing light like a scene from a horror movie and took the meat from the guy standing next to me. They took my meat, and I let them. I got

back by Sam, and we watched them eat the red meat
that had barely cooked around the edges. They stared
back at all of us, but said nothing. I wondered if
they'd forgotten how to talk. I got a package of steaks
from the freezer and pulled Sam out of there.

Sam and I stood in the doorway of the little,
one-room "hospital," in the flickering light of a candle burning on a windowsill. Eloise Hansdatter was
inside with her back to a wall and a knife in her
hands, and I thought, of course, she had to do this
with the wild guys in town and everybody else here
all together—she couldn't stand around a bonfire if
none of the other women were in town for her to
stand with, and her help couldn't stand the light of a
fire, couldn't protect her. Then I saw that it wasn't
just jitters and light that had kept Eloise and her
help away from the fire and the food. She had two or
three of her help in each of six beds made up in
white sheets, and the help lay there limp, not moving, breathing through their mouths. Eloise had put
wet cloths on their foreheads. Why had all the help
gotten sick? I hung onto Sam with one arm and held
the steaks in the other. The steaks dripped blood on
the floor. Eloise just sat where she was, looking at
us.

  "What do you want?" she asked.
  "Look at Sam," I said. "He needs help."
  "And I suppose you want me to help him?"
  "I don't want you to do anything," I said.
  She just looked at me.
  "Can we come in?"
  No answer.
  "Is there another bed?"
  "No," she said. No offer to move any of her help.
The floor was filthy—littered with trash and mud

blown in by the hurricane and puddled with water.
"Eloise," I said, "You know Sam and me—you know
you can count on us as friends. Sam needs help, and
I've got to try to help him. We're coming in." And
with that I pulled Sam to a table where the doctors
had evidently operated and leaned him against it,
slammed the steaks down on one corner. Sam winced,
tried to hold his leg and would have fallen over if I
hadn't grabbed him. Eloise stood up and stared at
us, then put her knife in her boot. Sam's leg was
black and swollen. I could see it throb.

"I don't want to lose this leg," he said.

I didn't want to have to cut it off for him. But the
infection looked that bad. He had to get help.

"Where are the antibiotics?" I asked Eloise while I
shoved all the trash off the table onto the floor. The
tabletop was filthy, but who was going to care? Sam
wasn't.

Eloise didn't answer. When I looked over at her
she was holding the wrist of one of her help, maybe
looking for a pulse. Her own wrist was bandaged like
mine and Sam's, dirty. She hadn't done anything to
take care of herself.

"Eloise," I said. "Where are the antibiotics?"

"I don't want these help to die, Jake," she said.

"Shut up about the help," I said.

"One doctor said he'd come back today and look at
my help. I've waited all day for him."

"Why didn't they take you?" Sam asked.

"American Nicoji would bankrupt them—impound
their ships for hauling contract breakers. American
Nicoji won't sell our contracts."

I pulled Sam onto the table, and he scrunched up
his eyes, grabbed his leg, and lay still. I picked up
the steaks and tried to brush the blood off the table,
but it just smeared in the dirt.

"Don't get your hair in this blood," I told Sam.

He didn't say anything. He was lying very still, not moving his head toward the blood.

I shoved the steaks in a cupboard to get them out of the way, then started looking through the cupboards. I didn't find any antibiotics, but I did find a box of syringes—clean in their sterile packaging.

"Eloise, I need antibiotics for Sam. Did you find any?"

"I couldn't bring all my help," she said. "They'd collapsed on my raft. I tried to carry them all up before the storm, but I couldn't. The wind—"

"Shut up!"

She looked at me.

"Shut up about your help. Mine are dying, too. I don't know what to do for them, but I can help Sam if I can find some drugs."

She carried a bucket of water to another bed of help, took the cloths off their foreheads and wrung them out on the floor, rinsed the cloths in the bucket and put them back on the helps' heads. I started looking through drawers, slamming them open and shut, finally found some antibiotics in the fridge. The fridge was dark, of course, no power for a day. The medicines were warm. I didn't know if they were any good.

"You want to try some warm antibiotics, Sam?" I asked. He didn't say anything, so I gave him a big shot of it. He looked at me when the needle went in his arm.

"Found the medicine, huh?" he said.

"Found it," I said.

I cleaned off Sam's table, washed his leg and rubbed it with alcohol, cut the filthy bandage from his wrist. Scabs tore off in the gauze, and the wound bled

again. I cleaned it and wrapped it in a new bandage.
Then I rebandaged my own wrist. It was healing,
scabs around the edge. "Eloise," I said, "let's
rebandage your wrist before you get leprosy or some
other noxious disease in that wound."

"I'm OK."

"Get over here."

She looked at me, then came and let me rebandage
her wrist. She kicked the bandages I'd cut from
Sam's and my wrists toward the door with the toe of
her boot. "Didn't you ever change those?" she asked,
disgusted.

Hers was nothing to brag about. Besides, the water we'd been in during the hurricane had actually
cleaned up our bandages somewhat. She should have
seen them before. "How long since you've eaten?" I
asked.

"I don't know. Long time. Couple days."

"Do you have your gun or any matches?"

"No."

"I'll go back to the bonfire and get some embers so
we can build a fire, cook the steaks I brought."

"Fine," she said.

Only the wild guys were left around the fire. I
stood back in the shadows, wondering what to do.
But I was in no mood to go sneaking around a
wrecked up town trying to find the other guys to see
if they had dry matches, so I walked straight ahead
as if I owned the place, pulled a burning branch from
the fire, and started back for the hospital.

One of the wild guys stepped out in front of me.
"What are you doing with the fire?" he asked.

"You can talk," I said.

He just looked at me. I heard some of the other
guys move up behind me. My dad always said being

a smart aleck would cause me more trouble than it was worth. But I'd get mad, hungry, and tired and not think about what I was saying—like the time back home when I asked a policeman if he hadn't met his monthly ticket quota since he'd pulled me over on the thirty-first. That made him mad, so he cited me for not wearing a seat belt, for not carrying an instant spare so if I had a flat I wouldn't have to spend more than two minutes at the side of the road where who knows what could happen to me, and for not showing respect to a public official—besides the speeding ticket I deserved. "I've got sick people to take care of," I said. "They need food. I'm going to go cook it for them."

"Where are these sick people?"

Somebody behind me laughed. "Are you down with that woman holed up in the hospital?"

I didn't like that. Eloise evidently had good reason to be afraid. I stood there and looked at the guy in front of me and wanted Raimundo to step out of the shadows with about sixty Brazis to help me handle this, but nobody came.

"You need help?"

Somebody behind me. I didn't turn to see who, but it had to be one of the wild guys. I didn't recognize the voice. I didn't know if he was talking to me or to the others around me, but I decided to act as if he were offering to help me.

"No," I said. "If I can get food to my friends and find some decent medicine in that wreck of a hospital I think they'll be OK."

Nobody said anything for a minute. My answer evidently took them by surprise. "Your partner didn't look too good," the guy who'd offered help finally said.

"He's not doing well," I said.

"You need some help taking care of him or whoever else you've got to look after. We'll do what we
can."

"Thanks."

"Let him go, Jeff."

I walked past the wild guys and out into the dark,
carrying my burning branch.

I smashed apart some drawers to get dry wood for
the fire and started cooking the steaks. Sam was half
asleep on the table. Eloise came out after a while
and stood looking at the fire. "The help can hardly
breathe," she said, when I didn't ask her anything.
"Something's swelling their esophagi shut. They
can only breathe through their mouths. And all I've
got are warm antibiotics, cool cloths for their fevers,
pillows to prop them up with so they can breathe
easier."

I wondered how my help were doing. I didn't like
to think of them down in a stinking cave with no
water and no food and nobody to prop them up.

"I don't know how to doctor help," Eloise said.
"I've lived with them for years, and I don't know
what to do when they're sick."

"Nobody does. You're doing the best you can."

She took one of the sticks and touched her finger
to the grease on a steak, sucked it off.

"How much antibiotic is left?" I asked.

"Five or six boxes of different kinds."

"I ought to go get my help and shoot them full of
it."

"In the morning."

In the morning. Me, alone, with thirty sick help in
a cave. I'd have to get some Brazis to go with me.

"Hold these," I said. I handed Eloise the steak
sticks, walked in the hospital, took the antibiotics out

of the fridge and put them in Eloise's bucket of
water where maybe they'd stay a little cool, a little
potent.

We ate, and Sam even kept down the few mouth-
fuls of meat he could chew. Afterwards, Eloise curled
up on a bed, at the feet of her help. She evidently
felt safe enough with Sam and me around to get
some sleep. I swept off the steps, then got a dry
blanket from a cupboard and spread it over the top
step outside to sleep on. I slept outside because the
steps were dryer and cleaner than the floor inside. It
was so hot we left the door open. I covered Sam with
a blanket because I didn't want him to get chilled. I
thought I'd hear him if he needed help.

I didn't. Late in the night, I opened my eyes and
saw Eloise holding a lit candle, standing over Sam. I
hurried in. Eloise just looked at me. Sam was red
and sweating, and his fever was higher. He'd kicked
the blanket off his leg. "My leg hurts so bad I can't
touch it," he said.

"How long since we gave you the antibiotic?" I
asked. None of us had a watch. None of us knew. It
had probably been hours. I pulled a vial out of the
bucket and got a syringe. "I'll shoot it right in the
leg."

"No! Don't touch it," Sam said.

So I gave him the shot in his arm and threw the
syringe in a sink. Sam's chest was covered with irreg-
ular splotches of black, as if he'd been bruised.
"How did you get these?" I asked. I touched one,
and he winced. His leg was black. Dark spots were
forming on his arms, one on the back of his left
hand.

"If I had something for the pain in the leg . . ."
Sam said.

I covered Sam with the blanket again. "Is there any aspirin?" I asked Eloise. I hadn't seen any when I was looking for the antibiotic.

"Didn't find any," she said.

But I thought of a Brazi who'd probably have some. "Keep him covered," I told Eloise, for want of anything more competently medical to say, and hurried out into the dark.

I found the Brazis sleeping in the workers' barracks. Raimundo was groggy, but he gave me what aspirin he had left. Then he handed me the medkit itself. "Take it," he said. "It's got alcohol, blood coagulator, I don't know what's left. Take it."

By then all the Brazis were up, babbling in Portuguese, Raimundo telling them Sam was worse.

"We've got to get a doctor down from a station," I said. "Either one—new company or old. Can we call out?"

"Storm smashed all the communications equipment. Besides, power's out—solar panels wrecked up."

"Somebody got power in that store to run the neon light."

"Battery ripped out of a truck. But it doesn't matter—no equipment, no calls. The new company people *are* supposed to come back. We expected them today."

I turned to go back to Sam, take him the aspirin, rub the alcohol on his leg. One Brazi stood up and started talking to me in Portuguese and broken English. He was one Brazi I tried to ignore, so I just kept walking, but Raimundo pulled me back. "Listen to Mauá," he said. "You should listen to him."

Mauá had set himself up as a Macumba lord. Most Brazis and some Americans—even some company boys—went to him with their physical or spiritual ailments, and he'd perform voodoo and take money or nets or nicoji for it. I'd had no patience with his scam.

"Not now," I said.

Raimundo pulled me back hard, slammed me against the door. "Listen," he said.

"Tell me what is wrong with Sam," Mauá said. Mauá was a tall, Valkyric Brazi with red hair that stuck out from his head as if it had electricity in it—blue eyes, peeling skin always sunburned.

"Tell him," Raimundo said. He knew I didn't believe in Macumba. But I thought of Sam and what I was going to be able to do for him till a doctor came, which was not much. Sam did love Japanese mysticism. Maybe he wouldn't mind Brazilian voodoo. I decided it couldn't hurt. So I told Mauá about Sam, tried to tell him in Portuguese, and when I didn't know how to say something I'd say it in English and if Mauá didn't understand, Raimundo would translate. Mauá listened till I was through, then knelt and started pulling things out of the pack he'd been using for a pillow.

"He can help," Raimundo said.

"What's he doing?"

Mauá tried to tell me, but he didn't know the words in English.

"He will wrap Sam's leg in leaves and powders that draw out poison," Raimundo said.

"A poultice?" I asked. "He's going to put a poultice on Sam's leg?" I'd expected chicken guts smeared on sacred stones—not a poultice.

Mauá made a little bundle of his stuff and stood up. "Let's go," he said.

*   *   *

We hurried to the hospital. Sam was groggy and breathing hard. While Mauá wrapped Sam's leg, I got some water and gave him six aspirin. I could tell Mauá's poultice hurt Sam, but Sam didn't make him stop.

"Thanks," I said when Mauá was done. "I'll find a way to pay you." And I would have, too. I would have paid him for a poultice. "Should we change it tomorrow?" I asked.

"I'll sleep here," he said. "Watch Sam."

He came out on the steps with me, but he didn't go to sleep. He moved my blanket, then spread out dried nicoji and shells in patterns on the top step and tossed white powder in the air. Here come the chicken guts, I thought. But what did it matter? It couldn't hurt. I'd tried everything I could think of.

When I opened my eyes in the morning, Mauá and Eloise were changing the poultice on Sam's leg. I couldn't believe I kept sleeping the way I did. I got up, stepped over the shells and dried nicoji, and walked in. "Did you give him any antibiotic?" I asked. My voice sounded terrible.

"Mauá did," Eloise said.

Sam was holding his head while Mauá worked on his leg. I hung onto his shoulder till Mauá was done.

"You going to go get your help?" Eloise asked.

"We take care of Sam," Mauá said, nodding at Eloise.

"The doctors should come back today," she said. "We'll see that Sam gets the attention he needs. So get your help—maybe the doctors can do something for them."

If my help were still alive. Eloise's looked awful, and they'd been getting some care.

"Go," Sam said. "I'll be all right."

So I went. It was foggy outside. All the trees were black in the white fog. A cold mist beaded on my skin, and I wished I had more to wear than just my shorts. I went back to get my blanket and wrapped it around me.

I couldn't find the Brazis. I had thirty help to carry back, and I couldn't find the Brazis. They weren't in the barracks. I walked back down through the town but didn't see anybody. I stopped in the ruins of the general goods store to look for a shirt, but all the clothes were blown into muddy heaps on the floor and I didn't want to put on the wet things I found. I did pull two plastic buckets out of the muck. I needed something to carry water in to the help.

Then one of the wild guys walked out of the last store and started picking through the freezer the Brazis had dragged into the street. Why not? I thought. What did I have to lose? I walked up to him.

"Good morning," I said.

He looked up at me but said nothing, then looked back down at the smelly meat.

"Bom dia," I said in Portuguese.

"I speak English," he said.

Great, I thought. This is going really well. "I need some help," I said. "One of your guys told me last night you'd help me if I needed it. I don't know if he spoke for all of you or just for him, but I need some help."

"What's wrong?"

"I have thirty help dying in a cave on the other side of the mesão. I've got to bring them here so when the doctors come they can maybe do something for them."

He straightened up and looked at me as if I'd been the one who'd spent too much time in the pântano.

"You want us to help you carry sick help back to this town?"

"Yes." I almost went on to say please, or yes sir, or yes, your royal majesty I'll be your slave forever just help me but I stopped with yes.

The guy looked at me. "Stewart," he yelled after a minute.

"Shut up!" somebody yelled back.

"Stewart, get out here."

A guy stomped through the store and came out on the steps. "What?"

"You promised this guy help if he needed it. He's asking for it now."

Stewart looked at me. I told him what I needed. By then some of the other wild guys had crowded out on the steps. Nobody said anything. "Look, if you're too busy I'll just do what I can on my own," I said. I picked up my buckets.

"I'll go," Stewart said. Six of the others said they'd go. That meant the eight of us could carry back maybe sixteen help. At least it was something. I put down my buckets, walked up to Stewart, and held out my hand. "Thanks," I said. "My name's Jake."

Stewart shook my hand and introduced me to the other guys who'd be going: Carlos, Lindoval, Scott, Todd, Dave, and another Dave. All of them had guns, knives, and shirts. I didn't ask if one of them had an extra shirt. I was asking for too much already. I'd get warm once we started walking, and I did have my blanket.

We set out, climbed up the road to the spaceport— and found the Brazis and some American guys clearing off the runway. "Somebody had to do it," Raimundo said. They all looked surprised to see me walking up with the wild guys. There was a pile of Coke cans around the door of the building, so I thought the Brazis had drank it all, but I walked in to check the dispenser anyway. Two cans were left. I gave one to Stewart. "Here," I said. "Pass it around. Share it." I kept the other for the help, thought maybe the sugar and caffeine in it would do them some good.

I found where Sam and I had rolled down the hill onto the runway, and we climbed up into the forest and started trying to follow the trail I'd left.

But the forest had changed.

The grass was black, and it crumbled like ash when we stepped on it. The trees had shriveled and stood leafless and twisted, their branches lifted to the sky. Some had become top-heavy and slammed to the ground, pulling out roots and dirt. Every tree had pustules as wide as my hand dotting the trunk. Sap oozed out from under the pustules and congealed on the trunk. Stewart punctured one pustule with the butt of his gun, and it stank of sulfur. We could hear trees falling around us, slamming to the ground.

"How far is this cave?" Todd whispered to me.

And whispering seemed the right thing to do. I didn't like the feel of this place, either. I didn't like being in the forest. Some plague was passing through it. The branches I'd laid out as markers were covered with leaves, and I had a hard time finding them. But I did find them. "I don't know if Sam and I took the most direct route," I said, after we'd walked some time without talking. My words sounded loud in the stillness around us. "We probably wandered—"

Stewart pulled me around to face him. "Shut up," he said. "You don't know what's out here. Noise scares away most things, but it attracts others."

I wondered what he'd seen, what had happened.

"Lead the way," Stewart said. "We'll follow."

*   *   *

The cave stank of vomit and help dung, and I could hardly stand to crawl into it. Lindoval had a light, and he let me take it in. I turned it to a soft setting so the light wouldn't hurt the helps' eyes too bad. "Kena," I said as I crawled in. "Kena. Ditha."

None of them stirred. The help lay in heaps on top of each other. I started looking at their faces, turning over the ones facedown. One was dead. She wasn't breathing. I grabbed her feet and pulled her away from the others. Her arms dragged behind her head.

Then I found Kena. He was lying on top of another help. I turned him over, and he threw up. None of the help he threw up on crawled away or even moved. They were all dying; I was sure of it then.

"Kena," I said.

He opened his eyes and looked at me. I laid him back and crawled out for the Coke. The wild guys had washed the buckets and filled them with water. I took them and pushed them ahead of me as I crawled back in the cave. I bathed Kena's face and hands, then popped the top of the Coke can. Kena opened his eyes. Some of the Coke fizzed down the side of the can, and I licked it off.

"No, Jake!" Kena's voice was barely a whisper, but his eyes were wide and he looked at me in utter disbelief that I was drinking a brown, fizzy liquid.

"It's good," I said. "Here—"

He turned his head away and let the Coke run down his cheeks. Some got on his lips, and he started spitting. Other help were watching me now, blinking in the light. One reached up and tried to knock the can from my hands.

"Jake, no," Kena said. "Jake, *no*."

I gave up on the Coke, put down the can, gave Kena some water, and carried him outside, laid him in the shade under the branches of a fallen tree, covered his eyes with leaves. He lay there, limp.

I crawled back in for Ditha. The help had knocked over the Coke can, and the Coke had run all over the muddy floor. I got Ditha out and went back looking for the help who had gone around with Sam and me. Stewart and Todd and Carlos screwed up their noses and crawled in, too. They sat on their haunches, looking at the help, not wanting to touch them. Stewart unstrapped the gun from his leg and turned it on. "Do you want me to put them out of their misery?" he asked.

"No!" I said. Didn't he think it would be murder? Hadn't he worked with other help long enough to know? We found two more dead help and pulled them out. Dave and Dave and Lindoval used rocks and sticks to dig holes in the ground and bury them.

"We can't carry two apiece," Stewart said. "It's too far. And two of us are going to have to keep guard, keep guns ready."

Paranoid, I thought. These guys are paranoid. "I'm carrying two," I said. Kena and Ditha.

So did Lindoval. That meant we carried back eight help, not even all the help who had gone around with Sam and me. Before we left, Todd and I gave water to the help we had to leave, then put fresh water in the buckets and left them by their heads.

"This world's going crazy," Todd said.

"Dying," I said.

"That's one reason we came here. We were out on a plateau in the mountains, growing vegetables— squash, beans, corn—but the native plants all started to die, and we wondered how long the plants from Earth would last. So we left. On the way in, it looked like the whole pântano was dying. We'd have starved out there."

I wondered how long it would take till we started getting sick ourselves, like the help. We weren't that alien to this world. The bacteria or virus killing the native life wouldn't take forever to adapt to our systems, figure out how to utilize our proteins, and tear us apart like everything else. I folded the blanket and put it under the head of one of the help who had worked with Sam and me. "Let's go," I said.

We took a shortcut across the top of the mesão and walked into a clearing where the red-veined plant grew in clumps. I made the guys stop to rest there, and we laid our help face down so their eyes would be out of the sun. I started picking leaves. They were dry and shriveling. "Does anybody have a rope or some string I can tie these up with?" I asked.

"What is it?" Stewart asked.

I told them how the plant worked and what the help had done to Sam. They laughed, softly, then looked guiltily around at the trees, afraid of their own noise. Nobody had any string. I tore a strip of cloth from the hem of my shorts, bundled up the leaves, and tied them to a belt loop. We picked up the help and went on.

It was dark when we got to the town. The Brazis had a big fire burning in the street again. Somebody's sack of nicoji sat open by the fire, and all the guys were roasting nicoji. "Meat in the freezer's rotted," Raimundo said. He smelled sweaty. All the Brazis did. They'd cleared off half the runway. We'd walked down it carrying the help. But nobody from the new company had come. No ship had landed.

We carried the help to the hospital and laid them on the table and counters. Eloise and Mauá had crowded up Eloise's help and put Sam in a bed. The wild guys went back to the fire. "How's Sam?" I asked.

"Not good," Eloise said. "I kept giving him antibiotics. He's been unconscious since noon."

Lagarto poison would send you into a coma. I knew that. But the red-veined plant had brought Sam out of it once before. I untied the bundle of leaves from my belt loop and put it down by the help. Mauá had shells and dried plants and nicoji in all the windows and hanging from the heads of all the beds. I walked up to Sam and pressed his shoulder. He didn't move. I pulled back the blanket and looked at his leg. Most of it was black, even his foot. I covered it back up. "Thanks for putting him in a bed," I said.

Eloise said nothing to my thanks. She was acting more like her old self now. A little sleep, a little food, and she was a nice person again. She carried Kena and Ditha to a bed and laid them at the feet of her help. Mauá and Eloise had swept and mopped the floor, scrubbed off all the counters. Somebody had even started washing one of the walls.

"Why did no doctors come down?" I asked.

"Nobody knows," Eloise said. "All the new company personnel should have been here yesterday."

We had to call out. We had to tell them we needed a doctor. "I'll be back," I said.

I hurried up to the fire. The neon light was buzzing on and off again, strobe light melodramatics. "Raimundo," I said, "you've got to take me up to the company house. I've got to look at that communications equipment."

"I've seen it, Jake. It's no good."

"Take me! We've got to try. We've got to call a doctor."

Maybe I looked desperate; maybe I looked like I'd take only the answer I wanted; but Raimundo pulled the roasted nicoji from his stick, got a light from Manoel, and we started up the street. Manoel took off his boots and threw them at me.

"Put them on," Raimundo said. "You don't want to walk in the company house barefoot."

I pulled them on. They were too big, so I laced them up tight. We kicked our way up the street, through the clothes and nets scattered from the store. Raimundo handed me a nicoji. I bit the meat off the back and chewed it and swallowed, but my stomach felt too nervous for food, though I'd been hungry and hadn't gotten anything all day except part of a Coke.

The company house stood up the mesão across from the workers' barracks on a narrow ledge, exposed. It must have had a wonderful view of the ocean. The storm had smashed in the front, and the whole building leaned back against the mountain. Raimundo pushed on the side of it and kicked the doorframe. The building didn't collapse.

"Let's go," I said.

Raimundo went first, with the light. The inside was damp and muddy. Water dripped from the ceiling. Raimundo shined the light around. "I found the communications room over here," he said.

He led me down a corridor strewn with plastic chairs and desks. Glass and biochips and bits of hard plastic crunched under our boots. The place stank of something dead, and I realized it could be the machines. If biochips got smashed open and left in the

air for a couple days, they'd smell like rotting flesh.
I'd been in the post office in Alma when the guys at
the Idaho National Engineering Laboratory out by
Arco had some experiment go haywire and send a
power surge over the lines no surge protector could
blink at. All the computers and appliances in a four-
hundred-mile radius were fried, and the post office
started to smell like some kind of weird barbecue. I
was glad to pay cash for my stamps and get out.

"Here," Raimundo said. He shined the light around.
We were in a room of smashed-up communications
gear. The floor had sagged, and the bigger pieces of
equipment had slammed into the depression and lay
there in two feet of water.

We wouldn't be calling out.

X

I leaned back against an outside wall of the hospital and closed my eyes. We had to wait. Wait till somebody on one of the stations decided that people left on a forsaken world might need medical attention after a hurricane. In the meantime, I didn't know what to do for Sam. Cut off his leg? Was it still lagarto poison killing him, or gangrene? I could probably find a saw in the wreck of the general goods store up the street. We had blood coagulator in Raimundo's medkit. But I didn't know if we'd have enough to stop the kind of blood flow that cutting through all the arteries in a leg would produce. Tie a tourniquet up high, have Eloise ready to spray the stump like mad once the leg was cut off, get eight or ten guys to hold Sam down? I didn't know.

Eloise was talking to somebody inside. I didn't want to walk in and have to talk to people, not then. So I stayed out against the wall.

"Blind female's eyes swollen, like the others. Pupils dilated."

What was she talking about?

"Rapid pulse, shallow breathing through mouth, swollen glands in throat constricting esophagus, fever—all the general symptoms of anaphylactic shock noted before on my help."

I looked through the window. Eloise was leaning over Ditha. No one else was in the room but Sam, and he was still unconscious. Eloise was talking to herself. For maybe a minute I watched her examine the help and listened to her talk about the similarity of their symptoms.

Then I realized she wasn't just talking to herself. She was making a recording.

I walked in and Eloise looked up quickly, touched her left temple.

"Who are you working for?" I asked.

She just stared at me.

"Are you with the government? Is somebody coming to help us?"

"Don't be a fool," she said.

Wishful thinking. I wanted her to be with somebody besides just another corporation, one that had paid the enormous expense of having her head implanted. "Is your equipment visual, or just audio?" I asked.

She said nothing. Biochips wired into the back of her brain could give her practically unlimited information storage.

"Can you transmit? Can you call down help for Sam?" Even just a talk-through link up with a doctor would be good if I had to cut off Sam's leg.

"Shut up, Jake," she said.

She either didn't want to blow her cover completely or she couldn't call out. I didn't think Eloise would let Sam die if she could help him, so I decided she couldn't call. "Why the interest in the help?" I asked.

She sat down on a bed, held one of her help's hands, and looked at me. I was getting nowhere. I walked over to Sam. "How long since he's had antibiotic?" I asked.

"We're out," she said. "We shouldn't have given any to the help, should have saved it for him."

But we'd thought the doctors would come. Warm medicine probably wasn't good anyway. All he'd need was a reaction to bad medicine on top of everything else.

"I can't call out," Eloise said. "I'd have done that for Sam if I could."

"I know. So who are you with if you can't call out?"

"Why do you care?"

Sam frowned with pain and turned his head to the side, but he wasn't awake. "I don't care," I said. "My friend is dying, and I thought maybe you could help him. If you can't, I don't care what you're doing here or who you're working for."

She stood, walked up to me, and spoke quiet and fast. "I had money to wire myself so I could come here and do solo research on help intelligence, Ph.D. I signed on as a worker so the company wouldn't suspect and interfere with my research. I thought I could make fast money harvesting nicoji, buy my way back to Earth after a couple years, be a big surprise to everybody—settle whether the help are intelligent or merely imitative."

I just looked at her.

"It would have been a scientific coup, studying the help in their native habitat, not in cages run by company-bought researchers."

Her plan would have bought her way into footnote heaven, if the company couldn't have bribed her first. But it hadn't worked. None of us had realized getting back to Earth would be so hard.

"One word of this to anyone and I'll kill you," she said.

The company would kill *her* if they found out. They'd arrange an accident, I was sure of it. It didn't matter if they believed she was a Ph.D. candidate or a corporate spy. They wouldn't want to lose either company secrets or this world—and the company could stay here only so long as the scientific debate about the help was left unresolved.

"I should kill you now," she said. "What I've found out is too important to jeopardize." She walked to the door and looked out. I wondered if she was checking to see if anybody was there to notice if she turned around and stabbed me.

"The help are intelligent, of course," I said.

"And the company knows it. Why do you think it's trying to kill all the help?"

"What?"

"Release a virus, kill the help—then reintroduce nicoji on a world no native sentients would ever challenge them for."

I didn't believe her, even knowing, as I did, that American Nicoji had the motivation to do such a thing. "I'm no friend of the company's," I said, "but it's not them. The help told me this happens every so often—the world dies and a lot of help starve, then most things grow back and the cycle starts over. It happened before when some of these help were young. We haven't been on this world long enough to see it."

She looked at me as if I were some kind of imbecile picking his nose on a street corner. Defender, studier of the help, but she wouldn't consider what they'd told me. After all, what could the help know about their own world? They only lived here. "If they come out of this, they'll tell you," I said.

"Fine," she said. "And what could cause something like that?"

"How should I know? You're the one getting an education."

"Smart aleck."

I thought for a minute. "The help told me the froth—all the sulfury things—come out when this happens."

"Cause or effect?"

I shrugged.

She walked over by her help again. "I don't want them to die," she said. "And I don't want them to lose their world if they live."

I didn't either.

"With the information I have, I could give them back their world, and they would never lose it. All I have to do is see that they live, then get out of here and publish my studies."

That was all. "Good luck," I said.

Raimundo, Manoel, and six other Brazis walked in. Eloise looked hard at me, but I had no intention of telling her secret. "How's Sam?" they asked. That night, all the guys started coming in small groups to see Sam, talk to me and Eloise. Some brought their help and put them in the hospital with ours. We soon had help all over the floor and the counters. Eloise told the guys they had to come take care of their help or she'd throw them out. She wasn't going to clean up after them all. I looked at the sick help and wondered if maybe Eloise wasn't partly right. The company wouldn't release something that would kill the whole world—kill the nicoji. But maybe they'd released something help-specific and it had gotten out of hand.

But that was too easy. Something like that could be traced. They wouldn't try something that obvious. It had to be what Kena had told me—a natural cycle, part of this world.

I mashed two of the red-veined leaves in clean water and tasted it. It made my stomach queasy but didn't numb my tongue or fingers. I didn't know if the juice would do any good without help spit, but I decided to give it to Sam just in case. Raimundo helped me lift Sam up, and I poured some juice in his mouth. It just ran back out. "Swallow it, Sam," I said. Raimundo tilted Sam's head back, and I poured in more juice. Sam coughed and sputtered, but swallowed quite a bit. I mashed more leaves and gave more juice to Sam. Then we all watched him to see if it would do any good. It didn't. He didn't open his eyes or throw up or get any better. I went to the door and threw out what juice was left. It was no good. Water didn't work. Eloise was wiping the juice off Sam's face with a wet cloth. I came back and let a sick help drool in the bowl.

"Jake," Sam said, hoarse. "I hate you."

I turned around, fast. Sam was awake.

"You were going to put that in my mouth, weren't you?"

Raimundo laughed. "The threat of drinking help spit woke him up."

"You just want me awake to feel all this," Sam said.

Fine, I wanted to say. We'll just leave you lying here in a coma, wouldn't that be great? But I didn't say it. Besides, did *he* now think he was dying? I didn't ask that either. I wondered, though, if it was only comfort to me to have him conscious when he was so sick.

Sam went to sleep, but it was just sleep. We could wake him up. "Let me sleep, Jake!" he said the second time I woke him.

"Come eat," Raimundo said to me. "We've got nicoji to roast."

"Bring me some," Eloise said.

So I went. The guys had six fires burning in the street. Raimundo took me to one with a bunch of Brazis I knew. They boa noitéd me but didn't say much else. I gutted two nicoji, rinsed them off in a bucket of water by the fire, shoved the nicoji on a stick, and sat down in the dirt, held the nicoji over the fire.

Stewart walked up. "How's your friend?" he asked.

"Not good," I said.

"How're the help?"

"Not good either." I wondered again why nobody'd come from the stations. They could look down and see the fires along this street. What were they thinking?

"Tomorrow is Christmas Eve," Raimundo said.

Great, I thought. Not much chance of snow, and nothing depended anymore on whether we'd been good boys and girls. Nothing at all.

Todd and Dave walked up. Lindoval and the other wild guys must have been out on watch. The Brazis looked nervous to have the wild guys come up to the fire, and I thought they were crazy. The wild guys had been a big help to me. Of course, I didn't know what had happened when they'd all first gotten into town. Something had spooked the Brazis.

Nobody said anything and I didn't feel like talking, but I couldn't stand the awkward silence. I decided that if I got them talking I could probably shut up and sit and listen or tune them out if I wanted to, but at least break the ice. So I looked up at Stewart. "What have you seen in the pântano?" I asked. "Where have you been?"

"To the mountains," he said. "And to the sea beyond them."

The Brazis who understood English translated that for their amigos. Todd started telling us about a plateau they'd found that looked like Kansas: rolling hills, wide rivers meandering through fertile land— straight west of us, three thousand feet up, across the mountains.

Then Stewart told us a story.

"My friend, Peter Rojas, and I once decided to follow a river to the sea," he said. "We made a raft and floated downstream for seven days. On the sixth and seventh days we could hear a distant, constant roar ahead of us, growing louder, and the eighth morning we didn't dare put out on the river. We walked up the riverbank and came to the end of the world, and the river plunged over it."

One Brazi heard that translated and crossed himself three times. I wondered what part of Brazil he was from that he could still believe the worlds were flat—after he'd even seen them from ships. But some men see things and do not believe. Ideas are stronger for them, and facts don't matter.

"The plateau doesn't slope down to the sea," Stewart went on. "It ends at a cliff two thousand feet high. The cliff runs north and south, broken every so often by white falls.

"We decided to find a way down, build a raft in the river below, and keep going. We spent days braiding ropes, getting food, scouting out the best way. Our first night over the edge we camped on a ledge four feet wide facing a sixteen-hundred-foot drop. In the night, a bug walked onto my face. I opened my eyes and brushed it off. It was a spider—and I had spiders in my hair, all over my shirt and arms. I sat up and started hitting them. They bit my hands, and the venom made my hands numb. Then I looked at Peter. Six little spiders were ringed around his right eye, sucking, and one big spider—maybe as big across as the palm of my hand—sat over his left eye, sucking hard, while littler ones tried to crowd in around its sides. I pulled them off of him, and he woke up, then, but they'd sucked out his eyes. His eyes were sunk back in the sockets, all bloody and—gone. He couldn't feel a thing. They'd bit his face and eyes and anesthetized them so he hadn't felt them sucking out his eyes. We sat up the rest of the night, and I kept hitting the spiders when they crawled on us. My hands went completely numb and were like sticks I kept throwing out at spiders to smash them. Peter kept putting his fingers back in his eye sockets one at a time as far as they would go—till he touched what was left of his eyes—then pulling out his fingers, fast.

"The venom started to wear off towards morning, and he started to feel what they'd done to him. When it was light enough, I told him we had to climb back out: he had the hands to pull us up, and I had the eyes to see to tell him how to do it. I guided him to the rope. He took hold of it but knocked a spider onto his face. He brushed it off, frantic, stepped back—and fell over the edge. I tried to grab him, but my clubs of hands didn't work and I couldn't hang on."

He stopped talking, the Brazis finished translating, and nobody said a word. I'd eaten my two nicoji and had had enough. I gutted five more, skewered them

on the stick, and held them over the fire, to roast for
Eloise.

"How did you get away?" Raimundo asked.

"The spiders were nocturnal. After the sun came
up, they left. Four hours later my hands got their
feeling back and I climbed out."

"You said you went to the sea," I said.

"A year later, with different guys, down a different
way. We wore eye coverings and kept a night watch."

I finished roasting the nicoji and took them back to
Eloise.

Kena was sitting up in bed, propped up by pillows.

I could hardly believe it, and I just stood there by
the bed.

Eloise took a nicoji off the stick and gave it to
Kena, and he ate it. "He told me what he told you
about this world," she said. "The periodic famines
and the sulphur-based life forms that seem to appear
only then—and I've been thinking about it. Connect-
ing those two events might actually fit together some
of the puzzle of this planet. Look."

She'd dug a block of sod out of the ground and
stuffed it in a bucket. She lifted up the sod and held
it out to me. I put the stick of nicoji on the bottom of
Kena's bed and took the sod. The grass was black on
the surface, dead, like ash if touched, but the roots
were very much alive—the dirt around them was
even warm—there was so much frantic life in the
roots. I broke apart the sod and could see the roots
bulging with life, covered with hundreds of shoots:
most shriveled, but some pale green, like they should
be before getting to the sun, and etched with blue
up the middle.

"Immunological experimentation," Eloise said. "At
least that's what I think we're seeing. These shoots

are each an attempt at immunological response to whatever attacked the adult plant."

Kena reached down toward the nicoji, so Eloise gave him one. She nodded at Kena. "It must be the same with the help. They've got all the symptoms of anaphylactic shock—allergic reaction: sudden collapse, difficulty in breathing, fall in blood pressure. Their bodies pulled back, shut down all but the essentials, channeled all available energy to their immune systems which experiment to find a way for the individual to survive. The attack from whatever causes this must be so fast and so deadly that only those systems that quickly produce the right antigens survive and pass on their trait for rapid immunological response."

Kena reached down for another nicoji. "Hungry, Jake. Got lot big hungry."

I put down the sod and let him pull the rest of the nicoji from the stick. His hands were shaking.

"Come with me," Eloise said.

I followed her outside and behind the hospital. She had sulphur-based creatures laid out on the ground: pustules cut from the trees; spindly, silvery stalks of a plant with a red sheen in the moonlight; flat, octagonal things the size of pancakes that oozed along the bottoms of two red plastic buckets.

"I've been gathering specimens from the forest just around this building," Eloise said. "I thought they were simply unobserved life-forms endemic to the mesão. It never occurred to me that they might be connected to what was killing this world."

I stepped back from an amorphous, white blob crawling toward my feet.

"There's a whole new ecosystem here, Jake," she said. "This world apparently has two ecosystems battling to control the same biosphere. We're seeing something more alien on this world than we dreamed of."

I thought Eloise wasn't thinking right anymore—this world was so much like Earth. I remembered when it was found, how all the news-ports had said we were lucky to find yet another world like our own. Nobody'd thought any farther than that after the surveys. Till now. Eloise's talk made me think of the anaerobic creatures at the bottom of oceans on Earth, and I realized that her idea could make some sense. "One beats the other down into the muck," I said, trying to think it through, trying to fit her ideas in with what Kena had told me. "But every seventy or eighty years it mutates enough to attack the other ecosystem again—"

"Not attack—no intelligence—just life trying to utilize the energy locked up in the life-forms of the prime ecosystem—but you're right, actually, kill it in the process, tear it apart. Not the creatures we can see, mind you, the things we can run from, but the sulphur-based bacteria or viruses—they must be truly deadly to the higher orders of oxygen-based life here. The members of the prime ecosystem have to collapse back and on an internal, individual level find a way to resist microbial attack within days or weeks."

"Or die," I said. I grabbed a stick and shoved back the silvery blob still trying to crawl over my feet. The stick broke through its side, and the blob curled around the end of it, tight, started inching up toward my hand, impaling itself. I threw it back in the trees. "It sucks the life out of anything that uses oxygen," I said.

"But us," Eloise said.

"So far," I said. At least on a microbial level. Sam and I knew the visible sulphur-based life forms *could* hurt us. I wondered how long we'd stay immune to the invisible, how long it would take the sulphur-based ecosystem to figure out a way to get to the energy stored in *our* bodies. But then I thought maybe it never would. Maybe we had a built-in immunity to cellular level attacks from sulphur-based life: when life evolved on any world maybe it broke out in all kinds of ways at the same time but one became dominant and eventually immune to the others' attacks and destroyed the others—or left them only niches it couldn't utilize itself, like the niche on Earth two thousand feet under an ocean around a hot vent. That just hadn't happened here. Two inimical forms of life had evolved. And rapid immunological response or no, the oxygen-based ecosystem on this world simply couldn't overcome the sulphur.

I thought, too, about the plants Todd told me they had been growing out on the plateau—and how the plants had seemed unaffected by the plague, at least when Todd left. I told Eloise about that, and about my idea on the evolution of life and the possibility of our immunity to attack from sulphur-based microbes.

"You could spend your life working on that one idea," she said. "I came here to do research for just one dissertation. I could do fifty."

So the help, if their immune systems were strong enough and inventive enough, would live, and there was nothing we could do for them. We had no way to help them—except maybe feed the survivors through the coming famine as their world tried to grow itself back. And who knew how long that would take and what would come back, if even the nicoji would—whole species could go extinct in days under these circumstances. I wondered how the help had lived through past famines, what they'd found to scavenge. Obviously they'd made it as a species, somehow. Then I thought of Sam.

"Could Sam be sick from what made the help sick?" I asked.

Eloise looked up at me. "No," she said. "He has all the symptoms of lagarto poisoning and infection. Quite a few of his symptoms differ from the helps'."

Which was true. And Sam had been sick before we'd run into at least the visible sulphur-based life forms. None of the other men were sick—and I wasn't sick. I had been exposed to the sulphur-based life forms more than probably anyone else. I'd had froth all over me more times than I cared to think about. It had made my skin red and sore, but that was all.

"Do you realize what this means, if we're right?" Eloise said. "Do you realize how quickly cures for human diseases could be found if we harness, say, the mechanisms driving the immunological systems of the plants here? Clone the immune system of the help?"

It could free all the worlds from disease. And for the help, it was a gold mine. It would make them rich, if they could keep their world.

"This is all theory—we could be wrong," Eloise said. "But clearly I've got to get out of here, establish that the help are intelligent, and only write about the rest of this once the world is declared theirs."

Good luck, I thought again.

"It could, after all, still be the company trying to kill the help," she said.

"You don't believe that," I said.

"No. Not anymore."

I fed Kena and the other three help who came out of their sickness that night. Eloise tried to help, but she kept thinking out loud about what she'd started to learn, coming up with theories, rejecting them, coming up with more but keeping to the basic ideas we'd talked about outside. Sam slept through it all. His hands were both black now, and his shoulders. His stomach was splotched with black. His leg was black all over. Mauá came and wrapped it and his hands and shoulders in a poultice. Sam opened his eyes but didn't say anything. I gave the help some leaves and tried to get them to chew some for Sam, but they wouldn't. "Not good now, Jake," Kena said. He held the leaves away from him at arm's length. "Not good, not work." So I quit trying with the leaves. These withered ones hadn't done much good anyway. I helped Mauá hang more shells and dried nicoji around Sam's bed and rattly nut shells in the windows outside.

In the night, I dreamed of the girl in the white dress. She took off her red shoes and held them out to me. "Go home," she said. "Put these on and go home."

I took them from her. "Thank you, Dorothy," I said.

She looked surprised. "You know my name."

"Of course," I said. "How else would I dream of you?"

I looked around for Sam. I wanted to put the shoes on Sam and send him home so his family could get him to a doctor. I found him lying out on the steps where I'd been sleeping, by the shells and white powders, but the shoes wouldn't fit his feet. I kept trying to put them on him, kept trying—

And woke up. Mauá and all the help were snoring. I wondered how anybody could sleep in that hospital. Something was tapping the window above the beds of help, so I tiptoed back there and looked out. Seven or eight sulfur balls were floating by the window, trying to bite the glass with their teeth. I'd been hearing their teeth tap the glass. The balls glittered in the red moonlight and hung in the air like delicate ornaments on a Christmas tree. I got Mauá inside and shut the door.

Early in the morning, when it was just coming light, I woke again. Sam was moving around on his bed, in pain. I went to him. He looked at me once and closed his eyes. I got him the last two aspirin from Raimundo's medkit, and he managed to swallow them and keep them down. Only then did I notice that Mauá was gone.

I went to the door, opened it a crack, and looked out. Mauá was crouched in the street, breaking nut shells off of strings and dropping them one by one into a little fire. He'd taken all the strings down from the windows. The top step was clean of charms. I stepped out and closed the door behind me. "Mauá," I said. "What's wrong?"

He didn't answer. I heard a tree fall below the town, then another, loud in the still dawn. I walked up to Mauá's fire. He'd spread the bits of dried nicoji and the strings of seashells and nut shells around the fire and was feeding them into it piece by piece—burning them up.

I knelt to look at them more closely. The nicoji bits were just chitin. The soft parts had been eaten. Even the seashells had been chewed on.

I stayed with Mauá till he put out the fire. He crushed the seashells to dust, then scooped up a handful of ash and crushed shell and let it sift out of his hands and blow away on the wind off the sea. We went inside to sleep while we could. Kena crawled over, put his legs on my stomach, and went to sleep. I had barely dozed off when all the windows started rattling, and the whole building shook. I tried to get up, fast, but by the time I got Kena's legs off me Mauá was already out the door, looking around. The hospital shook again.

"Explosions?" Eloise shouted. She pulled a butcher-knife from a drawer, and we ran to the door. Men and women dressed in olive-green bodysuits were running up and down the street, shoving Brazis and Americans out of buildings, shouting orders.

"It's the new company people," Eloise said.

I ran into the street and tried to stop one new guy. "Where are your doctors?" I yelled at him.

He shoved me away. "Get out of town," he said.

"We need a doctor!"

"Get out of town! We've got to tear this place down to bedrock. We brought no doctors."

Ecological restoration. Leave a world the way you found it, as much as possible. Boy Scout lore played with by adults. It meant the new company was abandoning this place, for good. Another explosion shook the ground, and we were peppered with rock and dirt blown on us from higher up. The company house collapsed in flames. The workers' barracks were already burning.

I knew this: if the doctors hadn't come here, I had to get Sam to them, to their station.

I ran up the street and shoved my way through a crowd of Brazis to a team of green-suited men scooping debris into piles and burning it. "Who's in charge here?" I shouted.

"Get out of town!"

"Who's in charge!"

One of them pointed up the street, so I ran in that direction. They'd pitched a tent in the road below the workers' barracks, and people inside it were looking at maps on tables. I figured these must be the people in charge. They'd set up a huge trash compactor and sterilizer behind the tent, and teams of new company boys were feeding it sheets of corrugated metal from the barracks. It ground away, making a screeching sound so loud I couldn't believe they'd pitched their HQ tent just below it, but the HQ people seemed to like it—the noise meant their work was coming along fine: press into one-ton blocks whatever metal, plastic, and glass they didn't want to take back up the gravity well, sterilize them, and bury them deep.

I pushed my way into the tent. "I've got a friend who's sick bad," I said. "Can you take him up to your doctors?"

"Get this guy out of here," a clean-shaven, showered man at a table said.

"My friend will die!"

He looked at me like so what. "We can't touch any of you," he said. "Your company'd impound our ships. They're coming for you later today."

Later today. Only later today.

Somebody started pulling me out of the tent, and I thought at first it was some of the green-suited company boys, but it was Raimundo and Manoel. "They're throwing the help out of the hospital," Raimundo said.

And Sam, I thought.

We ran down the street, shoving our way through the crowds, and got to the hospital. They'd dragged Eloise out, and three company boys were holding her. One had a bloody arm, and I realized she'd stabbed him. Help were lying all over the ground, in the mud, trying to crawl into shadows. One company boy carried two more to the doorway and dumped them down the steps. I shoved past him into the hospital. Sam was still in the bed.

"My friend's dying," I said. "You can't dump him out of here. Leave him a bed, at least."

"We've got to burn this place. Get out."

I didn't know what to do, but the more I thought about it, the more I realized there was nothing I could do. "I'll get some guys to help carry him," I said, and I started out.

But one of the HQ men walked in and looked at Sam. "Is this your sick friend?" he asked.

I didn't answer that.

He pulled the blanket off Sam. I grabbed it and tried to put it back. "At least leave him a blanket to die in," I said.

"What did this to him?"

"Lagarto poison."

"The lagarto might all be dead now," he said. He let go of the blanket, and I covered Sam. One company boy looked like he wanted to throw up.

"Leave this building till last," the HQ man told his boys. He turned to me. "We'll leave your friend a bed and a roof over his head as long as we can. Let's just hope your company comes for you, fast."

They shoved Sam's bed in a corner and started tearing out the cabinets, threw out the operating table and the fridge, jerked the glass windows out of their frames. Sam lay unconscious through it all. I found my bundle of red-veined leaves trampled in the mud out in the street and left them there. They let Mauá in to change the poultices on Sam. He put one string of living grass roots around Sam's neck—a new charm; one last try—before he left.

After the company boys took the door off its hinges and busted up the steps, they left, too. There wasn't anything else to dismantle in the hospital without attacking the walls, floor, and roof. They brought in tillers and started plowing up the street, loosening the dirt so they wouldn't leave it compacted. Teams shoveled the dirt by the latrines into plastic bags and dragged them to the compactor.

One company boy pulled himself up into the doorway. "Here," he said. He threw a sack of ice at me. I missed it, and it fell to the floor. "For your friend," he said.

I picked up the sack. "Thanks," I said.

"I'm sorry about him," he said.

"Why are you doing this? Why are you leaving?"

"Game's changed. Your company just announced it can build a nicoji growing station above Earth. Seems it had stocks of uncontaminated nicoji in its corporate HQ and can breed up to commercial levels from there. Got UNDA clearance for it two days ago. The plague killed nicoji harvesting on this world."

"What about us?" I asked.

He didn't know. He looked outside, over the pântano to the sea. "This place stinks," he said. "How could you guys stand it?"

I'd forgotten that the pântano stunk.

After the company boy left, I tore up a sheet, wrapped ice in the cloth, and put ice packs on Sam's forehead, leg, hands, and shoulders, then covered him with the blanket. Raimundo walked in.

"I'm sorry, Jake," he said.

How many people were going to tell me that? "For what?" I asked.

"For telling you about this place. For telling you to come here. It didn't work out."

I said nothing.

"I'm sorry."

"It isn't your fault. None of it: the company, Sam, none of it."

"I'm just sorry."

"OK."

"There's talk American Nicoji might keep us here. See what happens to this world and have us here just in case."

I could believe it.

Eloise came in later in the morning. She said the help were together in shadows down the mesão. "They're all awake now, weak and hungry," she said. "But they're going to be fine."

Till they starved. The ice had melted and Sam's bed was all wet. He wasn't awake to care about it, though.

In the evening, he did open his eyes.

"Sam," I said.

He tried to touch my arm, but his hand was so sore he couldn't close his fingers on it. "Jake," he said, hoarse.

I tried to give him some water, but he didn't want it, so I didn't make him drink it. I wondered what had woken him up.

"Where are the help?" he asked.

I told him what was happening and that American Nicoji was supposed to come get us. "At least they've got a doctor," I said.

He closed his eyes. I couldn't blame him for not being excited about that doctor.

"It's Christmas Eve," I said.

He looked at me and tried to smile. His cheeks were dark and sunken in, and he'd lost so much weight he looked like he'd been a prisoner of war in Popayan or up in the camps in Medellin during the Drug Wars.

"I wonder what they're doing back home," Sam said.

"Your family's eating the nicoji you sent," I said.

"Our cousins are probably out sledding down potato pits."

"Remember when you took Loryn and me skiing?"

I smiled, then. Neither Sam nor Loryn had ever gone skiing, and I thought how could these two live in Idaho and never go skiing? So I saved my money and gave them a one-day ski trip for Christmas. We went two days before New Year's. I took them first on the bunny slopes, showed them how to keep their balance, how to stop, how to slow themselves down. They fell quite a bit, but were catching on. After a while, I took them to the lift and we got on to go just to the top of the first little hill and ski down that, easy.

But Loryn couldn't jump out of her chair, and the lift carried her up past the next hill and all the way to the top of the mountain. We could see her up there, a little speck dressed in red. She sat in the snow and looked at how steep the slopes were and cried. People tried to coax her down, tell her she could do it. Finally she got up and skied down a little ways, but whenever she picked up any speed she'd make herself fall over. It took her an hour to get down to Sam and me. She was so cold we just packed up and drove home.

"Do you remember how the snow looked in the Arctic when we left?" I asked.

He nodded. We'd sat for hours in the little observation deck of American Nicoji's station orbiting Earth. The snow in the Arctic had shone so brilliantly white we'd been amazed. But we'd thought—coming from Idaho—that we'd never miss snow.

"We were crazy," Sam said.

To think we wouldn't miss snow or to leave Earth? I didn't know what he meant. Both, maybe. I didn't ask.

We started to smell roasting nicoji and smoke. It blew in through the gutted windows. Our guys were cooking nicoji down the mesão where the trees had all fallen and none were likely to fall on them. I was starving.

"Go get some food," Sam said.

"Do you want any?" I asked.

He shook his head.

"Maybe some nicoji would taste good to you."

"Maybe. Go, Jake."

So I went. None of the new company people were in sight, so I didn't think they'd pull Sam out of the hospital and start tearing it down in the few minutes I'd be gone. I started off through the bare trees. Dry leaves crunched under my feet.

"Jake! Jake!"

It was Kena, up in a tree.

"You're feeling better," I said.

He climbed down to me.

"Got lot big hungry, Jake. Lot hungry."

"Me too."

He reached up and held my hand, and we walked along toward the fire. Before we got there, Eloise started to sing "O Little Town of Bethlehem," and some of the Brazis with good voices hummed the harmony since they didn't know the English words. I stopped to listen.

> O little town of Bethlehem,
> How still we see thee lie.
> Above thy deep and dreamless sleep
> The silent stars go by.

I wondered if Sam could hear them singing. Kena looked up at me, all smiles. He loved to hear any human sing, ever, anything. The Brazis would trans-

fix him—like all Latin Americans I'd ever known—if
nothing else, they could sing. And Eloise could sing.
She had a husky, alto voice like my aunt Carolyn's—
who'd sing Hindi songs and never explain where or
why she had learned them.

"Why you and Sam not sing outside box water
falling on head?" Kena asked. "Why not?"

I kept hold of his hand and we walked closer to the
fire, to where we could see the guys.

> *How silently, how silently*
> *The wondrous gift is giv'n!*
> *So God imparts to human hearts*
> *The blessings of his heav'n.*

I couldn't go up to the fire, not then. I sat on a rock
and waited out in the trees. The Brazis went on to
sing "Away in a Manger," in Portuguese, and after
that everybody was quiet. Maybe they were eating. I
looked up at the stars that shone through the leafless
trees. A few stars were still in the sky. The moon was
just starting to rise, and its red light hadn't yet
blotted them all out. I could clearly see the bright
light that was our station.

"Get food, Jake. Nicoji."

"You go," I said.

He tried to touch my eyes, but I wouldn't let him.

"Jake, get food—food."

"Go to Eloise. She'll give you some."

He went. I decided to go back to the hospital and
wait for a little while. There'd be time to eat.

But when I got back, Sam was lying very still in
his bed, his eyes open, and his mouth. I felt his
wrist. No pulse. No breath. I closed his eyes and
held his mouth shut till it would stay shut on its own.

Then I heard the choppers from American Nicoji, landing in the street.

Now they come, I thought.

After a few minutes, Eloise, Raimundo, and Manoel rushed in. They stopped in the doorway. Then Eloise walked up to me and took hold of my arm.

"We've got to go," Raimundo said. "They want us in the choppers now."

"No," I said. "I'm going to bury Sam."

One of the company boys—one of our company boys—stepped in through the doorway and looked at us. Three more crowded in behind him. "Jake, the rest of you, out," the first one said. "Helicopters are waiting."

"Sam just died," I told him. He knew us, knew Sam.

"Tough, isn't it?" he said. "Out."

"I've got to bury him."

"Somebody will take care of his corpse when they tear down this building. Leave it."

The other three company boys snickered. A team of workers from the new company started pulling the metal sheeting off the sides of the hospital, and I suddenly knew how they meant to dispose of Sam's body—along with the metal.

"Bastards," I said. "I'm getting a shovel."

"Five minutes, Jake."

Most of the Brazis and Americans I knew were crowded in front of the hospital. I tried to shove my way through them, heading for the latrines where they'd been using shovels, but then Stewart was in front of me, with a shovel. He put it in my hands. I ran back to the side of the hospital and started trying to dig but hit rock under the thin layer of dirt.

Stewart pulled me back. "Try digging in the street," he said. "They've been plowing there."

It was easier in the street. But there was a lot of rock, and soon I was down to solid rock.

"We'll pile it over him," Stewart said.

There was nothing else to do. I kept digging at the sides and ends of the hole I'd made, to get it big enough.

"There was only one shovel," Stewart said. "They've packed up the others."

"We should have dug a grave today while we had a better chance," somebody said. I looked around to see who'd said it but I couldn't tell.

"Time's up, Jake. The rest of you—get to the choppers."

I kept digging. The guys moved off slowly, to give me more time. Stewart lay down in the hole, and it was two feet short. His legs wouldn't fit. I dug at the ends.

"Time's up, Jake. Where's the body?"

Raimundo, Manoel, and Lindoval came out carrying Sam, wrapped in the blanket off the bed. I kept digging, and they laid him on the ground. "Couldn't you find any plastic?" I asked. I didn't want to bury Sam in just a blanket. Things could get through a blanket too easily.

"No plastic, Jake."

"Go! Now! Shove him in and let's go!"

We lifted Sam into the grave. I'd wanted a deep grave, but it wasn't very deep. Stewart and the Brazis helped me push dirt and rocks over Sam, and we smoothed it out with our hands. When I stood up, somebody'd taken the shovel to pack it up. Everybody picked up rocks and dumped them on top of the grave.

It was all I could do for Sam, in the end. Nothing else. I hoped the new company would leave his body in the grave.

Eloise came up through the trees, her arms full of help, the other help following her. "We're taking them," she told the company boys. "We've got to feed them or they'll starve."

There was no arguing with Eloise. Somebody put Ditha in my arms and pulled me along toward the choppers. I was inside a chopper surrounded by terrified help—Kena and the others who had worked with Sam and me. Eloise was at my side with her help. Raimundo handed me Sam's pocketknife. "I got it out of his pocket for you," he said.

I put it in my pocket. We took off and flew out across the pântano. I could see nothing below us in the dark.

XI

We landed in the correction field and were made to stand there all night. Most of the guys came up to me and tried to say something about Sam, that they were sorry. The help sat around me, quiet, and took turns touching my legs. I thought I should want to kill them, that I should hate them, but I didn't. I just wished that Sam and I could keep working together. "We'd worked together since we were boys," I told somebody, but I looked up and didn't know who I'd been talking to, all kinds of people were standing around me.

Swarms of bugs found us.

"Feeding on carcasses in the pântano," Eloise said. "Breeding like mad."

They'd evidently won their immunological battles. I was amazed at the variety of insects out that night—even rare things came in great numbers: floaters, oval patches of toothy fluff that drifted on the air, never touching anything solid except to feed, tinged pink by their blood—or was it the moonlight?—para-quedas, that dropped like little, black parachutes into our hair and crawled down to bite our scalps. The Brazis thought they really wanted the oils there, not blood, that they hated blood, but I didn't care—I just wished them gone; Camas-de-nariz, odd things that thought a human nostril the best place to weave a trap for other bugs and made nose-picking an object of sympathy, not disgust. Nobody complained or asked for help. The company boys would be glad to know we were uncomfortable. We just stood there and swatted the bugs.

"Behind you, Jake," Eloise said. "Turn around."

I turned and faced one of the transparent, sulphur balls, bobbing on the air.

"I was afraid it would bite your neck," she said.

I knocked it away from me but it bobbed back up to my face. I could see three floaters inside it and even two ants trying to crawl through a sticky liquid and choking on the sulphur. It had swallowed the bugs nearly whole. I knocked it away from me again, and it stayed away.

Hundreds of balls shimmered in the air behind us, like bubbles rising out of the pântano. They frightened away the bugs, and the balls followed them, hunting. I pulled one last para-queda out of my hair. The gravitational wind started blowing off the land.

"Jake! Jake!"

It was Maria, the Vattani's girl, carrying three cups in each hand. Her hair was wet so the para-quedas wouldn't want to get in it when she went out in the dark—I knew that—but for a minute I thought she'd started swimming again, and I wondered how could she stand to do that after she'd nearly drowned the day Sam had had to save her.

"Where's Sam?" she asked.

I just looked at her. What was I supposed to say, and how? I didn't know. I didn't know what to do. I let her start to run off, looking for Sam, but Eloise stopped her, knelt down by her, told her. Eloise was the one who hugged her, then. The cups fell in the mud.

"Maria!" Senhora Vattani yelled. She'd come up with her husband, carrying a steaming pot. Marcos and Fabio put down a crate, and the Vattanis put their pot on it. Senhora Vattani marched up, snatched the cups from the mud, and tried to rub them clean on the towel tied around her waist.

"Sam, he is dead," Raimundo said. "Eloise just told Maria."

Senhora Vattani blinked once, walked back to the pot, took off the lid and started stirring inside it.

"We had to bring you some tea," Senhor Vattani yelled.

Had to? I didn't understand.

"Come and get it or I'll throw it out," Senhora Vattani yelled. "This is your breakfast."

Guys started forming a line. When one finished his tea, Senhora Vattani would wipe off the cup and fill it for the next. They had only six cups to pass around.

Somebody held a steaming cup of tea up to me. It was Maria. She had tears in her eyes. "Why aren't you crying?" she asked.

I took a sip of tea. It was brewed from one of Senhora Vattani's combinations of native leaves and barks. The cup was warm in my hands.

"Can't you cry, Jake? Didn't you cry at all?"

"Maria," Eloise said. "Get me some tea."

She took hold of Maria's left hand, and walked her off to the pot.

No, I thought. No. I hadn't had time to cry when Sam died, and I couldn't now standing in the chill in the correction field, drinking weak tea. But I couldn't stop thinking about Sam, who had been my friend, and about his life and mine. What did it matter, the things we did? We worked hard for years trying to make our dreams come true, dreams that in the end could never come true. We were too much a part of a system, living lives that served the expectations of others, not ourselves. And perhaps we dreamed the wrong dreams.

Kena took hold of my arm. "Tea, Jake," he said. "Tea."

I gave him the cup. He took a big swallow, then held open his mouth because the tea had been hot.

"Oh, Jake," somebody said, disgusted. "You want us to drink out of that cup now?"

Kena handed me the cup back, empty. I carried it to Senhora Vattani. "Thank you," I said.

She took the cup and started wiping it. "How did it happen?" she asked.

I told her, some of it: lagarto attack, infection, lost medicine. She didn't say anything, didn't look at me after that, just filled the cup with tea and handed it to somebody else.

I walked back to where I'd been standing. It seemed to be my spot. The Vattanis left when the tea ran out, and somebody said they'd signed up to cook for us to make extra money, and somebody else said they'd lost everything in the storm, had barely been evacuated up to the station before the waves hit the town. The company'd loaned them money to start again somewhere else, but that meant they were just in deeper like the rest of us and when they reopened a store their prices would be higher and they'd be more exacting, more demanding, more interested in a worker's paydays, and they wouldn't get ahead anyway.

It started getting light, and the help ran off to the trees and the shadows. "Move out!" the company boys shouted, no warning, no hint that we were going anywhere but the correction field. We started walking down into what was left of the town. The garbage flat had been washed clean. It was only a black mud flat now. Sam's and my house was gone, but the freeze-shack was still there.

"Inside," a company boy ordered. I pushed open the door and walked in. The people around me followed—a lot of Brazis, Eloise and some of the other Americans, the wild guys. They took the rest off to other buildings.

The shack stank so bad I could hardly breathe. Some of the guys started coughing. "Something's dead in here!" I said.

"Then bury it," a company boy yelled back. He pulled the door closed.

I got the window open. The company boys came around to look at the open window but didn't try to close it. It was still pretty dim outside, but getting lighter and at least we had some light and a little fresh air in the shack. I started kicking through the muck by the walls, looking for our shovel. Sam had put one together from a metal lid and a straight stick we'd found floating on a bayou, and I thought if I could find it we could bury whatever was dead like the company boy had said.

And I saw what was dead.

"It's the nicoji," I said. The nicoji Sam and I hadn't processed. We'd left them hanging in sacks on the wall, and they'd rotted there.

"Get them down from the wall," Eloise said.

Two Brazis tried to lift down one of the sacks, but

it burst open and spewed rancid nicoji over the Brazis' legs and feet and all over the ground. The Brazis swore in Portuguese, and the smell was so bad that nobody laughed at them. I found the shovel, dug a shallow hole, scooped the nicoji into it, and covered them up with muck.

"We can't stay in here," Eloise said.

We couldn't even sit on the ground, it was so muddy. But the company boys wouldn't let us out. They got us another shovel, though, which surprised me. Raimundo started digging, and we got the rest of the nicoji down from the wall and buried without breaking open the sacks. But it smelled only a little better.

"At least my nose doesn't hurt when I breathe," Eloise said.

I wondered if I could ever eat a nicoji again, but thought, yes, I probably could. Fresh nicoji wouldn't taste like what I was smelling now.

Some Brazis found a stack of empty sacks covered in mud, and the wild guys used them to rub mud all over the walls where the sacks of nicoji had hung. That helped. The smell got better then.

Towards noon, a group of company boys shoved open the door and started handing out papers. "You're being taken out of here to new jobs," one company boy told us. "No choice. Just work out your contracts somewhere else. These papers explain the kinds of work available. Pick what you want; we'll process your requests, get you up to the station and out of here."

We crowded around the open window and tried to read. Raimundo translated for the Brazis who couldn't read English. American Nicoji had affiliates that offered mining jobs on six different airless asteroids. I'd read of mining companies that made their miners

cut so close to the outer edge that sometimes it
crumbled away and the guys got sucked out into
vacuum. Great work. But it paid well, and it had a
good miners' union that hadn't been bought off yet.
It actually looked out for miners, and after a few
years of hard, dangerous work, would retrain you in
some other mine-related field, maybe get you back
to Earth where you could pick up family. If you
survived, you'd go home. There were also decent,
in-dock jobs repairing solar sails on the various intra-
solar system mining fleets and some jobs working
construction on a new station at Sirius. That didn't
sound too bad, except that I was a farmer. I hadn't
had much construction experience—and none in zero
gravity. Most of us were like that. Which meant
most guys would want to repair solar sails. Which
meant most guys would end up working in mines.

Some of the guys started clamoring at the door
about this job or that. The company boys took their
papers. One would hold them up and read them in a
deep voice. "Construction worker," he'd say. Then
they'd all laugh. "You'll end up in the mines." It
became a chant with them. "Repairer of solar sails,"
he'd read. "But you'll end up in the mines." I marked
my papers and turned them in.

"What did you mark?" Eloise asked.

"Construction worker, not that it matters," I said.

She looked scared. "I don't want to work in the
mines," she said.

I thought maybe she wouldn't have to because she
was a woman, but then I thought no, they'd take
her. She was big and strong.

I didn't want to go, either, even if it was a chance
to go home someday. I worried about the help. What
would happen to them when we all left and took our
food with us?

"Jake," one of the company boys yelled from the door.

He handed me a paper that told me the life insurance payoff on Sam had been applied to our debts and various unpaid fines. I was left with three hundred dollars in my account—not enough to fly me to the company station above us. I threw the paper on the ground.

"What is it, Jake?" Eloise asked.

"Sam's insurance," I said.

She picked up the paper and all the guys crowded around to look. The Americans started pounding me on the back. "Wow! Three hundred dollars," Cliff laughed. Raimundo grabbed the paper out of Eloise's hands and translated it for the Brazis. Then *they* started pounding me on the back.

Towards evening, just as it was getting dark, some of the help came up and climbed into the open window. "Jake," they said.

I walked up to them.

"Hungry, Jake. Hungry."

"Me, too."

If the Vattanis were supposed to be cooking for us, they weren't doing much.

Eloise came to the window and looked for some of her help, but only mine had come up. They knew this place.

"House gone, Jake. House."

"I know."

One held out his hand to me and unexpectedly gave me a handful of gagga raisins. Another handed me some uncooked rice. Kena gave me more raisins. They'd obviously robbed the Vattani's, and I wondered how they'd done that. Senhora Vattani would hate them for it.

And I wondered why they were giving me food, when they themselves were hungry.

They crawled through the window and up into the rafters. "Eat, Jake. Eat," Kena said. They all sat in the rafters, looking down at me.

I just stood there, holding the food in my hands. "I can't give you anything in return," I said. "I can't do anything for you."

The help looked away as if they were disgusted with me for saying something so stupid.

"Thank you," I said. I ate the raisins and sucked on the uncooked rice.

"What will happen to the help?" Eloise said. She was touching the sides of her head. I knew what she had stored there, what she couldn't get out to anybody, at least not then.

"They'll starve," I said. "Most of them."

Ditha would starve. I wondered who among the help I knew would live—and how they would live if they did.

One of the help pulled a can from the nail we'd hung it on and shook it. Nothing rattled. I took the can from him.

It was the can Sam and I had put the peach pits in, and they'd sprouted. Water had gotten in the can. In our rush to leave for the mesão, Sam and I'd forgotten to take the pits with us and here they were. We'd meant to plant them at a higher elevation. I held one pit up in the light by the window and looked at the little green shoot coming out the end of it. The pit was bulging with life.

I took the other pit out of the can and set them both on the ground. I scooped moist dirt into the can, put the pits on that, packed dirt over the top of them.

Planted them.

And knew, then, that I could not go work in mines or help build a new station—or ever see home again.

I looked up at Eloise. "I'm not going," I said. "I'll stay and teach the help agriculture, see them through the famine. I can do that. I know farming."

Eloise crouched down by me. "I'll stay with you," she said.

"You can't," I whispered. "You have to get your information out."

She looked at me.

"We both said we didn't want the help to lose their world," I said. "Neither of us wants the help we know to die. So we'll play different parts in this. You do yours. I'll do mine."

She leaned back against the wall and closed her eyes. I started thinking of where I could take the help to farm. I wouldn't want to do it here. It was too low. A hurricane would come again, someday. The mesão was too rocky. I'd have to go to the mountains—to the plateau that looked like Kansas. The wild guys had been farming there. Maybe their squash and corn and beans were still growing and ready to be harvested—they were plants from Earth, after all. Everything Terran was still immune. For now.

"This could take years," Eloise said. "If I have to work out my contract, it could be years before I get anywhere useful."

"I know that." And I thought of Loryn. I would never see her again. I wished that I could talk with her, make her understand what I had to do, why I had to give up my other plans. I wished Loryn could be here with me, but there was no way for that. For her sake, I hoped she'd forget me, marry somebody nice and have good kids, live a good life.

"You'd be alone. They'll take the station and demolish the town. There will be nothing left here from Earth but you."

But staying was something I could not turn away from. I'd be giving life and knowledge to the help where there would have been only death and ignorance before.

"I have to do this," I said.

The company boys pushed open the door, and Senhora Vattani walked in carrying a pot of something that smelled wonderful. Marcos and Fabio came behind her with the crate, and Senhora Vattani put the pot on top of it. Maria came through carrying loaves of bread wrapped in towels. Senhora Vattani had a sack tied to her waist. She untied it. "I've got eight bowls for the stew," she said. "And six spoons. Line up."

Eloise and I ended up in the back of the line, so we had a long wait while the guys ate their stew and passed the bowls to someone else. Maria tore a loaf of bread in two and walked back to me, handed me the bread.

"Bread," Kena said, reaching down from the rafters. "Bread, Jake."

I tore off a piece and gave it to him.

Senhora Vattani banged the side of her pot to get my attention. "I didn't bring enough food for them," she said.

We eventually got up to the pot. Senhora Vattani scraped the last of the stew into bowls for Eloise and me. "Do you have any seeds?" I asked her, quietly.

"What?"

"Do you have anything from Earth I could plant?"

She looked at me as if I had completely lost my mind, put the lid on her pot, and started to pack up.

Eloise put her hand on Senhora Vattani's arm.

"The help are going to starve," she said. "Jake is going to stay and teach them to farm."

Senhora Vattani looked at me differently, then, as if I were some kind of new creature, something maybe acceptable, not just scum.

"You were a farmer on Earth, weren't you?" she said.

"Yes."

"Sam was, too, wasn't he?"

I nodded.

"They're flying you guys out tonight. You've got to go now."

"But do you have any seeds?"

"I've got more than that. Meet me by the rocks where I did the wash."

She gathered up her things and left, her children behind her.

"What are you doing, Jake?" Raimundo asked.

They'd all been listening. I told them what I was doing.

"What if the Terran plants don't live?" Stewart asked.

"I'll die, then, a few years early," I said. I wasn't really that nonchalant. I didn't really know what to expect, but I knew I didn't want to starve. Some help had survived in the past, though. They could help me survive now till we got our first harvest.

Todd walked up and handed me a pair of eye guards. "For the spiders," he said. Stewart explained how to find their farms on the plateau.

"Eloise," I said. "I've got to talk to you."

I took her back by the window where there was still a little light. "I've got to send a message to Sam's family," I said. "Can you record it?"

She nodded and touched her temple. We looked like we were just talking, but I was really trying to tell Sam's family about their son, and brother. And I said a few words to my family, and Loryn.

"Go," Eloise said.

I climbed out the window. The company boys were in front and never heard me. Eloise handed me the shovel and the can with the planted peach sprouts. The help followed me out.

Senhora Vattani brought me a rubber raft. It was all muddy—it had evidently been lying in the muck on the floor of their store—but it would get cleaned up in the bayous. I knew it would never last, it would get punctured too soon, but there was plenty of fallen timber out there to build rafts with. It would last till then.

Maria handed me her father's gun.

"Take it," Senhora Vattani said. "He'll be mad as a lagarto in a drought, but you won't be anywhere to care about that."

She'd stocked the raft with enough canned and packaged food to last us maybe a month, boxes of water-purification tablets, three med kits, ropes—one case of peanut butter. Fabio came running up and handed me a wet, muddy blanket. I could wash it and dry it.

Senhora Vattani started explaining the food. "Cut the potatoes around the eyes. The eyes will start sprouting on the way to wherever you're going, so I've given you these boxes to plant them in." Marcos had even put dirt in the boxes. I wanted to laugh because she was explaining to me, a guy from Idaho, how to grow potatoes, but I didn't laugh. What she had done for the help and me was wonderful. Our rafts would be little arks of life floating over a dying world.

"These carrots and onions can be planted. Let

them go to seed. Here's a dried tomato that will be filled with seeds. I have apple cores in this bag."

She had dried peas, and corn, and wheat that had sprouted because it had gotten wet, but it would grow in a box like the potatoes.

"Thank you," I said.

"I did it for Sam."

There were all kinds of branches wedged in the rocks. I found a branch that would work as a pole, then climbed in the raft. The help climbed in with me. "Go find the other help," I told Kena. "Bring them with us. Get Ditha."

Kena left. He'd find us out in the bayous. It suddenly struck me as odd that the help and I were talking in English. I was staying on their world, but we talked in my language. If I had been an anthropologist, I'd have learned their language and never spoken English to them, but I was hardly here to leave their culture uncontaminated. I wasn't going to start worrying about English now.

"Good luck," Senhora Vattani said.

Marcos, Fabio, and Maria waved to me. I waved back. Doing that gave me one moment of vertigo as I realized I was turning my back on Earth forever. I thought of my grandparents eight generations before me who had turned their backs on Switzerland to come to the wilderness that was Idaho, then, looking for Zion. Maybe they'd found it, I don't know. But Zion wasn't in Idaho anymore. The promised land was gone from the Earth. Maybe I was going to find a kind of Zion on this alien world with the help.

"Good-bye," I said.

For two weeks, as required by law, the company shined a light over the pântano in the international symbol of planetary evacuation: alternating flashes of red and white. But early one morning, just after the moon had set and it was very dark, the help started patting my face to wake me up. "Not got light, Jake," they said. "Not got light."

The company wasn't shining the light over the pântano anymore. I hurried to climb up in the dying tree I'd tied our rafts to, as high as I could go, till the help and I were swaying back and forth on little branches near the top, and I looked at the stars. There were no artificial lights among them. The station was gone.

Epilogue

Eloise came back thirty-one years later, two years after Jake had died. She had found six old help in a zoo that flew among the new worlds displaying curiosities. The zookeepers hadn't known what the help were, at least that's what they said, till Eloise saw them and identified them and brought them home.

The help, of course, did not make her go through customs in Jake Station, the elegant station they were learning to run above Nicoji, built by medicines all the worlds blessed them for. They took her, as the Great Lady—the Lady whose work had given them unalterable rights to their world, who had spent years advising the first two help ambassadors to Earth—down corridors and through waiting rooms all named *Jake* (the help had named every nameable thing on the station *Jake*—Jake 10 or 12 [corridors], Docking Bay Jake 3, Jake's [a restaurant]) to a suite of reception rooms paneled in dark woods from the

new forests below, and gave her gifts: peaches spar-
kling in rainwater, books written in the script Jake
had devised for the help language, platters of nicoji
on ice. Not one of the help dared speak.

"Talk to me," Eloise said. "I can't stand this quiet."

"How did you lose your arm?" one help asked.

Eloise smiled, thinking how the help hadn't really
changed. They still asked questions a human might
never ask. "I had to work eleven years in an asteroid
mine," she said. "My arm was crushed off there, in a
cave-in, but losing it got me to a hospital that got me
home."

That got her to a place where she could publish
her studies on the help. They knew that part of the
story, so she didn't repeat it to them.

"Come with us to Oz," they said, and they handed
her a book with pictures of Oz, their city: built down
the edge of a cliff in Novo Kansas, between two great
falls, looking out across the pântano to the sea.

"That is part of what I came for," she said.

And they went.

Paksenarrion, a simple sheepfarmer's daughter, yearns for a life of adventure and glory, such as the heroes in songs and story. At age seventeen she runs away from home to join a mercenary company, and begins her epic life . . .

ELIZABETH MOON

THE DEED OF PAKSENARRION

"This is the first work of high heroic fantasy I've seen, that has taken the work of Tolkien, assimilated it totally and deeply and absolutely, and produced something altogether new and yet incontestably based on the master. . . . This is the real thing. Worldbuilding in the grand tradition, background thought out to the last detail, by someone who knows absolutely whereof she speaks. . . . Her military knowledge is impressive, her picture of life in a mercenary company most convincing."—**Judith Tarr**

About the author: Elizabeth Moon joined the U.S. Marine Corps in 1968 and completed both Officers Candidate School and Basic School, reaching the rank of 1st Lieutenant during active duty. Her background in military training and discipline imbue The Deed of Paksenarrion with a gritty realism that is all too rare in most current fantasy.

ELIZABETH MOON

THE DEED OF PAKSENARRION

Anne McCaffrey on Elizabeth Moon:

"She's a damn fine writer. The Deed of Paksenarrion is fascinating. I'd use her book for research if I ever need a woman warrior. I know how they train now. We need more like this."

By the Compton Crook Award winning author
of the Best First Novel of the Year

Sheepfarmer's Daughter
65416-0 • 512 pages • $3.95 _____

Divided Allegiance
69786-2 • 528 pages • $3.95 _____

Oath of Gold
69798-6 • 512 pages • $3.95 _____

THE TRUTH
BEHIND THE LEGEND!

FRED
SABERHAGEN

Once upon a time, King Minos of Crete angered the Sea God, Poseidon. And Poseidon in revenge, sent a monster to plague him. And that monster was— But everybody knows the story of the Minotaur, right? Wrong—not the true story! Here's an exciting new look at an ancient Greek myth—a look through a uniquely science fictional lens.

"Fred Saberhagen is one of the best writers in the business."—Lester Del Rey

The brilliant craftsman, Daedalus, and his young son, Icarus, haven't been at King Minos' glittering court very long when the realm is disturbed by strange visitors from the sea: a menacing man of bronze and an eerie, white-furred creature, half man, half bull. Little do the Cretans know that this minotaur, this White Bull, is no supernatural being sent by an angry Poseidon. Instead, he's actually an extraterrestrial, come to Earth with a thankless job: administer to the stubborn Greeks the principles of a liberal, high-tech education. But the Greeks aren't the best of students. Daedalus finds himself in the middle of things, trying to keep the peace between King Minos, hot-blooded Prince Theseus of Athens, and the White Bull. But the Minotaur himself must learn that it's not wise to meddle in the affairs of primitive peoples. After all, they just might take offense . . .

December 1988 • 69794-3 • $3.95

AN OFFER HE COULDN'T REFUSE

They were functional fangs, not just decorative, set in a protruding jaw, with long lips and a wide mouth; yet the total effect was lupine rather than simian. Hair a dark matted mess. And yes, fully eight feet tall, a rangy, tense-muscled body.

She clawed her wild hair away from her face and stared at him with renewed fierceness. Her eyes were a strange light hazel, adding to the wolfish effect. "What are you *really* doing here?"

"I came for you. I'd heard of you. I'm . . . recruiting. Or I was. Things went wrong and now I'm escaping. But if you came with me, you could join the Dendarii Mercenaries. A top outfit—always looking for a few good men, or whatever. I have this master-sergeant who . . . who *needs* a recruit like you." Sgt. Dyeb was infamous for his sour attitude about women soldiers, insisting that they were too soft . . .

"Very funny," she said coldly. "But I'm not even human. Or hadn't you heard?"

"Human is as human does." He forced himself to reach out and touch her damp cheek. "Animals don't weep."

She jerked, as from an electric shock. "Animals don't lie. Humans do. All the time."

"Not *all* the time."

"Prove it." She tilted her head as she sat cross-legged. "Take off your clothes."

". . . what?"

"Take off your clothes and lie down with me as *humans* do. Men and women." Her hand reached out to touch his throat.

The pressing claws made little wells in his flesh. "Blrp?" choked Miles. His eyes felt wide as saucers. A little more pressure, and those wells would spring forth red fountains. *I am about to die. . . .*

I can't believe this. Trapped on Jackson's Whole with a sex-starved teenage werewolf. There was nothing about this in any of my Imperial Academy training manuals. . . .

**BORDERS OF INFINITY by LOIS McMASTER
BUJOLD
69841-9 • $3.95**